Birthright

Also by E.J. Stevens

IVY GRANGER PSYCHIC DETECTIVE

Birthright

E.J. STEVENS

Published by Sacred Oaks Press
Sacred Oaks, 221 Sacred Oaks Lane, Wells, Maine 04090

First Printing (trade paperback edition), July 2015

Stevens, E.J.
Birthright / E.J. Stevens

ISBN 978-0-9894887-1-6 (trade pbk.)

Printed in the United States of America

PUBLISHER'S NOTE
This is a work of fiction. Names, characters, places, and
incidents either are the product of the author's imagination or
are used fictitiously, and any resemblance to actual persons,
living or dead, business establishments, events, or locales is
entirely coincidental.

PRONUNCIATION GUIDE

Pronunciations are given phonetically for names and races found in the Ivy Granger series. Alternate names and nicknames have been provided in parentheses. In some cases, the original folklore has been changed to suit the city of Harborsmouth and its environs.

Ailinn: ah-lynn
Aleya: uh-LEE-yuh
Arachne: uh-RAK-nee
Athame: ah-thaw-may
Banshee: ban-shee (Bean Sidhe, Bean Sìth)
Barguest: BAR-guyst (Bargheist, Black Dog)
Bean Tighe: ban tig
Béchuille: beh-huh-IL (Bé Chuille)
Bema: BEE-muh
Bheur: ver (like air)
Blaosc: BLEE-usk
Bogey: BOH-gee
Boggart: BOG-ert
Boitata: boy-TAH-ta
Brollachan: broll-ach-HAWN
Brownie: BROW-nee (Bwca, Urisk, Hearth Faerie, Domestic Hobgoblin)
Bugbear: BUG-bayr (Bug-a-boo, Boggle-bo)
Bwca: BOO kuh (see Brownie)
The Cailleach: kall-ahk (The Blue Hag, Cailleach Bheur, Queen of Winter, Crone, Veiled One, Winter Hag)
Cat Sidhe: KAT shee or kayth shee (Faerie Cat, Cait Shith, Cait Sith)
Ceffyl Dŵr: keff-EEL dore (Kelpie King, Ceff)
Chir batti: CHEER bhut-TEA
Clurichaun: kloor-ih-kon (clobhair)
Cu Sith: KOO shee
Daeva: DAY-va
Demon: DEE-mun

Djinn: JIN
Draugr: DROW-ger
Duergar: doER-gar
Each Uisge: erk OOSH-kuh (Water Horse)
Elphame: EL-faym
Emain Ablach: EH-van ah-BLAH
Faerie: FAIR-ee (Fairy, Sidhe, Fane, Wee Folk, The Gentry, People of Peace, Themselves, Sidhe, Fae, Fay, Good Folk)
Fear Dearg: far DAR-rig (The Red Man)
Fionn mac Cumhaill: FIN mac COO-will
Forneus: FOR-nee-us (Demon, Great Marquis of Hell)
Fragarach: FRAG ah roch
Fuath: FOO-ah
Gaius Aurelius: GUY-us aw-REE-lee-us
Galliel: GAL-ee-el (Unicorn)
Ghoul: GOOL (Revenant)
Glaistig: GLASS-tig (The Green Lady)
Gnome: NOHM
Goblin: GOB-lin
Griffin: GRIF-fin (Gryphon, Griffon)
Grindylow: GRIN-dee-loh
Gwarwyn-a-throt: GWAR-win-uh-THROT
Hamadryad: ha-ma-DRY-ad (Tree Nymph)
Harborsmouth: HAR-bers-MOUTH
Henkie: HEN-kee
Hippocampus: hip-po-CAM-pus
Hob-o-Waggle HOB-oh-WAG-gul (Brownie, son of Wag-at-the-Wa)
Hy Brasil: HY bra-ZIL
Ignus fatuus: IG-nus FATCH-you-us
Inari: i-NAH-ree
Jenny Greenteeth: JEN-nee GREEN-teeth (Water Hag)
Kelpie: KEL-pee (Water Horse, Nyaggle)
Lamia: LAY-me-uh
Leanansídhe: lan-awn-shee (Lhiannan Sidhe, Leanhaun Shee, Leannan Sìth, Fairy Mistress)
Leprechaun: le-pre-khan (leipreachán)
Loup garou: LOOP guh-ROO
Mab: MAB (Unseelie Queen)
Manannán mac Lir: MAH-nah-nahn mac leer
Mauthe doog: MOW-thee DOO
Melusine: MEL-oo-seen

Mermaid: MER-mayd (male Merman)
Merry Dancer: MER-ree DAN-ser (Fir Chlis)
Murúch: mer-ook (Merrow, Moruadh, Murúghach)
Nixie: NIX-ee
Nuckelavees: NOOK-uh-LAY-veez
Oberon: OH-ber-on (Seelie King)
Peg Powler: PEG POW-ler (Peg Powler of the Trees, Water Hag)
Peri: PER-ee
Pixie: PIK-see (Pisgie)
Pooka: POO-kuh (Phooka, Pouka, Púca, Pwca)
Redcap: RED-kap (red cap)
Roca Barraidh: ROH-ka BAR-rah
Saytr: SAY-ter
Selkie: SEL-kee
Shellycoat: SHEL-lee-cote
Sidhe: SHEE (see Faerie)
Succubus: SUK-you-bus (male Incubus)
Tech Duinn: tek DOON
Tezcatlipocan: tehs-cah-tlee-poh-cahn
Tir na nOg: TEER na NOHG
Tir Tairngire: TEER TEARN-geer
Titania: ti-TAY-nee-uh (Seelie Queen)
Troll: TROHL
Tuatha Dé Danann: tootha DAY da-NAN
Tylwyth Teg: TILL-with TEEG (Seelie Court)
Unicorn: YOU-ni-korn
Unseelie: un-SEE-lee
Vampire: VAM-pyr (Undead)
Will-o'-the-Wisp: WIL-oh-tha-wisp (Gyl Burnt Tayle, Jack o' Lantern, Wisp, Ghost Light, Friar's Lantern, Corpse Candle, Hobbledy, Aleya, Hobby Lantern, Chir Batti, Faerie Fire, Spunkies, Min Min Light, Luz Mala, Pinket, Ellylldan, Spook Light, Ignus Gatuus, Orbs, Boitatá, and Hinkypunk)
Ynis Afallon: un-NIS AH-fuhl-on
Yue Fei: yweh-fay

INTRODUCTION

Welcome to Harborsmouth, where monsters walk the streets unseen by humans…except those with second sight.

Whether visiting our modern business district or exploring the cobblestone lanes of the Old Port quarter, please enjoy your stay. When you return home, do tell your friends about our wonderful city—just leave out any supernatural details.

Don't worry—most of our guests never experience anything unusual. Otherworlders, such as faeries, vampires, and ghouls, are quite adept at hiding within the shadows. Many are also skilled at erasing memories. You may wake in the night screaming, but you won't recall why. Be glad that you don't remember—you are one of the fortunate ones.

If you do encounter something unnatural, well, you are currently out of luck. Normally, we would recommend the services of Ivy Granger, Psychic Detective. Unfortunately for you, Miss Granger is recently deceased.

Perhaps, we can interest you in local real estate. With Miss Granger dead, it is likely you may become one of our permanent residents. We kindly direct you to Harborsmouth Cemetery Realty. It's never too early to contact them, since we have a booming "housing" market. Demand is quite high for a local plot—there are always people dying for a place to stay.

CHAPTER 1

I grimaced at the noodles currently taunting me with their salty broth and rubbery texture, and pushed the steaming bowl away with gloved hands. My stomach growled, but I ignored its rumbling and grabbed a mug of coffee instead.

"Girl, if you keep drinking that sludge without any food in your stomach, you're just asking for total coffee rotgut," Jinx said, leaning a hip against the counter and pointing a red lacquered fingernail my way. "Eat your dinner."

Jinx wasn't my mother, but sometimes she acted like it. Normally, I put up with her bossiness without too much grumbling. Well, maybe some grumbling, but when it came to eating, I usually did what she said. Jinx was my best friend, which was why we were roommates and business partners.

Until recently, Jinx was also the only person in my life who cared if I lived or breathed—or so I'd thought. So when she fussed over me, I secretly felt all warm and fuzzy inside. I wasn't a touchy-feely person, being saddled with the curse of psychometry made sure of that. Over time, objects, including people, collect psychic residue and all of those strong emotions—mostly traumatic—sit there just waiting for someone like me to reach out and make contact.

So normally, that meant I ate what Jinx put in front of me, no questions asked. Not today. If I had to eat one more bowl of ramen or plate of mac and cheese, I'd puke.

"I'd rather wrestle with a smelly, pulsating jincan queen," I muttered.

"Well, you won't be wrestling with the fae anytime soon," she said. "Not with you being dead and all."

I sighed, and glared at the bowl of ramen noodles, but ignoring Jinx didn't make what she said any less true. As far as the fae were concerned, I was dead. Last month, the faerie courts sent their assassins, the Moordenaar, to terminate me as my punishment for crimes against the fae. It was against fae law to go around letting the general public know about the existence of Otherworlders.

Faeries are immortal, but they can still be killed if the human masses became aware of the monsters in their midst and decide to take up arms against them. It was why the ability to glamour ourselves was so important.

So when it came to the faerie courts' attention that I was breaking their law, intentionally or not, they ordered my execution at the hands of the Moordenaar. The Moordenaar are very, very good at their job. They'd shot poisoned arrows into my heart, kidney, and liver, and then left me to die.

Humphrey was one of the reasons my assassins hadn't waited to witness my death, and therefore weren't around when my friends force fed me a magic apple that brought me back to life. I'd have to thank him for that someday, though I didn't like the idea of being in a gargoyle's debt. Talk about a rock and a hard place.

"Fine, I'll make you a box of mac and cheese," she said, rolling her eyes. "But just so you know, we're out of milk and butter. It's probably going to taste nasty."

"No, don't waste it," I said. "I'll eat the mac and cheese tomorrow."

I had no intention of eating another box of the stuff tomorrow, or ever, but Jinx didn't know that. Mab's bones, I'd rather starve.

"I have a protein bar in my bedroom," I said with a one-armed shrug.

"That's not dinner," she said, eyes narrowing.

"Neither is this," I said, pushing the bowl farther away. "You want it?"

Jinx stared at the bowl, lip twitching.

"Hells to the no," she said.

I snorted, and shook my head. Jinx had been oohing and ahhing over her meals all week, but she was just as sick of ramen as I was. My best friend was tricksy like that.

"Sparky!" I yelled. "You hungry?"

The little demon came tearing out of our bathroom, streaming toilet paper from his long ears, and climbed the rungs of the bar stool beside me. With a gleeful squeak, he hopped onto the counter and danced a squirmy little jig.

"Yes, yes, yes, yes!" he sang.

I reached for the package of plastic cutlery we kept on hand for Ceff—my boyfriend the local kelpie king—but Jinx shook her head.

"Wait," she said. She narrowed her eyes, and aimed a ladle at Sparky. "What have you been up to? Have you been playing in the toilet again?"

Forneus claimed that Sparky would someday grow to become a massive demon lord, but that was hard to believe. The little guy was the size of a potbellied Chihuahua and got into just as much mischief. Last week he'd started tossing "treasures" into the toilet to be salvaged by Sparky the great spelunking explorer. Unfortunately, one of those treasures was Jinx's toothbrush.

"Nooooo," he said.

He blushed and gave Jinx a shy smile.

"Then how did you get toilet paper strung up in your ears like garland?" she asked, reaching over to pluck the paper from his ears.

"No toilet, silly," he said. "Trash can!"

I rubbed a gloved hand over my face, and tried not to laugh. Sparky had found the wonders of the bathroom trash can. Oberon save us all.

"Oh my God, ewww!" Jinx squeaked, dropping the toilet paper as if it scorched her fingers.

"Ewww!" Sparky yelled, smiling as he parroted Jinx.

"If it's anything like his game with the toilet, he was probably putting the toilet paper into the trash can, not the other way around," I said. "The toilet paper is most likely clean."

It also meant that he'd probably been adventuring inside the trash can, sifting through who knows what with his bare hands. Apparently, Jinx had come to the same conclusion.

"Go wash your hands," she said, pointing to the bar sink. "And no more playing in the bathroom."

"Then food?" he asked.

"Then you can eat Ivy's ramen noodles," she said. "Now hurry up, before they get cold."

Sparky skipped over to the sink. He leaned out to turn on the faucet and pretty soon he was playing under the running water as if running through a lawn sprinkler. Jinx scowled at the mess the demon was making of her kitchen, but I shook my head and smiled.

"Let him have his fun," I said. "We can always heat the ramen up again later."

"You shouldn't feed him all that salt," she said. "If he were a dog, he'd have hypertension by now."

I shrugged. The kid looked fine, not that I could tell if he had high blood pressure or not. His skin was always tinged red.

"He's a demon," I said. "That food will probably kill us before it does anything to him."

I eyed the bowl of ramen as if it were about to reach out its noodle tentacles and attack.

"If you want to eat real food again, we have to start making some money," she said. "Either that, or we dip into the emergency fund. Oh wait, we can't do that. Someone already spent it."

I sighed. She wasn't entirely wrong to be angry with me, but I hadn't had a choice.

"You know I have to find my father," I said. "He's the only hope I have of gaining control over my wisp powers and clearing my name with the faerie council."

Until I could prove that I wasn't a walking menace to fae society, I had to remain dead. Something we soon discovered meant a huge blow to our income. It's hard to work cases when you're supposed to be six feet under the ground.

"Let me start taking cases," Jinx said. "I can do the legwork, and you can consult from home. If I need your magic touch, I know where to find you."

I shook my head, and waved my hands.

"No way," I said.

"Look, I'll just meet with the clients and get the deets on the job," she said. "If I wear faerie ointment, I'll be able to see if they're not human."

The ingredients to make faerie ointment were expensive. If Jinx was willing to use up the last of her ointment, I knew she was serious about landing a job. That made arguing with her that much more difficult.

Not that I was willing to give up yet. What Jinx didn't know, what I was forbidden to tell any human, was that I had a key to one of the secret gates to Faerie. The only pathway to that gate revealed itself on the summer solstice—a date that was fast approaching. If we took a job now, I'd only be able to help work the case for a few more days. After that, Jinx might be without backup, permanently.

"Faerie ointment doesn't work on the undead," I said.

Vampires have their own glamour, one that faerie ointment doesn't penetrate. I let out a deep, gratifying sigh. I was sure to win this fight.

"I'll only do business during the day," she said.

Crap. I hadn't thought of that. I cleared my throat, trying to think of another reason my best friend shouldn't put herself at risk. I was pretty sure that telling her "food is highly overrated" wouldn't work.

"It's dangerous," I said.

She lifted her chin, eyes shining, and shoulders back and leaned toward me, her palms spread out on the counter.

"Let me do this," she said. "Please."

Damn it. I slumped forward, and put my head in my hands. It was the "please" that did it. Over the past month, Jinx had been trying to prove that she was the same tough-as-nails woman she was before her attack. The fact that she'd show any sign of weakness now, proved how much this meant to her.

"Okay, fine," I said. "But I'm not letting you do this alone. No meeting with clients without me."

We'd have to work overtime to meet my solstice deadline, but it wasn't like I hadn't worked a case round-the-clock before. So long as Jinx kept pumping me full of coffee, we might wrap up a job before I did my disappearing act.

"You can't come to the office," she said with a frown. "It's too dangerous."

"Then I guess, I'll just have to make sure nobody sees me," I said.

CHAPTER 2

I elbowed myself in the kidney and winced. I'd insisted on accompanying Jinx to Private Eye for her meeting with a client. Too bad our office was small and there weren't many places to hide. I shifted my weight, catching my ass on a loose screw that protruded from the wall of the cupboard I was currently crouching in. I frowned, hoping the sharp metal hadn't snagged my jeans. The last thing I needed right now was to be dragged down into a vision.

I sighed. I should have thought this through a bit more. I was wedged in here so tight, I already had a crick in my neck and my legs were going numb. Another twenty minutes of this and I wouldn't be able to move at all, which meant that if some big, bad supernatural nasty came striding into our office, I wouldn't be much help. Maybe the cupboard wasn't the only thing with a screw loose.

I was being paranoid, and I knew it. Jinx had met with our clients in the past. She was good at flying solo, that bossy streak of hers keeping the meetings on track and a steady cash flow into our bank accounts. But she'd never done this under the guise of running the place herself.

That's the part that worried me. She'd always been my paper pushing partner, the helpful administrative assistant. Now she was putting herself out there as a psychic detective—a job that attracted its share of nut cases. Walking in my shoes might just put her in danger, a fact that had me wishing she'd stick to answering phones and bossing me around. Was food so important that we really needed to swap jobs?

Jinx's role in the office wasn't the only thing that had changed recently. Until last summer, our clientele had been mostly human. But after a battle with flesh-eating faerie horses that made kelpies look like My Little Pony, our client base had shifted. The fae now knew that I could be a valuable ally, or a powerful enemy.

Unfortunately, they also thought I was dead. That left my human partner on the front lines with some potentially deadly nasties, monsters who thought she was here without backup. I was just about to extricate myself from my self-imposed prison when the bell above the office door rang out.

I held my breath, and tried not to move a muscle. If we were lucky, Jinx's client would just be some helpless human here with a mundane job. The bell over the door only chimed once, which meant we were likely dealing with only one opponent, um, client.

"Welcome to Private Eye..." Jinx said, voice faltering. I couldn't see anything through the narrow crack that I was squinting out from, so I inched the cupboard door open further. I shifted my weight, preparing to come to her aid—or at least fall on her assailant—when the next word out of her mouth stopped me in my tracks. "Dad?"

I'd never met Jinx's father, but from what I could see, he was a large, burly man with a dark beard and more tattoos than his daughter. He pulled a baseball hat from his head, running grease-stained fingers over a bald spot, and sighed.

"Sorry to bother you at work," he said. "Especially after all that's happened. I'm sorry for your loss, sweetheart."

Jinx froze, and blinked at her father, for once at a loss for words. I'd known that going into hiding and perpetuating the story that I was dead would be hard. What I hadn't planned on was what keeping that secret would cost my friends and loved ones. Jinx paled and looked down at her desk, straightening the pens and stacks of paper that were already lined up with military precision.

Her father mistook her discomfort for grief and closed the distance between them, pulling Jinx into a hug. My friend stood there, face going red, and I knew I needed to do something. Unlike the pureblood fae, humans can tell lies, but that didn't mean that lying to her father would be easy.

"Um, that's okay," she said, gently pushing her father away and putting her desk between them. "Is that why you're here?"

This was my mess. I had to do something to fix it.

Jinx continued to stare at her desk and I eyed the door, wondering where our client was. Someone, or something, had asked for a morning meeting. Maybe if I was fast enough, I could reveal myself to Jinx's father, give him a quick explanation of my current situation, swear him to secrecy, and wedge myself back into this tiny wooden box before our client arrived. Okay, it wasn't good odds, but I couldn't just leave Jinx hanging out to dry.

"Actually, sweetheart," he said. "I'm your ten o'clock appointment." He rolled his hat in his hands and blushed, nose going bright red. "I need your help."

With a crash, I tumbled out of the cabinet and onto the floor at Mr. Braxton's feet. It wasn't a graceful entrance, but then again he seemed more concerned with the fact that a dead woman had just rolled out of our office cupboard.

I winced and came to one knee, waving to Jinx's dad. I glanced at the large window that faced the street, but there were no monsters lurking there, and the desk kept me mostly hidden from view. I pulled back the hood from my sweatshirt and stuffed my gloved hands into my pockets, but I kept my face turned away from the windows that faced the street.

"Pardon me if I don't shake your hand," I said. "It's nothing personal."

"No offense taken," he said voice shaky. "My daughter told me about your...affliction."

Good. If Jinx told her father that I was a psychic and he believed it, then he might be more receptive to what I was about to tell him.

"Jinx, can you pull the shades and lock the door?" I asked.

"Sure," she said, eager to have something to do to keep busy.

"I'm sorry that I was eavesdropping, but I didn't know who would turn up for this meeting," I said. "And I couldn't leave Jinx on her own. There are dangerous people out there, monsters who don't value human life."

"These dangerous men, they why you've been playing possum?" he asked.

I nodded, taking in the man's muscled body and grease stained coveralls. There was dirt under his fingernails and his hands and arms were crisscrossed with tiny scars. He was a man who worked with his hands, but the most impressive thing about him was the intelligence in his sparkling, blue eyes. I imagine it would be easy to underestimate a man like that, if you didn't look him in the eye. Judging from his size, most people probably didn't.

I smiled and gestured for him to take a seat.

"There are people who want me dead," I said. "It's better if they think they got their wish, for now anyway."

"People wanting you dead usually put you in such a good mood, Miss Granger?" he asked.

"No," I said. "I'm just happy to finally meet Jinx's father. Coming out to your business hasn't really been an option. Old and used things have a tendency to bite me in the ass, so to speak."

He chuckled and took a seat, slapping his tree trunk-sized thigh with his hat.

"And here I thought you just didn't like junkyards," he said.

"Only for their complications," I said.

A scrap yard filled with the detritus of hundreds, perhaps thousands, of lives left me shaking in my boots. Some people fear death, but me? I was terrified of the potential for madness that lurked within old items, the memories of their previous owners waiting to pounce and claw away at my sanity.

"Okay, Dad," Jinx said, taking a seat behind her desk. She'd locked the door, and dropped the shades. "So why are you here? What's wrong?"

"Someone's been breaking into the junkyard," he said with a frown. "And I don't think they're human."

I brushed paper dust and toner from my jeans and rocked back on my heels. We'd hastily removed the shelving and office supplies from the cupboard this morning, but hadn't bothered to wipe it down before I crawled inside. I frowned at a dark spot on my jeans. That smudge of toner was going to be a bitch to get out.

Too bad that wasn't all I had to worry about.

CHAPTER 3

"Why don't you think the thieves are human?" I asked.

The question was directed at Jinx's father, but as he pondered the question, I raised an eyebrow at his daughter. She mimed fangs and horns with her fingers, nodded, and shrugged. Apparently, she'd shared some of her knowledge of paranormal creatures with her father. While I could commend honesty, that kind of information was dangerous. Most of the fae and undead would go to great lengths to guard that secret, and many of the long-lived weren't bothered with things like morals or consciences. They'd snap Eben Braxton's neck, and pat themselves on the back for a job well done.

I'd need to remind them both of that, but for now, I had a job to focus on, one that I was already beginning to dread.

"Wait, can you repeat that?" I asked.

"I said, they lured my night guard away with some kind of floating lights," he said, scraping a hand through his hair. "It was unnatural."

I bit my lip, trying to ignore the churning in my gut. I told myself that I'd had too much coffee and not enough food. That was all. But a tiny traitorous voice inside my head was already drawing connections between the unnatural floating lights and my wisp brethren.

I shook off the growing sense of dread, and focused on the job. Any number of things could cast strange lights throughout a junkyard. It was probably just moonlight reflecting off pieces of metal, or lightning bugs, or a trick of the weather. It was breezy yesterday. Maybe the winds had shifted some of the junk, making the light bounce and dance.

"How long has this been going on?" I asked.

"Around about two weeks," he said.

Well, that ruled out the recent windy weather. But that still didn't mean we were dealing with wisps. There are other nocturnal creatures that enjoy toying with humans.

"It all started when Bruce's dog went missing, though we didn't put two and two together until what happened later," he continued.

"Bruce?" I asked.

"Dad's best night watchman," Jinx said.

"You sure this Bruce isn't in on it?" I asked. "Maybe he staged the loss of his dog, and lied about the lights?"

"No," he said with a shake of the head. "He's a good man. Plus, I got no proof any thieving's been going on. It's beyond peculiar."

"Nothing has gone missing?" I asked.

Due to all the scrap metal in the junkyard, I'd been starting to suspect we were up against gremlins. I'd never dealt with the pests myself, but from what I'd heard they were one of the very few fae races that could handle iron. Some people claimed they even had a love for technology, or at least the airplane engines of the early twentieth century. More than one WWII pilot came home with a tale of gremlins sabotaging their aircraft.

If gremlins weren't the ones messing around in the junkyard, then who was? Vampires? Ghouls? If we were looking at ghouls, I didn't have much hope of finding that dog alive. Most vampires wouldn't lower themselves to feeding off the blood of dogs, but ghouls had no such aversion. Ghouls may prefer human flesh, but they'd feast on whatever carrion they could find.

"Nothing of value has gone missing, just Bruce's dog," he said, running a hand over his beard. "Like I said, Bruce is a good man, and he'd never do nothing bad to that dog. He loved that mutt like his own kin."

Jinx nodded.

"Bruce has worked for my dad for so long, he's practically family," she said, fists on her hips as if daring me to argue.

"Damn," I said through clenched teeth.

I didn't like where this was going. Not at all.

"What?" Eben asked.

He frowned in confusion, but I could see Jinx's eyes widening as the same realization crept in.

As much as I wanted to rail against the possibility, I had to face the facts. The glowing unearthly orbs, floating through the night to lure man and beast to their doom sounded an awful lot like my wisp brethren.

"The ones causing trouble at your junkyard aren't part of your family, but they just might be part of mine," I said.

CHAPTER 4

I climbed over a pile of car parts, careful not to snag my legs on the sharp metal. My caution wasn't for fear of wrecking my clothes. I didn't need a trek through a junkyard to accomplish that. No, I was more worried about puncturing the armor of my jeans and leather, allowing my skin to come into contact with the stacks of metal and plastic. People loved their cars—they lived in them, had sex in them, fought in them, and died in them.

I'd rather eat ramen for the rest of my life than touch those car parts.

I swallowed hard, and stopped to survey the junkyard from my new vantage point. The place was a sea of memories, waiting to dig their claws into my skull. Experiencing visions was bad enough, but that wasn't my only concern. My biggest fear was being pulled down into the abyss, and the psychic impressions never letting go.

I shuddered, but pushed on. I couldn't turn away from this job. If I was right, and wisps were involved in the mischief at the junkyard, I'd not only have to take on this case free of charge, but I'd also owe Jinx's family a debt.

Sparky let out a whoop, making me jump, and I almost lost my footing. I turned to watch the tiny demon as he ran around the junkyard, chasing seagulls with glee. At least someone was having fun.

I couldn't bring any of my fae friends along, not with the high iron content of all this metal, but Sparky was a demon. There wasn't much here that could bother the little guy. So long as we didn't dig up any crosses or holy water, he'd be fine.

"How much farther to where you found your night watchman?" I asked, turning my attention back to the case.

The dog hadn't been the only one to wander off and get lost, though he'd been the first. A watchman, a guy who filled in on Bruce's night off, had gone missing for two days. When he returned with stories of following strange lights through the junkyard, lights that led him on a merry chase that resulted in him lost and terrified for two days out on the marshes, his friends thought he'd gone on a bender.

Eben didn't believe the gossip. He claimed that his guard, a man named Mitch Keane, hadn't touched a drink in six years. Eben suspected something unnatural was going on in his junkyard, and I had to agree with him.

"Just down there," he said, pointing to the base of the pile of junk we were balanced on. I raised my eyes at the walled in patch of ground, and Eben shook his head. "It's not part of his regular circuit. My guys stick to the paths. A man can break a leg, possibly even his neck, out here in the dark. No reason for him to be in this deep."

"What if he caught someone stealing?" I asked.

"I don't pay Mitch enough to risk his hide," he said. "He'd make sure it wasn't some fool kids out here partying, and then he'd call for backup."

"You get much of that up here?" I asked, picking my way down the hill. "Kids partying?"

"Kids will be kids," he said with a shrug. "But the fence, guards, and barking dog usually keep them out. If they do show up, a flashlight in the face and a threat to call the cops sends them packing."

I took in the high, barbed fence that circled the junkyard, and nodded. I had to agree with Eben. That fence wouldn't be easy to climb, and cutting through it with the threat of security guards and dogs would be more trouble than it was worth. No matter how you sliced it, there were easier places for kids to go party.

The spot where Eben had found Mitch Keane also wasn't an easy place to access. Three towering piles of tires and scrap metal converged, forming a ring, leaving a patch of ground no larger than my kitchen.

"Stay here," I said.

I slowly made my way down over twisted pieces of salvaged vehicles. If it wasn't for my newly developing faerie fast reflexes, I probably would have made the trip head first. As it was, my breathing was ragged when I reached the bottom.

I waved at Eben to let him know I'd survived the trip down in one piece, and began walking the patch of ground in a grid pattern. My boots sent up little puffs of dust. We hadn't had rain all week, a fact that I was hoping would work in my favor. If there were clues to be found, they wouldn't have been washed away. The wind, on the other hand, had been less helpful.

There were no footprints or drag marks. I spun in a circle, letting my eyes go soft as I tried to clear my mind. A good detective knows not to give up just because there's nothing to see. I breathed deep, and let my subconscious chew on what I knew, but the only answer it kept spitting back at me was the one thing I didn't want to hear.

After another search of the ground, I turned and made my way back to where Eben Braxton waited.

"You find anything?" he asked.

I could tell by the rigid way that he held himself that the answer was important to him. I could understand that. Two men had suffered here on his property. I could relate to feeling responsible for the safety of your friends and allies. I chose my words with care.

"There's no evidence that this is your fault, Mr. Braxton," I said. "That fence should keep all but the most determined riff raff out and, from what you've told me, you have good safety protocols in place for your men."

"So how do you explain one man nearly dying of exposure, and the other losing his dog out from under our noses?" he asked.

"I'm not ready to answer that, not yet," I said.

"When do you expect an answer?" he asked.

"I'll know more after tonight," I said.

I sent up a silent prayer that I was dealing with something simple, like a swarm of fireflies and a couple of drunk security guards. But deep down, I knew better. My life was never simple.

CHAPTER 5

Eben wasn't happy about letting me wander around the junkyard at night, but I hadn't given him much choice—neither had Jinx. In fact, my rockabilly friend had stubbornly refused to listen to either of our arguments against her participating in tonight's stakeout. So now I crept along the moonlit dirt pathways with Jinx and Sparky at my side.

"Ouch!" Jinx griped, tripping over a piece of plastic that jutted out from one of the nearby piles.

"Ouch! Ouch! Ouch! Ouch!" Sparky parroted, skipping circles around Jinx, and flashing a wide, gap-toothed grin. His long ears kicked up dust as he bounced along, like a lop-eared Tasmanian devil on happy pills.

Sparky had lost another baby tooth this week, and I tried to ignore the fact that his adult teeth were coming in razor sharp and deadly. Forneus had warned me that my innocent little ward was actually a Tezcatlipocan demon—the very rare and extremely dangerous offspring of a fallen angel and a demon. According to Forneus, if Sparky had remained in Hell, it would be the kid's birthright to grow up to enslave other demons. Heck, he'd have his own plane of Hell to rule over.

But the kid chose to stay here in Harborsmouth with me and Jinx. So long as Sparky wanted to be a part of our dysfunctional family, he was welcome here. None of us can choose the nature of our birth. Being born with certain powers didn't make us monsters—it's what we did with those powers that counted.

If I stopped believing that, I might as well slit my own throat.

"Come on, buddy," I said, waving the kid along. "Leave Jinx alone. She's looking murderous."

"Am not," Jinx said, glaring from beneath bangs that contained so much hairspray, they were practically bulletproof. I cocked an eyebrow, folding my arms across my chest, and she rolled her eyes. She rubbed her ankle and sighed. "Okay, maybe just a little. You'd think my dad would keep these walkways clear of junk."

Yeah. Like her tripping didn't have anything to do with her penchant for bad luck, or her choice of footwear. Platform sandals were not the best choice for a stakeout, even if they did match her dress.

"We don't have much farther to walk," I said. "There's a clearing up ahead. We can wait behind that bulldozer, and see if anything turns up."

I led the way, Sparky skipping along at my side. It didn't take us long to reach the spot I'd spied during my daylight tour of the junkyard.

Careful not to touch anything, I spread an old towel over a steel barrel and settled in for a whole lot of waiting. I wasn't overly fond of stakeouts—I wasn't the most patient person on the planet—but they were a necessary part of detective work. That didn't mean I had to like it.

I tapped my gloved fingers on the tops of my knees, and sighed.

"Do you really think it'll be wisps?" Jinx whispered.

I frowned, and flashed a sidelong glance her way. She settled on the edge of an overturned milk crate, and concentrated on her skirt as she picked nonexistent lint from its hem.

I shrugged, and turned my attention to the clearing where three of the pathways intersected just beyond the bulldozer that sheltered us from prying eyes.

"I hope not," I said.

I crossed my fingers in the darkness, and sent up a silent prayer. Too bad no one was listening.

*****

I'd been staring so long into the dark clearing, that I no longer trusted my eyes. I'd started seeing tiny sparks of light, even behind my eyelids, after the first hour. It might have been fatigue, but my guess was a side effect of high blood pressure. Keeping Jinx awake, and Sparky from dancing and singing, was trying my patience.

And I had been living on ramen noodles and mac and cheese for the past few weeks—food that fell firmly in the high sodium food group. High blood pressure was a very real possibility. I told Jinx that stuff was evil.

Four hours into our stakeout, a familiar glow appeared off to my right. It winked out, only to appear a second later off to my left. But no, it wasn't just one glowing orb. Lights began winking on and off throughout the junkyard, zipping through skeletal car windows, and hovering over piles of refuse. That was no optical illusion, no ramen induced side effect.

The wisps were here.

Jinx gasped, and clamped a hand over Sparky's mouth, hugging the demon to her chest. Another second, and the little guy would have run off to chase the twinkling lights…and we all know how well that would end. If I'd given it more thought, I'd have put the kid in one of those toddler harnesses you see at the mall and tied him to my belt so he couldn't run off.

I motioned for Jinx to stay here with Sparky, as my knives hit my gloved palms. She set her jaw, and nodded once. Jinx wouldn't let anything happen to Sparky. She'd wanted to come, to prove that the monsters hadn't stolen her courage, that she wasn't broken. Protecting the kid would give her something to focus on—it would give her strength.

I turned my attention back to the swarming wisps. A low buzzing sound was building, as if the entire planet had started humming. Within minutes, wisps flooded the clearing. Their movements were jerky, not the smooth, graceful dance of the wisps I'd met during the Danse Macabre.

These wisps may fly about like drunken pookas, but it was clear that they were all moving with a purpose. They were hunting someone, and I had a good idea who.

I stepped out from behind the backhoe, and the buzzing stopped. Silence fell on the clearing, and I held my breath. The wisps I'd met previously had been happy to help the daughter of their king. But my father had been wandering the world of men for a long time, leaving his people without a leader. These wisps might greet me with open arms, or I could get blasted with tiny fireballs. I had no idea what to expect.

I just knew that I couldn't walk away.

"Come, my kin," I said, taking a calming breath. "I am Ivy Granger, the daughter of Will-o'-the-Wisp. I don't mean you any harm."

That wasn't entirely true. Unlike pureblood fae, I can lie, at least for now. And though I didn't want to hurt any of my people, I would do what was necessary to protect the citizens of Harborsmouth—even if that meant taking down a pack of wild wisps gone feral in my father's absence.

Oberon's eyes, please don't be a pack of tiny killers.

"All I ask is that you refrain from harming innocent people...and animals," I said, remembering the missing dog. "I'm sure this has all been a big misunderstanding."

I set down my silver and iron blades on the dusty ground at my feet, raised my hands, and smiled.

"Ivy?" Jinx asked.

A glance over my shoulder revealed Jinx stumbling toward me, a glowing wall of wisps at her back. In larger numbers, it was obvious that these wisps were different from the ones I'd met in the past. These wisps pulsed with a sickly, jaundiced hue. They started to zig zag nonsensical patterns in the air, and the buzzing began again, this time a discordant whine that made me grind my teeth.

Jinx paled, her grip tightening on Sparky. The little demon was singing a nursery rhyme about hugs and love, oblivious to the potential danger.

Jinx had her crossbow in the bag slung over her shoulder, but she'd never get to it without dropping Sparky. That was not an option. The kid was already reaching up toward the sparkling lights, and trying to wiggle out of Jinx's death grip.

"I am your princess," I said, raising my voice so that it carried over the cacophony of buzzing. "These are my friends. None of us are here to harm you. We just want to talk."

"Pretty," Sparky said, wiggling in Jinx's arms. He reached up toward one of the wisps, and yelped. "Ouch!"

"Ivy," Jinx hissed. "It bit him."

Shit. This was not how this was supposed to go down. The wisps weren't playing nice.

"Okay, start heading toward the exit, while I distract them," I said.

"And how do you plan to do that?" she asked, inching toward the same path we'd taken to get here.

I retrieved my knives, and spun, shooting one last glance at Sparky who was shaking in Jinx's arms, and sucking on his finger. Mess with my kid, eh? I let the fear and anger take over, flooding my body with power.

"Show them my angry side," I said.

"You mean flash them your headlights," she said, stumbling away from the clearing. I snorted, and she sighed. "God, Ivy, you know what I mean."

I did know what she meant. I may not know how to control my wisp powers, but I'd learned one way to let them out. If I got mad enough, my faerie half took over, unleashing a rush of fiery magic.

"Your eyes are glowing," she said.

"Good," I said with a nod, feeling the tingle of magic searing my skin. It prickled along my scalp, down my arms and legs. More than just my eyes were glowing.

I waved my blades toward the wisps, and tilted my head back, letting them get a good look at my glowing eyes and skin. I was their liege and, by Mab, they would listen to me.

"No. More. Games," I said, biting out the words. My teeth hummed with energy, the strain of holding so much wild power making my vision waver. "No more harming innocent people and animals. You are mine, and you will obey."

For a moment, the glow of the wisps closest to me began to shift into the healthy spectrum of light—a yellow like sunlight on a spring day—but it faded in a flash. In an eye blink, the wisps were twitching, bodies jerking back and forth, their color taking on a sickly green hue.

There was something terribly wrong with these wisps.

"What happened to you?" I asked, the words barely a whisper beneath the dissonant notes of wisp song. Rather than a melodic chirping and humming, this song was tortured and strained. These wisps, my people, were in pain.

I slid my knives back into the sheaths strapped beneath my leather jacket, and shook my head. Making threats and demands wasn't getting through to them, and it was no wonder. Something was making them sick, and in their weakened state, I was just another threat.

With my ignorance of the wisp language, and their agitation, I could think of only one way to get the answers that I needed. I'd rather walk away. Hell, I'd rather run, but instead, I stripped off my glove, and held out my hand.

Sweat trickled down my spine, and my hand shook. It felt like I stood there for an eternity, but it was only a second before a wisp dove in to bite my hand.

I staggered forward, falling to my knees. It wasn't because of the pain of the bite—that was nothing more than a bee sting. No, what brought me to my knees was the vision sucking me down into the vortex of another being's memories, moments of such raw emotion that they'd left psychic impressions on this wisp.

Before I lost myself completely, I managed one last scream. The air in my lungs laced with fire.

"Run!"

I just hoped that Jinx and Sparky made it out of the junkyard alive.

CHAPTER 6

For a happy moment, I basked in the warm glow of my father holding court, but in this vision, he wasn't my father. He was my king.

Visions blur the lines, making it difficult to retain my sense of self, but I dug in, clawing at the fragments that remained of Ivy Granger. I knew that if I lost myself in a vision for too long, finally letting go and succumbing to the power of the vision, then I would never fully return to my body. My mind would shatter, leaving a shell of my former self behind.

"Father," I choked.

But he was already gone. The warmth and safety of the wisp court was replaced by a bog. It was peaceful here—birds sang, frogs sat on lily pads, and wisps floated lazily above the water—until the construction crew came. Men with chainsaws and dynamite changed the surrounding landscape, rending it into a wasteland.

We hid in the remaining vegetation along the water's edge, waiting for the men to leave. Instead, they brought in monstrous dump trucks and backhoes to loom over the swamp hole. When the excavation reached the middle of the swamp, encroaching further on our hiding place within the cattails and bog grass, we decided to flee.

Frightened and starving, we flew away from the men and their noisy machines. But in every direction more men blocked our way, driving in their monstrosities of iron. And where there were no men, there were fae unwilling to share their territory.

At last, we settled in a quiet place where no other fae had settled, and for good reason. It was ringed in iron, its metal fence reaching high to defend against our wingless brethren. We moved to the center of our new territory, as far from the iron fence as we could manage, to a shallow pool of water.

We struggled to retain our strength, to fight against the iron madness that threatened our sanity and our survival. More iron was brought into our territory, but we held out. We fought the iron sickness—until the water dried up.

Now, we just fight.

*****

I gasped, air wheezing through my burning lungs with an unhealthy rattle. I came back to myself in a sudden rush of memories, struggling to pull back from the brink.

Every vision was a danger to my sanity, but touching the wisp had been worth that risk. I now knew why these wisps were behaving so strangely. Their homes had been threatened and they were hungry and suffering from iron sickness.

It was making them rabid.

"Ivy?" Jinx asked. "Ivy, wake up!"

"Jinx?" I asked, blinking away the last of the vision. What was she doing here? I'd made one hell of a diversion. Jinx and Sparky should have been in the next county by now. "Where's Sparky?"

"Back at the gates," she said. "He thinks he's playing a game of Houdini."

"You tied him up?" I asked.

I stood up too fast, and the junkyard started spinning. It didn't help that the wisps were still buzzing around like drunken fireflies.

"You got a better idea?" she asked.

Jinx was holding a loaded crossbow in one hand and a can of hairspray in the other. At least, it looked like Jinx's hairspray. It might have been roach killer. Not that insect spray would kill wisps, but it might slow them down.

I started to shake my head, but thought better of it. I needed all my senses if we were going to make it out of here in one piece. Jinx and I weren't likely to become wisp led, but I was sure my people had other weapons up their sleeves—most likely some hardcore magic ones. I just hoped they were too to iron sick to realize that.

"Nope, you did good," I said. "Let's get out of here."

I reached into my leather jacket, pulled out a heavy round object, and lobbed it into the opposite side of the clearing.

"Run!" I said.

Jinx's eyes went wide, but she ran, only stumbling once or twice. I was pretty sure that was a record for my unlucky friend.

"What did you throw?" she panted, running at my side toward the gate. "A grenade?"

"Nope," I said with a smile. "Honey."

Most fae have a sweet tooth, and I knew from my vision that these wisps were starving. The jar was supposed to be a gift for Marvin, a teenaged bridge troll who I owed with my life, but I'd buy him another jar. Maybe I could afford a jar if I scrounged up enough bottles. The redemption center was probably getting sick of the chick in dark sunglasses and hoodie. I practically lived there lately. Being broke sucked.

We reached the gates where Sparky was singing and spinning around the gate post, wrapped in a ribbon, as if dancing around a Maypole.

"So what was that all about anyway?" Jinx asked, running a hand over her hair.

Not that her hair was messy. She hairsprayed it within an inch of its life.

Jinx slung her crossbow over her shoulder like it was a new fashion accessory, and started untying Sparky. Not that the kid needed much help. The little demon had already worked his way through most of the knots.

"Is that the bow from your dress?" I asked, pointing at the ribbon.

"Ivy," she said, rolling her eyes. "I'm not giving up that easily. We almost got nuked by a gang of crazy, hung over wisps with bad attitudes. I'd say I've earned an explanation."

I sighed. She was right.

"They're not hung over, but they're definitely volatile," I said.

"So they're a group of psycho rogue wisps?" she asked, taking Sparky by the hand and giving the kid a lollipop. I really hoped that demon diabetes wasn't a thing, because the two of us were spoiling that kid.

I recalled what I'd learned from my vision, and shrugged. The wisps had reverted to the primal urges of wisps—and one of those instincts was to hunt their enemies by leading them away to the edges of battles, where they were often drowned or became lost in an unfamiliar landscape. Wisps are small fae, but no less deadly. I feared that Eben's watchman Bruce would not be finding his dog again, not alive anyway.

I explained my fears to Jinx.

"I need to find a way to move these wisps somewhere away from iron, somewhere safe," I said. "If I understood the wisp language, and knew how to command them, I'd be able to save the wisps, and the junkyard."

"Yeah, but you'd need your father, the king of the wisps, for that," Jinx said. "Last I knew you still didn't have any solid leads on where to find him."

"I may have one lead," I said, not meeting her eyes.

"Ivy?" she asked, waving a hand at me from head to toe. "Did body snatching aliens come and take you to their mother ship? 'Cause last I knew, my best friend shared important shit with me, like, you know, leads on finding her long-lost father."

"I can't talk about it," I said. "But if it pans out, you'll be the first to know."

"Fine, whatever," she said, stomping toward the street with Sparky on her hip. "Since you're so great at doing things on your own, I'll just leave you to inform my dad that his junkyard is crawling with iron sick fae."

Wisps don't actually crawl, not even sick ones, but I didn't correct her. She tossed me a "have fun with that" look over her shoulder, and kept on walking.

"Thanks a lot, Jinx," I muttered, but I couldn't blame her for being upset. I'd spent nearly every dime we had on locating my father. If I'd learned something new, she should have been the first to know. Too bad faerie law forbade me from telling her.

I sighed and trudged up the steps to the trailer Eben Braxton used as his on-site office. This wasn't going to be fun.

CHAPTER 7

Unlike Jinx, who could sweet talk an angry bugbear, I've never been all that good with people. It probably had something to do with growing up seeing monsters at every turn, and having seizures when someone gave me a hug.

The gifts from my father's side of the family—second sight and psychometry—had left me a bit prickly when it came to social situations. I'd rather work from the shadows than the limelight, and I'd rather be anywhere right now than inside Eben Braxton's tiny work trailer.

Eben's onsite office was an eight foot by twenty-eight-foot metal can with a desk, shelves, and file cabinets in the front, and a small bathroom and cot in the back. The entire place was filled with stacks of paper, plastic binders, and discarded work gloves, safety gear, and tools.

I shoved my hands in my pockets and stood before Eben's desk, avoiding the folding chair he used for guests. I wasn't about to touch the hardhat and walkie talkie that someone had left there, and I didn't feel much like sitting. The faster I got this over with the better.

"I'm finished with my assessment of the situation, for now," I said.

"That fast?" he asked.

He lifted dark eyebrows, and came around the desk. He started to reach out to shake my hand, but thought better of it. Good man.

"Your problem falls into my realm of expertise," I said.

That sounded better than saying he had a junkyard full of iron crazed faeries. Most humans, even the ones who thought that they were open minded, would have trouble wrapping their head around that claim.

"So Mitch wasn't off the wagon then," he said, stroking his beard. "Then what now?"

"This isn't something you and your men can handle," I said. "Stay out of the junkyard."

"Until when?" he asked, frowning down at me, his hands fisting at his sides.

Most people probably cowered beneath that glare. Not me. Not today.

"Until I say so," I said.

"Now listen here..." he said.

"No," I said, stepping into his personal space.

He stepped back, eyebrows raised. People don't expect a touch phobe like me to move into their guard. It puts them off balance. Off balance was good. I could work with that.

"No?" he asked.

"I'm done listening," I said. "We all have shit to whine about."

"Missy, you don't know the first thing..." he said, beard quivering.

"About what?" I asked. "Running a business? Funny, your daughter and I do just fine with that. Thank you very much. Or maybe you were going to say I don't know the first thing about loss? Responsibility? Sorry to disappoint you, but I've got those in spades."

"Fine," he said, rubbing a hand over his face. "I'll close up shop, and give my men a few days off. But this can't go on for long. I need an end date. When will this nightmare be over?"

"Soon," I said. "Give me until next week to sort things out. But Mr. Braxton? I need your word that no one enters that junkyard until I say it's clear."

"A week?" he asked, sputtering.

"Your word," I said, voice going icy.

"Fine, you have my word," he said. "But I expect you back here next week with an explanation."

"I'll do my best," I said, walking out the door.

I tipped my head back to look at the clouds rushing past the moon, and sighed. I just hoped I'd be alive to keep that appointment.

CHAPTER 8

My only chance of fixing the problem at the Braxton's junkyard hung on the slim hope that I'd find clues that would lead to my father, or another way to control my wisp powers, when I entered Faerie three days from now. The very thought sent a thrill of shivers up my spine.

If I could survive the trip through Tech Duinn and find my way into the wisp court, I may finally discover a way to communicate with my wisp brethren. If my father had left me any clues as to how to fulfill my destiny as wisp princess, it would be there at the seat of his power.

"I will make this right," I said, voice soft. "I promise you."

I turned, and started making my way back to the Old Port Quarter. Jinx had left without me. I just hoped she was back at the loft when I got there. I only had a few more days to patch things up with her. I didn't want to leave on bad terms with my best friend.

Just a few more days.

Oberon's eyes, one way or another, everything would change on the solstice. I could feel it in my bones.

At least I didn't have long to wait. It was nearly the summer solstice, the day that the druid Bechuille's prophetic words promised to lead me through Tech Duinn and into Faerie.

I shivered, pulling my jacket close around me. I'd replayed my trip to Mag Mell, and the druid's words, over and over again these past few months. Recalling that day was nearly as vivid as one of my visions.

"Good, now let me prepare the bones," she said.

Béchuille lifted her hand to the bird on her shoulder. I thought she was going to stroke its feathers or pet its head. I gasped as she grabbed the bird roughly in both hands and deftly broke its neck. I'd bought into the Hollywood image of druids as peaceful, animal loving, hippie types who commune with nature. I chided myself for being a fool.

The druid dropped the bird to the ground at her feet and poured a ladle of steaming liquid from the cauldron over its broken body. My eyes widened as the bird was quickly reduced to bone. Whatever was in that cauldron had eaten away all sign of feathers and flesh. So much for Mag Mell being an idyllic paradise; just try telling that to the bird.

"Béchuille's cauldron contains waters taken from the Fountain of Knowledge in Tír Tairngire," Torn whispered.

A bit late for him to be informing me of that now. I inched away from the fire, putting Torn between me and the cauldron.

While I changed my position, Béchuille stuffed the bird's bones into a leather pouch. She tied the pouch and shook it, making the bones rattle inside. I bit the inside of my cheek, and tried not to think about the pretty bird that had perched on the Tuatha Dé's shoulder mere seconds ago.

The druid stepped to an area beside the cauldron that was void of moss and flowers, and used a wooden staff to draw a circle on the bare ground. She tossed her head back, chanting, arms lifted to the sky. Her green eyes rolled back in her head, and I wondered idly what would happen if the woman fell into her own cauldron. Torn had claimed there was no such thing as death in Mag Mell, but I'd already witnessed the bird's demise.

Béchuille tossed the bones onto the ground with a clatter, and I snapped my eyes back to the circle. A low moan escaped the druid's lips, and Torn sidled up to me, chomping on his apple.

"I love this part," he said.

A breeze stirred the woman's golden hair, and her face paled to a sickly hue. She pointed a shaking finger at me, and a chill ran up my spine to creep into my scalp.

"The door you seek is one that hides," she said. "You must await midsummer tides. Upon the summer solstice when the moon doth wane, the wisp princess shall sit upon her throne again."

"Riddles?" I muttered. I should have known this wouldn't be easy.

"Shhh," Torn said.

"Muster your allies and gather your power," she said. "You must reach Tech Duinn's steps by the witching hour."

"Oh shit," Torn said.

"Shhh," I said.

"Brandish the key and do not lose heart," she said. "On solstice night the ocean shall part. Go to Martin's Point at final light of day, and the stones of Donner Isle will lead the way. Not by sea, but by land. You all will take your stand. To the house of Donn you must carry, king Will-o'-the-Wisp's key to Faerie. Inside Donn's hearth, bend your knee, close your eyes and turn the key."

The druid lowered her head, shoulders shaking, and scratched her foot across the edge of the circle. Once the circle was broken, the bones pulled together and began to sprout flesh and feathers once again. I gaped at the bird as it chirped and took wing.

Maybe death truly couldn't touch this place. After witnessing the bird's apparent death and rebirth, I didn't find that very reassuring. I was pretty sure that having your neck broken and the flesh boiled from your bones was unpleasant whether death followed or not.

"So I have to bring the key to Martin's Point at dusk on the summer solstice?" I asked.

The seer didn't answer. At closer scrutiny, I realized by the rise and fall of her chest that she'd fallen asleep on her feet.

"Let's go, Princess," Torn said.

The cat sidhe started walking toward the pathway from which we'd come. The bones and feathers adorning his leather clothing rattled as he sauntered away from the ring of standing stones. He swaggered confidently, but I wasn't fooled. Torn's face had paled at the mention of Tech Duinn.

"What is this Tech Duinn?" I asked. "And who is Donn?"

"Tech Duinn is the house of Donn," he said. Torn rubbed his chin and grimaced. "Celtic god of the dead."

For once I was in agreement with Torn. Oh shit.

I shook my head at the memory. I wasn't any more comfortable with the idea of sneaking into the house of Donn now than I'd been that day in Mag Mell. Too bad I was fresh out of options.

CHAPTER 9

It took me over an hour to walk from the junkyard to the Old Port Quarter. Jinx and Sparky probably took the bus. They didn't even have to worry about freaking out the other passengers with Sparky's appearance. The little demon could glamour himself whenever he wanted, the lucky devil.

Last time they went out shopping, Jinx carried Sparky in her purse, and he looked like a toy poodle. Humans with second sight were rare, so there wasn't much risk taking the kid out on the town. Not many people can see the true faces of the monsters that walk our streets. I was just one of the very, very unlucky ones who could.

Unlike Jinx and Sparky, I didn't like public transportation. I avoided the city bus and taxis like the plague. To me, they carried something worse than disease. Taxis and buses were infested with memories, making them a volatile place for the rare individual with a psychometric gift. Your average car or truck wasn't much better. No, I'd rather take my chances walking the dark streets.

By the time I reached Madam Kaye's Magic Emporium, I had a stitch in my side and my calves were aching. I worked out daily, moving through the self-defense moves and katas that Jenna, my Hunter friend, had taught me, but I'd cut back on my normal runs along the harbor. It's hard to keep up your usual routine when you're playing dead.

I still would have been fine, if it hadn't been for the dog that chased me for six blocks. Some dogs could sense that I was other, and this one didn't want a monster in his territory. I couldn't blame him. The dog was just protecting the ones he loved, so I ran until he gave up.

All that running got me back to Harborsmouth faster than I'd planned, which meant I was on Kaye's doorstep well before normal business hours. I could keep on walking to the loft apartment that I shared with Jinx, or I could take my chances with a grouchy witch. Either way, I was likely going to face a fight. At least here I might get some answers as to what

I could expect on my trip to Faerie, a subject that was still off limits with Jinx.

I tilted my head back, studying the stone building until I saw a familiar silhouette atop the roof.

"Hey, Humphrey!" I shouted, cupping my gloved hands around my mouth. "How's it hangin'?"

Anyone walking or driving by would think I was another of the countless drunks, walking off a night of bar hopping through the Old Port Quarter. After two in the morning, the streets filled with the inebriated, and those who preyed upon them. If someone or something decided that I was an easy mark, they'd be in for a few surprises—including Sharp and Pointy. I hadn't yet used my silver and iron blades tonight, and I could use the practice.

I heard the scrape of stone claws a split-second before Humphrey's face came within inches of my own.

"Don't look now, but you left your eyes burning," Humphrey said, his voice like rocks in an avalanche.

Crap. Humphrey was right. His face was lit with a yellow glow that wasn't coming from the nearby streetlamp. I ducked deeper within the shadows of my hoodie, and angled my face away from the street.

"Thanks for the tip, Humphrey," I said. "As always, you rock."

The gargoyle laughed at my lame attempt at humor, and I tried not to wince. Humphrey's laugh was like an earthquake. Thankfully, due to his glamour, I was the only person who could hear him. Anyone else would just see a normal stone gargoyle perched above the occult shop's door. No one seemed to notice or care that the gargoyle wasn't always in the same place.

Maybe they thought Kaye liked to mess with her customers by moving the statue around. It was definitely the kind of thing she'd do. The witch did like to screw with people.

"Come in, dear, the door's open," Kaye's voice came from Humphrey's mouth, which was beyond unsettling.

The door clicked open, and I sighed and shook my head. Case in point. There was no reason for Kaye to use the gargoyle like a hand puppet, other than trying to mess with my head.

Humphrey shuddered, and cleared his throat. I was suddenly glad of my hood, or I would have been pelted in the face with dust and pebbles. When a gargoyle coughs, it's best not to be too close to his face.

"You okay, Humphrey dude?" I asked.

"Fine, fine," he muttered. He waved his hand like it was no big deal, but his ears were pressed against his skull like a pissed off cat. For the millionth time, I was glad that I wasn't one of Kaye's employees. "Go on in."

"I better not keep Kaye waiting," I said, passing beneath the gargoyle and through the open door. "I don't want to rock the boat."

I was running out of witty ways to use rock and stone in a sentence, but the gargoyle seemed amused. I smiled, and walked inside the shop, careful not to stumble into anything in the dark. My fae blood gave me better night vision than a regular human, but it still took my eyes a few seconds to adjust.

Humphrey's laughter cut off as the door slammed shut behind me. Flames shot up from every candle in the store, which was an impressive number with this being an occult shop, and I blinked at the sudden brightness. More of Kaye's parlor tricks.

I shook my head, and angled off to the right, passing the registers and heading into the back of the store. Kaye's shop was filled with occult bric-a-brac—tarot cards, packets of herbs, polished stones, plastic skeletons, brooms, and pointy hats—all the usual suspects. What you wouldn't find displayed for the general public were any truly powerful occult objects. Those were safely hidden behind closed doors.

Kaye was mischievous as a pixy, but she wasn't a fool.

The witch was not only wise, she'd also recently regained the full strength of her powers, thanks to dying and being brought back to life with a magic apple supplied by yours truly. I wasn't the only one who'd recently pulled that stunt, but since the island of Emain Ablach had been flooded, and the apple tree destroyed, I was pretty sure we were the last.

I'd obtained two magic apples, and Kaye and I had died—her from willingly imbibing poison, and me from assassins' arrows in my vital organs—and were resurrected. The reason for my rebirth was obvious—I was bleeding out and my friends had tried to save my life. Kaye had gone through all of that because of a bargain I'd been tricked into that required me to kill her. It was that or Jinx would die.

If it hadn't been for the magic apples, I would have been stuck between a rock and a harder rock. Humphrey would appreciate that.

Thankfully, in Kaye's case, resurrection had the beneficial side effect of removing the tattoos that marked her skin and kept a stranglehold on her powers. The witch was given a clean slate—a fact that gave me chills when I thought about it too hard. Kaye was my friend, but that kind of power was dangerous.

I'd heard stories of Kaye's exploits from her youth, and I'd been impressed. She'd partnered with the Hunters' Guild, and brought down some badass supernatural beasties. But she'd been more innocent then. I wasn't sure what the older, wiser woman would do with that kind of power.

Magic has checks and balances for a reason.

I reached for the latch on the back counter, the entrance into Kaye's lair, and jumped as a dark, furry shape landed in front of me. Midnight, Kaye's cat, started to purr, and I gave him a quick scratch behind the ear. I wasn't too worried about getting visions from Midnight. It takes strong emotions to leave a psychic imprint, and cats usually didn't care enough about the world around them to give me visions.

I'd explained that once to Torn, and he'd taken it as an invitation. I'd introduced his man parts to Sharp and Pointy, and he backed off. I don't mind cats, but I wasn't about to let their sociopathic immortal lord touch me. I wasn't suicidal.

Plus, I was courting the local kelpie king, which meant that I was off limits. Not that my relationship status ever curbed Torn's flirting, much to Ceff's chagrin. My boyfriend would also be frustrated with where I was right now, which was why I hadn't told anyone about my plans to make a detour on the way home. There was no sense giving the poor guy an ulcer.

Ceff worried about the faerie courts discovering that death was an affliction that I'd recovered from, and he'd warned against frequenting my usual haunts. I'd avoided the Emporium lately, but I needed to ask Kaye a few questions. Not that information was the only reason why I was here.

I knew better than most just how fragile life was. I'd died once, and we were fresh out of magic apples. If it happened again, I wasn't coming back.

I needed to say goodbye to my friends, just in case.

I gave Midnight one last scratch, and started toward Kaye's spell kitchen.

"Better move quick, dear, unless you want a kiss," Kaye shouted from somewhere inside the kitchen.

My boot had barely crossed the threshold when a set of large, hairy lips descended toward me. A kiss? Those lips were big enough to swallow me whole.

I ducked, and rolled between two legs the size of tree trunks. My knives hit my palms as I sprung to my feet, making Marvin and Hob stop dead in their tracks. Marvin's eyes were wide with surprise, but Hob's twinkled. The brownie must have put my bridge troll friend up to this nonsense, I just knew it.

"What are you two doing?" I asked, voice ringing loud in my ears.

I could have stabbed my friends with iron, the fools.

"Mistletoe," Marvin said, pointing a large hand toward a sprig of something green hanging above the door.

I gave an involuntary shudder, and stepped further from the door. Mistletoe was pure evil. Not only was the plant poisonous if eaten, but most people thought it meant mandatory kissing, which was a nightmare for a touch phobe like me. Even worse, mistletoe reminded me of the sacrificial murders I'd witnessed on the winter solstice.

I'd seen enough of that damn plant to last a lifetime.

"Don't worry, dear," Kaye said. "It's not the real thing. Only a plastic ornament that Hob found while dusting and sorting the solstice decorations."

Yeah, I was sure he just innocently came across that ornament. Mab save us all from bored hearth brownies and gullible bridge trolls.

"Should e seen ye face, lass," Hob said, slapping his knee with his hat, and letting out a whoop of laughter.

"No kiss?" Marvin asked.

The teenaged bridge troll blushed, and ducked his head. He was well over six feet tall and wide as an ox, but the kid was still shy, even around his new friends. I wasn't good around people either, but make no mistake, Marvin was a friend. One of the best.

I'd witnessed the beating that the kid had suffered at the hands of the *each uisge*—that vision still haunted me—but I'd never touched Marvin. I'd managed to get that vision off a carnival token, and since then I'd given the kid a wide berth. Marvin had survived one of the worst beatings I'd ever seen, all while trying to survive on the streets after his father's death left him an orphan. He'd suffered a lot of pain, and I hadn't wanted to relive that.

I'd been a selfish fool.

It's funny how clear things seem when you're facing down death. Love and friendship, those were the things that were important. My own selfish fears no longer mattered.

"I think someone owes me a kiss," I said.

I forced myself to smile, and walked up to Marvin, standing on tiptoe so the kid wouldn't have to kneel to kiss my cheek.

"On the lips, lad, on the lips!" Hob heckled.

Marvin shook his head, and rubbed the back of his neck.

"Nah," he said. "Don't want a rash."

Wait, what?

Marvin didn't give me any more time to think about his comment. He leaned in, and gave me a big, wet kiss on the cheek. I had enough time to think that the kid needed some practice kissing girls, and then the vision dragged me under.

Except for a few fond memories from Marvin's childhood, the vision was predictably sad. He'd lost his father, his home, and been beaten to within an inch of his life by vicious water fae. The beating went on forever, and I bit the inside of my cheek to keep from losing my sense of self. As it was, I'd never forget the feeling of being a child alone on the streets, my blood leaking into the ground as the *each uisge* knocked out my teeth, and broke my bones.

Hot tears leaked out of my eyes, and I remembered that I had a body of my own, one that wasn't beaten and torn. I fought my way to the surface of the vision, struggling to keep my sanity—struggling to stay me. I caught one last glimpse of memory, this one a proud moment when Marvin launched a pixie nest at a man who was making other children suffer.

I knew from Marvin's steely determination that he would never let another child suffer like he had. The pride and fear I felt for Marvin helped to pull me back to myself, a separate being with my own mind and body.

I gasped, eyes flying open to see Marvin's worried face. I gave him a thumbs up, and he lifted his chin and beamed from ear to ear. Let the kid think the kiss had knocked my socks off. He could use the ego boost, and it wasn't a total lie. It had certainly been one hell of an experience.

He thrust out his chest and strode over to where Hob perched wide-eyed.

"Why didn't ye kiss the lass on the lips?" Hob asked.

His furry brow was furrowed, and his knobby hands were fisted on his hips. Honestly, I think the curmudgeonly old brownie was just ticked off because his little game hadn't turned out the way he wanted. Hob probably expected Marvin to end up with a tongue lashing from Kaye, or a fist in the face from yours truly.

Hob and Marvin were friends, but brownies were mischievous, Hob more than most. If I had to guess, I'd say it was from living beneath Kaye's hearth. The old witch was rubbing off on him.

Marvin shook his head, and smiled.

"Didn't want poison ivy," he said. "Itches worse than pixie spit."

Clever kid. Poison Ivy was Marvin's nickname for me, and he never tired of making jokes about my prickly nature. It was his way of making light of my touch phobia, and giving an excuse for not getting too close. Now he'd used it as a reason to avoid kissing me on the lips, to which I was grateful. I thought of the kid like a younger brother. It would have been creepy if he'd tried to kiss me on the lips, not that Hob cared a wit.

"Okay now," Kaye said, the bells on her skirt jingling as she bustled across the kitchen. "You boys have had your fun. How about we let Ivy sit down, and we can all enjoy a cup of tea."

I raised an eyebrow, but took a seat on the bench that ran down one side of a long, wooden table. The table straddled the modern kitchen that was the witch's domain, and the old world style room that held Hob-o'-Waggle's hearth. I set a shiny toy airplane that I'd made from a piece of aluminum foil on Hob's side of the table.

It would be foolish to enter a hearth brownie's territory without providing a gift. You just have to make sure not to give the gift of clothing, or the diminutive faerie might take offense. A pissed off brownie was likely to tie your hair into pixie locks while you slept, and leave you with a cold, empty hearth. I didn't want to be on a receiving end of Hob's wrath, or Kaye's either, for that matter. I was pretty sure forgiveness

would be low on her to-do list, if I sent her hearth brownie
packing.

"Here ye go, lass," Hob said.

A cup of tea appeared before me, as if by magic, and
with a flash the tiny plane disappeared into one of the pockets
of Hob's patchwork coat. Brownies can move faster than the
human eye, even faster than my enhanced sight, making them
nearly invisible when they wanted to be. Jinx once commented
that Hob was like a kitchen ninja, and I had to agree.

"Are you prepared for the solstice?" Kaye asked, sitting
on the opposite side of the table and sipping her tea.

"I was born ready," I said with forced bravado. Fake it
'till you make it, right?

"You haven't told that human girl, have you?" she
asked.

I sighed, and rubbed a hand over my face. Kaye never
cared for Jinx, but her attitude toward my best friend had
tipped into open disdain when Jinx started dating Forneus.
She thought that Jinx was nothing more than a silly, clumsy
human who made bad decisions. In other words, Kaye saw
Jinx as a liability. In the past, I'd tried to argue that Jinx
couldn't be held responsible for being unlucky, but Kaye
wouldn't listen.

I considered explaining that Forneus was actually a
good match for Jinx, but I'd rather choke on my own tongue.
Forneus had vowed to protect Jinx, and his love for her was
obvious, but I still had a hard time accepting the troublesome
demon. I wasn't quite ready to become his staunch defender,
though I'd already given him a letter to open if he didn't hear
from me in a week's time. I'd left him strict instructions that if
I didn't make it back from Faerie, he was to take care of Jinx,
or I'd come back from the grave and kill him myself.

"No, Kaye," I said. "I haven't told *Jinx* about Faerie.
And I don't plan on it. I'm not going to paint a target on my
best friend's back."

I also didn't need to get any higher up on the faerie
court's shit list. No matter how much I wanted to let my best
friend in on my plan, telling Jinx about my father's key to
Faerie was not an option.

"Good," she said. "Now drink your tea before it gets
cold."

I gulped my tea, and grimaced. I didn't recognize the bitter taste, never a good thing when drinking tea in a witch's kitchen. I just hoped that Hob hadn't intentionally tried to poison me. Maybe he didn't like the gift I'd given him after all.

"Hob, is there anything you want me to bring you back from Faerie?" I asked.

I wasn't opposed to a little bribery, if it kept our resident hearth brownie happy.

"Just bring yeself back in one piece, lass," he said, shaking his head. "And get this mess with the courts straightened out. Olga says that the gnomes can't sleep for all the hollerin and singin the pookahs be makin over your death."

Olga was Hob's sweetheart. The female gnome was one of a clan I'd helped to relocate to my mother and stepfather's garden out in the suburbs. I'd also given a pack of pookahs my old tree house in return for helping us fight the *each uisge*. I wasn't sure if the party loving pookahs were really mourning my death, or just wanted an excuse for one of their drunken orgies. With pookahs, it might be a bit of both.

"Sorry," I said with a wince. "You haven't told anyone that I'm alive, have you?"

"No, lass, not even dear Olga," he said. "Though it pains me to keep a secret from her."

I fidgeted with my teacup, staring at the leather gloves covering my hands. I knew from experience just how difficult it was to keep secrets from the people we loved. Some days it seemed like I'd spent my entire life living a lie.

I pushed aside the tea and stood, every muscle protesting as I slowly came to my feet. I ran a hand through my hair, wondering what to say next. I wasn't going to kid myself. This might be the last time I saw my friends. Faerie was a dangerous place where the local flora and fauna would likely kill me and then fight over who got to eat my corpse and pick their teeth with my bones.

"I'm no good at goodbyes," I said, rubbing the back of my neck.

"Till next time then, lass," Hob said.

"Until we meet again, dear," Kaye said.

"Yeah, um, I'll miss you guys," I said.

"You're coming back, right?" Marvin asked, looking back and forth, watching our somber faces in confusion.

"I..." I said, my throat choking on the words.

Somehow, after all he'd been through, Marvin remained the most innocent of us all. I loved him for that. He had a way of seeing the beauty in a world that I'd long ago decided was too ugly to look at.

Saying goodbye to Marvin was the hardest of all.

"I'll try, big guy," I said.

For Marvin, I would try. That kid had lost everyone, and I refused to add to his pain. I'd fight to survive, and I'd wear my hands to bloody stumps digging my way out of the grave, but there were no guarantees that Marvin would see me again. I couldn't promise to return. I refused to lie to the kid—he deserved better than that.

"Remember, dear," Kaye said, pretending not to see my tears. "Your father's key leads to a back door, a secret entrance to his demesne. Entry will not be easy."

"No, I don't expect it to be," I said. I wiped my face, and shook my head. "Nothing associated with Faerie is ever easy."

"At least you've learned that, if nothing else," she said with a satisfied nod.

"So this back door, you think it'll dump me in my father's study—like a hidden entrance behind a bookcase?" I said.

I forced a laugh, but it came out flat.

This wasn't an episode of Scooby Doo, and we both knew it. Hidden doorways wouldn't open behind a bookcase into a nice, safe office, and the monsters wouldn't just be bumbling thieves wearing Halloween masks. The closest I'd come to jumping out from a secret tunnel behind a bookcase and unmasking my enemies, would be using my second sight to see through their glamour—to see monsters who wanted to eat my face. A tidy mission that wrapped up without someone shedding blood was a happy fantasy.

"I don't know where the portal will spit you out, how close or how far away from the wisp court, but be wary of Mab's minions," she said. "The wisp court is in Nithsdale, within the shadow of the ice palace, Mab's seat of power."

"But Mab left Faerie over two hundred years ago, along with Oberon and Titania," I said.

"The queen of cold and darkness doesn't need to be within the Faerie realms to be a threat," she said. "Her influence is widespread, but nowhere is she so revered as the

Unseelie lands of Faerie. Heed my warning, and stay away from the Ice palace and the Forest of Torment."

"With a name like, 'Forest of Torment', how can I resist?" I asked with mock bravado.

"Ivy," she said, eyes hard.

"I'm kidding, sorry," I said.

"Good," she said with a sigh. "The Forest of Torment is said to be sentient, and steeped in evil. The frozen trees guard the way to the Ice palace, keeping unwanted guests out by dismembering intruders, and drinking the blood of Mab's enemies."

Got it. No trips to the Ice palace.

"So, what do you know about Nithsdale?" I asked.

"Only that it is a dangerous place, as all the Unseelie lands are, but the Wisp Court is said to be a kind of paradise for the smaller Unseelie creatures," she said.

"A paradise?" I asked.

That didn't sound so bad.

"So long as you don't mind being surrounded by a bog that belches poisonous gas, and swallows men whole," she said.

Of course, it had a deadly bog. We were talking about a wisp paradise after all.

"Sounds like fun," I said. "Home sweet home. Anything else I should know?"

I ducked quickly beneath the mistletoe and into the passageway outside the spell kitchen, but shot Kaye one last glance over my shoulder, eyebrows raised. The witch stared back, lips in a tight line, and I knew the answer was grim.

"Humans who enter Faerie rarely return," she said. "In the Wisp Court, you will need to rely on the power within your blood, if you ever wish to see Harborsmouth again."

I sighed, and waved one last goodbye as I made my way to the exit. Needing to embrace my fae half was not a comforting thought. I wanted to go home—to the loft, not some fae infested swamp—crawl into bed, and hide under the blankets. Either that or go count my weapons. Instead, I readied myself for what might be one last night with my boyfriend.

I'd died once before, and faced death a number of times in the past. I knew all about regrets. This time, I was going to make the best of what time I had left.

CHAPTER 10

I brushed my hair, getting ready for my date. I didn't usually take the extra effort, but tonight was different. I wanted to make it extra special.

I had even managed to sneak in a few hours of beauty sleep this afternoon. Maybe I was still dreaming.

Jinx was leaning against the door to my room as if we never had our fight in the junkyard. In fact, she was acting as if I'd never told her about the lead I had on finding my father. I was happy to put our fight behind us, but the way she ignored the entire conversation put me on edge.

I was sure she was just waiting for a chance to get me back for keeping secrets. Oh well. If those secrets kept her safe, I was willing to cope with the awkwardness, and her eventual revenge.

"You should see if that hot piece of kelpie king you call a boyfriend has any new leads on your father," Jinx said, waggling her eyebrows.

The waggling was for Ceffyl Dwr, not my father. At least I hoped she didn't have the hots for my dad. For a moment, I was actually happy she was dating Forneus. Jinx had a thing for bad boys, and my father's curse put him squarely in bad boy territory.

"I'll ask Ceff when I see him tonight," I said.

"Tonight?" she asked.

"Yes," I said, tilting my head to get a better look at her. "It's date night, remember?"

"Oh crap," she said. "I haven't even decided what to wear."

Jinx ran to her room, and I frowned. She must have been more worried about the wisp infestation at her father's junkyard than I'd thought. Either that or she was really distracted plotting her revenge. With my luck, it was probably the latter.

Date night had been her idea. It had been difficult to see Ceff lately, since with me being dead he had no reason to come by the apartment. A kelpie king had no business with a human woman, not unless he decided to drown her, eat her flesh, and pick his teeth with her bones. Thankfully, Ceff didn't make a habit of eating my friends, but it didn't help with a cover story.

So Ceff and I slunk around, meeting in dark alleys and ritzy hotels. The dark alleys were all I could afford, but they weren't very romantic. They also tended to be crawling with the prying eyes of the fae and the undead. That meant that occasionally, Ceff managed to talk me into dressing like socialites and meeting in classy hotels.

I didn't like that the hotels were on his dime, but I also couldn't risk the kinds of visions that ran rampant inside the seedier dive hotels that were within my budget. For tonight, he'd picked a new swanky place uptown.

That meant shimmying into a long, red cocktail dress and donning satin opera gloves. For once, I looked like the princess that I was.

I'd have preferred my leather gloves, but they wouldn't have gone with the dress. My new, Clurichaun crafted leather jacket—a gift from Ceff to replace the one I'd lost in the Otherworld realm of Emain Ablach—was another story. I shrugged it on over my dress and slid on a pair of dark sunglasses. Maybe people would think I was a celebrity out for a night on the town.

Of course, most celebrities didn't go out armed to battle monsters. If my Hunter friend Jenna had taught me anything, it was to never go unarmed. In addition to the anti-fae charms I kept stashed in my jacket pockets, I wore iron and silver throwing knives strapped to each thigh. This dress wouldn't be easy to run in, but the slit up the side gave me access to my weapons. I piled my dark hair on top of my head, and held it in place with two sharp, wooden hair sticks that would double as stakes.

The fae were the ones gunning for me, but you couldn't be too careful. As Jenna was fond of saying, a good vampire is a staked vampire. My Hunter friend may be on another continent, but I still listened to her advice.

Satisfied that I was dolled up enough to enter the Stanton Hotel without getting kicked out and, more importantly, that I didn't look a thing like myself, I grabbed my keys and headed for the door. But at a knock from the other side, I froze.

I may be in disguise, but it wouldn't be hard to guess who I was while standing in my own apartment. I tiptoed to Jinx's bedroom, and ducked my head inside.

"Someone's at the door," I said.

"I'm sure it's just Forneus," she said. "I'll get it."

Jinx was wearing a retro style mini dress that managed to look both cute and sexy. She'd used hot rollers to give her black hair old-school movie star waves and her lips were coated in glossy, red lipstick that matched her nails and her shoes. Her bangs, of course, were curled under and sprayed within an inch of their life.

Forneus was in for a night of drooling.

"You two going out?" I asked.

"Nope," she said with a wink.

I shook my head, and tried not to look around her bedroom while I waited for Jinx to get the door. I did not need fodder for my nightmares. Forneus' comments were usually bad enough. I peeked out into the loft in time to see Jinx open the door for her date.

I'd rather it was a horde of assassins.

"Darling, you look ravishing," Forneus said as Jinx stepped aside to let the demon into our home.

I wasn't keen on Jinx's main squeeze being of the Hell persuasion, but then again, I couldn't cast stones. I'd welcomed Sparky into our home, so I couldn't very well tell Forneus he wasn't welcome. Not unless he did something to hurt Jinx. Then all bets were off.

"Good, because I intend to be ravished," she said, tilting her head back to stare up into Forneus' dark gaze. "It is date night, after all. A girl has expectations."

He let out a barely contained growl, and bent down to pull my roommate in for a kiss. I coughed, and stepped out into the loft before the two of them went any further.

"Hey, Forneus," I said.

He stiffened, pulling away from Jinx.

"Miss Granger," he said.

"Ivy's on her way out," Jinx said. "Right, Ivy?"

"Yeah, yeah," I said, striding across the loft. "You two have fun. You too, Sparky."

Sparky's reply was a round of snores coming from the dog bed beside the couch, but Forneus' words made me cringe.

"Oh we intend to, Miss Granger," he said, licking his lips.

I swallowed hard, stepping through the door and into the stairwell, Forneus' laughter ringing in my ears. If I took the stairs two at a time, who could blame me?

CHAPTER 11

The Stanton Hotel was Ceff's grandest choice yet. We stood at the front desk while Ceff convinced the receptionist that he'd scanned the credit card and paid for the room in full. The "card" was a dried piece of kelp, but for once, I wasn't going to argue faerie morality. We could do that over dinner, another thing we'd likely pay for with seaweed and driftwood.

I didn't like fooling innocent mortals, but I was a supposedly dead half-breed wisp princess who really needed a night out with her significant other. My life was beyond complicated right now, and I was hungry. Faeries may not have to worry about high blood pressure, but low blood sugar was raising hell with at least one of my halves. Dinner and a romantic evening in a brand new five-star hotel sounded like just the ticket for regaining sanity.

I was admiring the fish tank that rose from the center of the marble floor that took up half the room, while Ceff finished "paying" for our room. At first, I thought the fish tank may have been why Ceff picked this place, until I noticed his scowl.

Ceff gave the tank the stink eye, and I sighed. He wouldn't care about the fish swimming inside the tank. He was a predator of the sea, after all. No, that look probably meant that some poor water faerie had managed to get caught in a fisherman's net, eventually being deposited in this gilded cage of an aquarium tank.

I took a deep breath, and tamped down my disappointment. By the look on Ceff's face, we'd be spending our date night trying to free a captured water fae. Oh well, if that's what he wanted, I was in. It's not like we could be having hot sex in our suite if a cute sea monkey of a faerie was trapped down here in the lobby fish tank. Even though both of us were Unseelie fae, the kind of faeries with ties to the dark side, neither of us was wired like that.

Ceff had moved closer to the glass, and I sidled up beside him.

"So which one are we rescuing?" I asked.

I had the rare gift of second sight, the ability to see through both vampire glamour and faerie glamour, but the creatures in the tank all looked like tropical fish. To me, a lot of things from the sea looked alien. I was half land fae and I'd grown up human. I hadn't even known about my fae blood until recently, although it explained some of my more unusual abilities.

Staring at the aquarium didn't give me any answers, so I focused on Ceff. His forehead was damp, either from sweat or water magic, but his lip curved in a light grin and he raised an eyebrow at my question.

"There are none who need rescuing here," he said.

"Then what do you see?" I asked. He tilted his head at me, as if wondering if I was toying with him, but I just shrugged. "They all look like weird fish to me."

It probably wasn't the nicest or most eloquent thing for someone who was dating a water fae to say, but oh well. Ceff was used to my brusqueness. He said my candor was as refreshing as a northern tide. I suppose when you deal with scheming water fae clans all day, the rude half-human's honesty might make up for her bad manners. Pureblood faeries cannot tell an outright lie, but that just meant that over the past several millennia they'd perfected the art of talking around the truth.

As I suspected, Ceff didn't take offense. Instead, he tilted back his head and laughed. The melodic sound ran over me like dancing fingers, and I shivered with pleasure. There were few things as beautiful in this world as the laughter of the water fae.

"Do you see that one there, the creature hiding in the shadows of the pirate ship?" he asked.

"The black spiny one?" I asked.

The thing looked like some kind of sea anemone, and it seemed to be emitting a cloud of darkness similar to squid ink.

"Yes, that is no fish," he said. "That one is fae."

"What kind of fae is he?" I asked.

Okay, I had no idea if the faerie was male or female, but with all those spines I defaulted to the male pronoun.

"That one is so old, we no longer sing his name," he said. "But some call him Ship Breaker."

The water fae, though spread out across the world, all shared the same back yard. The oceans may be vast, but water was connected. It bound them in a way that I hadn't yet seen in the air or land fae, and helped them pass along knowledge from one clan to the next. If Ceff didn't know this faerie's name, it was because it was long forgotten or the creature was particularly tight-lipped. In a world where names held power and most creatures were immortal, either was a possibility.

"Well, all he has in there is a ceramic pirate ship," I said. "The management may not like it if he breaks it, but it doesn't make him a menace."

"Ship Breaker is known for living on the rotting hulls of shipwrecks, the carcasses of his most recent kills," he said. "He often sleeps for centuries at a time, but when he awakens...he hungers."

Okay, that did not sound good. My hand went to one of the blades strapped beneath my dress and my mouth went dry.

"Is it safe for the hotel's humans?"

Heck, I wasn't sure if that creature was safe for the city. Ship Breaker may be small, but size was deceptive with the fae. I didn't doubt that he got his name dragging ships down into the darkest depths of the sea where he devoured their men and cargo. There was something about the sleeping beast that, now that Ceff had drawn my attention to it, sent a chill racing up my spine.

"The hotel's guests and staff should be fine, but whoever cleans the tank could be at risk," he said. "Saltwater tanks take more finesse than freshwater. They must hire someone to come in and maintain it for them."

"Do you think you could persuade a water fae to come take the job?"

"Perhaps," he said. "I know a selkie woman who might do so for the chance to spend time in the city."

"Ask her," I said. "And let me know if you need help convincing the hotel to change vendors. My stepfather works for the city. Maybe one of his friends can do something."

My stepfather didn't know about the fae, but my mom did. Together, we could figure something out. Of course, with me dead, getting together to conspire would be difficult, but I never let a little obstacle like fae assassins stop me. Well, except for the ten minutes I lay dead in Kaye's spell kitchen.

I took a shaky breath, and pulled Ceff from the fish tank. When we were a few feet away, I blushed. I was wearing my gloves, but the satin made me feel naked.

"I am sorry," he said. "Before the receptionist saw to securing our room, you mentioned that you had a question for me."

I reached out, running one satin finger along Ceff's lips, and let a hungry smile spread across my face.

"We can talk later," I said. "Right now, there's something else I want to do."

Ceff's eyes glowed green behind his glamour and he bowed his head, kissing my hand through the thin glove. Warmth spread down my arm and to other places and, before I could blink, we were in the elevator.

Even in his human form, Ceff could move fast when he wanted to. And right now, we both really, really wanted to be in our hotel suite.

Thankfully, there was no one sharing the elevator with us, since right about then my eyes began to glow. Even if Ceff hadn't sucked in a sudden breath, I would have known by the two shining balls of light reflecting off the metal elevator wall.

"I'm glowing, aren't I?" I asked.

He nodded, and I sighed. I fished my sunglasses out of my jacket pocket, thankful we hadn't crushed them. A few minutes more and they'd have been pulverized. I slid the sunglasses on just as we reached our floor.

Ceff held the door for me, even though the iron content in the metal must have burned, and we hurried to our room. Ceff fumbled with the door key, a magnetic swipe card, swearing something under his breath about new technology, and then we were inside.

As the door closed behind us, I licked my lips, taking in the hot tub set into the floor. I should have balked at the extravagance, and a small inner voice chastised me for risking visions in a strange, albeit new, hotel, but I slipped off my sunglasses and shrugged out of my jacket. Next, I unzipped my dress, letting it pool onto the floor at my feet.

In three days time, we would risk our lives attempting to enter Faerie. This might be our last chance to be together. I planned to make it memorable.

With a Jacuzzi and a sexy water fae in the same room, it was memorable indeed.

CHAPTER 12

I floated in a haze of happiness, tracing patterns across Ceff's muscular chest. His body was marked by scars, physical reminders of his time in captivity, but he no longer flinched away when I touched the raised, waxy skin. We'd come a long way, he and I, me with the touching and him with the not flinching.

For a moment, I forgot about faerie assassins and Celtic gods of the dead. I watched the rise and fall of Ceff's chest, and imagined a lifetime of waking up with this beautiful man at my side.

Ceff gripped my hand, stilling its path along his skin and rousing me from my daydream. I tilted my head back, expecting a kiss, but instead, he sat upright. The motion did mesmerizing things to his abdominal muscles, and it was with herculean effort that I pulled my attention away from his rippling stomach. When my eyes finally met Ceff's, I flinched.

Rather than the passion or playfulness I'd expected to see, his face showed only signs of worry. Frown lines creased his forehead, and his lips were tight.

"What's wrong?" I asked, pushing myself up on one elbow.

It wasn't easy, not with the death grip Ceff still had on my hand, but I managed. When we were alone together, we often went out of our way to remain touching. I was used to it. It was the only way to avoid unnecessary rounds of visions. But something about the way Ceff was holding my hand seemed different this time.

For one thing, he didn't normally cut off the circulation.

"Ceff?" I asked, trying to keep my voice light.

"I...we...I fear we may be underestimating the dangers of entering your father's court," he said.

Was that a tremor in his voice? Even while being tortured with cold iron, Ceff hadn't shown fear. Not like this.

"I know the risks," I said. "I'm not stupid. I just don't see any other choice."

"No, of course, you are not stupid," he said. He looked pained, or constipated. Since he was searching my face as if I held the secret of life, I was going with pained. "I am doing this all wrong."

"Doing what?" I asked.

He looked away, suddenly absorbed with the shape of my hip. It was a nice hip, according to Ceff, but I got the feeling I was missing something. Usually, when he ogles my body, he looks alive with passion...not ready to throw up.

If this went on much longer, I was going to get a complex.

"Before we face certain death, there is something I must ask you," he said.

"You can ask me anything," I said. "You know that."

He nodded, but didn't look up.

"As you know, I have only courted you these few short months, an eye blink in our immortal lifespan," he said.

I waited, but he didn't continue. Sweat beaded on his brow, and a sliver of fear began twisting my insides.

"I know it is unfair of me..." he said.

Oh, Mab's bloody bones. Was he breaking up with me? I mean, I know the last few months hadn't been easy, what with one dangerous situation after another, but I thought our relationship was good. I thought we were good. When all of my beliefs had been turned upside down—who I was, what I was—my relationship with Ceff had been unwavering. I had come to believe that he was the one solid, true thing in this crazy, new life I was living.

I was a fool.

"Ivy," he said.

I looked up, as if against my will. There is power in a name, especially for those of us with fae blood, but that's not what lifted my chin like a marionette on a string. The husky sound of Ceff's voice when he said my name was like a drug. I was an addict, and if this was to be my final fix, I would savor every last painful moment of it.

Damn, I was in over my head.

"Does it pain you so much to consider it?" he asked, reaching out to cup my chin with his free hand.

I frowned. Of course, it pained me. He was leaving me, the bastard.

"How did you think I'd react?" I asked, pushing myself up and punching him hard.

It wasn't easy with Ceff still holding my other hand to his chest. Oberon's balls, I could still feel the rapid beat of his heart beneath my palm, though my fingers were going numb from the vice-like grip.

"I had hoped that our love was more important than mere etiquette," he said.

I clenched my fist, wishing I had something more than pillows to beat the man with. Too bad I'd shed my knives with my clothes. Wait.

"Did you say that you love me?" I asked.

"Yes, of course," he said. "I love you more than the tides love the moon. You are the center of my universe. You are my gravity. Without you, I float aimlessly, lashed at by volatile currents—a man with no heart and no purpose."

His eyes flashed green with passion, lending truth to his words. Not that I needed his eyes as confirmation. A pureblooded faerie cannot tell a bald-faced lie.

"You love me," I said.

"Yes."

"Then why?" I asked. I shook my head. "What etiquette are you talking about?"

"My love, the guidelines are very clear on rules of matrimony," he said. "But in our current situation, and after having lost you once already, I had thought you might be willing to ignore the impropriety..."

I held a finger to his lips, cutting off his words.

"Are you asking me to marry you?" I asked.

"Yes," he said, eyes searching mine. His muscles tensed, as if readying himself for a painful blow, but he continued on. "Ivy Granger, daughter of Will-o'-the-Wisp, princess to the wisp court, and my consort, will you take me, Ceffyl Dwr, king of the kelpies, to be your husband, soulbound for all eternity?"

Ceff wasn't trying to leave me—he was asking to marry me, even if it did go against millennia of fae tradition. I considered his proposal, thinking seriously about all that he promised and all that we risked.

"Well, you know," I said, lips curling into a smile. "I do love to break the rules."

"Is that a yes?" he asked.

His eyes were shining painfully bright, but I refused to look away.

"Yes, Ceff, yes," I said.

If we survived our trip to Faerie, I was going to get married. I'd pledged my love to an immortal. If someone told me a month ago that I would accept a marriage proposal, I would have stabbed them in the eye. Now I'd agreed to marry a kelpie king. I wasn't sure which one of us was the bigger idiot, me for wanting to be with the same man for eternity, or Ceff for willingly subjecting himself to my stormy moods and proclivity for danger. Oberon save us all from crazy, lovesick fools.

CHAPTER 13

I tiptoed into the loft, careful not to wake anyone as I closed and locked the door. Sparky was already up, but the little guy was currently mesmerized by cartoons. He sat in front of the television, with the sound turned down low.

"Come on kiddo," I said, keeping my voice low. "Give me a hug."

I sat down, and patted the threadbare couch cushion beside me. Sparky jumped up, launching himself from the floor and onto my lap, his cartoon forgotten.

"Ivyyyyyyyyy!" he squealed.

I winced, and cast a glance at Jinx's bedroom door, but no sounds came from within. With any luck, she was still asleep. Actually, I was probably being overly cautious. That girl could sleep through the apocalypse.

"How was your night?" I asked. "Did Forneus bring you some new movies to watch?"

On date night, Forneus usually brought over food and movies to keep Sparky busy. Nothing ruined the mood faster than a bored demon toddler.

Sparky nodded, and chattered on about the movies he'd watched. His weight on my lap was comforting, and I nearly fell asleep. Just another one of the many things I would have sworn was impossible not too long ago. I wasn't the most affectionate person, but Sparky was a hugger, and I'd learned early on that the only visions he gave me were brief.

It didn't hurt that his one terrifying memory ended with me as his hero. I'd rescued him from the cat sidhe, and that vision reminded me that I hadn't screwed up everything in my life. I'd managed to get a few things right over the past year, and standing up for Sparky was one of those things. I wasn't sure yet if bringing a demon child home was smart, or the very definition of stupidity, but I'd come to love the kid.

So had Jinx, and for that reason, I knew that Forneus would use his resources to help Sparky as he matured into his powers. That was a relief, since I no longer knew if I'd be here to help, and I doubted Jinx could handle demonic growing pains on her own.

I remembered the loneliness of my teen years, and tensed, nearly crushing Sparky in a tight hug. Those years had been hell. I couldn't imagine what they'd be like for an orphaned Tezcatlipocan demon. Maybe Marvin could help talk the little guy through it.

"You sad?" Sparky asked, pointing at a tear that had somehow escaped to run down my face.

"Nope," I said, forcing a smile. "Those are happy tears. I'm glad to see you."

"Happy!" he squealed, squirming in my lap, and tugging on one of his ears.

"Good," I said, setting him down, and patting his head. "Now watch your cartoons, while I get dressed, and I'll find you some snacks."

Sparky clapped his hands, his eyes going to the television screen where cartoon animals sang and danced.

I made quick work of changing into my leathers. I tugged reinforced leather pants, boots, vest, arm guards, weapon sheaths, and jacket on over a black body suit. The body suit provided a base layer that wicked away moisture, prevented chafing, and gave me an extra layer of protection against unwanted visions. Considering where I was going, the latter might just save my sanity.

I strapped on my blades, slid an extra dagger in my boot for good measure, and started loading up on anti-fae charms. Once my jacket pockets and the pouches on my military style utility belt were full, I started sliding wooden stakes into the back of the belt, and two smaller stakes into my hair which I'd twisted into a tight bun. Next, I unlocked the trunk where I kept my demon fighting tools, and grabbed a silver cross and a few vials of holy water.

I was an equal opportunity slayer of monsters.

Once I was wearing a full arsenal, I carefully locked the trunk and hid the key. Since allowing Forneus into our lives, and bringing Sparky home, we'd locked away most of our anti-demon charms and weapons. I'd kept my stash under lock and key in my bedroom, but not today. I might be focused on my journey to Faerie, but in order to reach the wisp court, I had to pass through Tech Duinn. I could imagine all sorts of nasty things living in a land ruled by the Celtic god of the dead.

Encountering unfriendly demons was a possibility, and it was always best to be prepared.

I also hadn't left Jinx unarmed. She had her trusty crossbow, the loft and office had magic wards that could be activated with one word—that had cost a hefty portion of our depleted savings, but I refused to leave my friend unprotected—and she knew where I kept the key to my trunk of charms. She was also dating a powerful demon.

That certainly had to count for something.

I tiptoed to Jinx's room, and silently pushed the door open a few inches. Jinx was in bed, face relaxed in sleep. Forneus had his arms around her, their bodies entwined, but his eyes were fixed on me.

"It's time," I whispered. "Take care of her."

He nodded once, and closed his eyes. I slid the door shut, and made my way to the kitchen. I found a granola bar, which I stashed in an already packed jacket pocket, and went in search of snacks for Sparky. If he had food and cartoons, he'd likely stay out of Jinx's hair for a few more hours.

I grabbed a bag of chips from the counter, and set them down on the coffee table. Forneus must have brought them over for Sparky, since Jinx and I could no longer afford the luxury of junk food.

Sparky was back watching his cartoons again, an ear in one hand, and the thumb of his other hand in his mouth as he sat curled up in the corner of the couch. I sent up a silent prayer that I would get to see the kid grow up, and then I was out the door, hurrying down the steps like the coward that I was. I'd told myself that I was protecting Jinx by keeping her out of this mess, but deep down, I knew there was more to it than that. I was also too afraid to say goodbye.

Jinx and Sparky were my family, and I was risking their happiness by going on this mission. Finding a way to control my wisp powers was important—especially if I ever wanted to come clean with the faerie courts and admit that I was still among the living—but Jinx wouldn't see it that way.

My best friend understood the sacrifices we made to help others. She'd risked her own life to save innocent people from harm, and she knew I'd continue to do the same whenever the chance arose. We'd made a habit of facing down danger to help people, but if she found out I'd risked my life in the search for my father, she might never forgive me.

That was one chance that I wasn't willing to take.

CHAPTER 14

Ceff and I stood waiting for Torn, who was, I hoped, being fashionably late. If the cat sidhe didn't show up in the next fifteen minutes, it would be just me and Ceff on this mission. My gut told me we'd need Torn's help, even if he was one of my more irritating allies.

"You look stressed, Princess," Torn said, melting out of the shadows. *Show off.* "Worried I wasn't going to come?"

In fact, I had been worried. I guess I should have had faith in the fact that cats are curious creatures. Torn knew about my father's key to Faerie, and was intrigued by the possibility of a portal that bypassed the faerie king and queens' seal on those lands. He was here bright eyed and bushy tailed, ready for danger and mayhem.

Of course, if the opportunity arose, he wouldn't hesitate to create his own mayhem. Torn loved chaos like a pixie loves salt, it was in his nature.

"Nope," I said. "This is my happy face."

Torn laughed, the sound beginning in his chest and gradually shifting into a purr. Glad someone was happy. I sure as Hell wasn't. I grit my teeth, facing the expanse of water between our position at the tip of Martin's Point and the island floating in the distance.

"What if the sea doesn't part like in the prophecy?" I asked, pacing back and forth.

"Do not worry, I can carry you both," Ceff said.

He started to strip off his pants, and Torn clapped.

"Nice show, fish for brains, but I'm not riding you," Torn said. "Ever."

Ceff sighed, and raised an eyebrow at me. Great. This was up to me to settle.

"Cats are sissies when it comes to water," I said, getting in a hit to Torn's pride. "If it's the only way over, he'll catch a ride. He's too curious about Tech Duinn and my father's derelict court not to come with us."

Ceff shrugged and began to shift into his water horse form. He didn't have to strip off his clothes to change shape. He'd been trying to get under Torn's skin. I'm not sure who insulted whom first, but if they kept this up, we'd be lucky to all survive this trip.

Not that I was much help. I never could miss a chance to goad the cat sidhe lord.

"You wound me, Princess," Torn said, hand flying to his leather clad chest. "Though I should warn you, I do have my limits. Do not push me."

His eyes went steely, and I knew the kidding was over. It was time for the claws to come out.

Oh yeah? Two could play at that game. I crouched down as if to tie my boots, and reached my gloved hand into the water at my feet. In one smooth, lightning fast move, I uncoiled, straightened, and flicked my fingers at Torn. Droplets of water hit his chest, and he hissed. The hissing turned to a yowl that raised the hair on my neck, and Torn arched his back.

"Hmmm, yes, you do oh so well with water," I said. "Come on, Torn. If we have to swim for it, let Ceff carry me, and I'll carry you in your cat form."

Torn relaxed, leaned one hip against the railing, and licked his lips.

"Ah," he said, eyes alight, trailing fingers along the beads of water trickling down his skin. "You just want me in your arms. Admit it."

Ceff let out an angry snort, and stomped his foot. He'd finished shifting, and was now an imposing, beautifully muscled creature. Torn should know better than to mess with him like this, especially when he was going to be shifting into a teensy, little kitty cat.

Then again, I knew better than to antagonize Torn. Our chances for success were greatly reduced if I pissed off our one ally on this mission, but I just couldn't resist. We hadn't even left Harborsmouth, and we were at each other's throats. I shook my head, and sighed.

We were all doomed.

CHAPTER 15

I shouldn't have worried about the doorway to Tech Duinn remaining under water. The druid Béchuille was a lot of things, but a liar wasn't one of them.

At the strike of the witching hour, my ears popped as magic pressure built and crashed around us. My skin tingled as the sea parted, exposing sandy ocean floor that ran like a ribbon from Martin's Point to Donner Island.

"Wow," I said, letting out the breath I'd been holding.

That's me, always the eloquent one.

"Now this is more like it," Torn said, rocking back on his heels.

"I would have preferred to swim," Ceff muttered, narrowing his eyes at the churning sea.

I'd convinced him to shift back to his human form after he'd tried to nip at Torn's shoulder, and got a claw across the snout for his trouble.

The water parted unnaturally to our left and right, revealing a pathway that led out to the island. The pathway was narrow, walls of water towering over our heads, and I suddenly wished that Ceff had brought a few of his water fae friends along. Ceff could use his water magic to keep me from drowning in the short-term, but it was a long walk to the island.

Too bad we were keeping this mission under wraps. Revealing a secret backdoor to Faerie, and the fact that I had my father's key, would put a price on our heads that none of us needed. Plus, the general fae population still thought I was dead. Now was not the time to reveal the truth of my survival.

No, for better or worse, we were on our own.

"Ladies first," Torn said, waving a hand at the magic pathway.

I frowned, but strode forward.

"Thanks a lot," I said, breaking into a jog.

The faster we got this over with the better.

"Always the gentleman," he said, following me when the magic held.

I snorted, shaking my head. *Yeah, right.*

I kept a wary eye on the water as we picked our way over rocks and debris. Some of this debris was wreckage from ships lost at sea. If the ocean could do this to a ship's hull, what would it do to flesh and bone? I had a newfound respect for Ceff's home as I continued on.

I ran, Ceff scouting ahead and Torn on my heels. There were no spotlights or the sound of news helicopters. If the spell that parted the waves was like most magic, humans would subconsciously avoid this area, never realizing that something existed outside their normal lives.

I frowned, glancing again at the creatures swimming alongside us. Although the creatures were aware of us, they couldn't reach us on the pathway. That didn't keep me from running with a blade in each hand. Aside from the claustrophobia, this seemed too easy.

"Anyone else wondering when we'll hit quicksand, or get swallowed up by a sharknado?" I asked.

"Can someone remind me why we didn't just rent a boat?" Torn asked.

"Kaye said we should stick to the druid's prophecy as much as possible," I said.

I flashed him a hard smile, but I had the same doubts. What did make sense was the witch's argument about the entrance into Tech Duinn. The pathway would lead us to an underground doorway that was only revealed on the summer solstice. If we took a boat or had Ceff swim us across, it was plausible that we'd never find the way inside.

Of course, I was cursing Béchuille's prophecy as we ran. She'd mentioned the spell lasting until the waning of the moon, which wasn't the most accurate timetable. The seas parted on the witching hour, but even keeping one eye on the moon, there was no way to know just how much time we had left.

"We must hurry," Ceff said.

Within seconds, the sound of hooves hitting rocks and hard packed sand pounded in my ears. Apparently, my boyfriend was also concerned about our timetable.

Trident in hand, he'd been ready to stand and fight if this was some kind of trap. But now that our biggest enemy was time, with the threat of the spell collapsing tons of water on our heads, he shifted into the better known kelpie form. In his horse form, he was nearly as fast on land as he was in the water, which meant he was our best option for hauling ass out of here.

He stopped in front of me, pawing impatiently at the sand. I hesitated, but Ceff was right. We were running out of time. I slid my knives into their wrist sheathes, and leapt onto his back.

"You coming, Torn?" I asked.

"Fish breath isn't the only one who can shapeshift, Princess," he said, a glint in his eyes.

His flesh rippled, and he sprung forward, a scarred tabby cat landing beside us. He flicked an ear, and started to run, leaping over rocks and debris with ease.

Ceff's muscles tensed, and then we were galloping so fast, I had to close my eyes against the vertigo that threatened to knock me over. Apparently, it was possible to get motion sick while riding a horse through a cavern of moving walls of water. Who knew?

When we came to an abrupt stop, I cracked my eyes open and smiled. The rocks that made up the base of Donner Island were so large that they may have been put here by giants. I swung down from Ceff's back, striding forward to run my gloved hands along the boulder at the end of the path. It didn't look any different from the other hunks of rock, but I could feel the magic that pulsed beneath its cool surface.

"This is it," I said. "The doorway to Tech Duinn."

"So what are we waiting for, Princess?" Torn asked, shaking as his fur became smooth flesh once again. His face lit up like a kid on Christmas morning. "Let's go visit the Dark One."

I nodded, raising my gloved hand. I wrapped my knuckles on the stone three times, and took a step back. With an ear shattering grinding of stone against stone, the boulder lifted to reveal a dark void.

I hesitated, squinting into the darkness. I took a deep breath, preparing to ask Ceff if he was ready, when a roaring was met with the smell of saltwater, and the ground tried to knock me off my feet.

Mab's bloody bones, the walls of water were falling. Tons of water came crashing down, and a sleek, muscled

shoulder barreled me through the portal. Then everything
went black.

CHAPTER 16

"So this is Tech Duinn?" Torn asked, spinning in a circle. "I hope there's more to it than this."

I knelt on the ash-covered ground, coughing up a gallon of seawater. Ceff had used his water magic to hold most of the crashing ocean water back long enough for us to make it through the portal, but it had been a close thing. Now he sat beside me, shaking off the last of his transformation from horse to man.

He moaned, and I grit my teeth. It didn't normally take this long for him to shift, but he'd used up a lot of magic getting us all to safety. Not that Torn was about to say thank you. He gave Ceff a disdainful look similar to the ones cats give their human companions when they're impatiently waiting for their dinner.

Something roared to our right, and flames shot up through the darkness.

"You just had to say that, didn't you?" I asked, flashing a scowl at Torn.

He smiled, his teeth gleaming in the darkness.

"Now that looks like something interesting," he said.

He started walking, and I shook my head. I coughed one more time, and stood.

"We should probably keep an eye on him," I said. "You okay to walk?"

"I will be," Ceff said, coming to his knees.

He looked pale, but he didn't wobble when he finally stood.

"Is there anything I can do to help?" I asked, fidgeting with my gloves.

If I was careful, I could give Ceff my shoulder to lean on. So long as our skin didn't touch, I'd avoid any visions. Although I'd become used to experiencing Ceff's memories in private, visions were incapacitating, and we didn't have time for that. Not with Torn running off to poke the nearest pixie nest.

"Tell me you love me, and that you will never come that close to dying on me again," he said.

"I love you," I said. "But you know me better than to stay out of trouble. I may not seek it out like Torn, but danger has a way of finding me. All I can promise is to do my best."

"I don't want to lose you," he said.

"That's why we're here," I said. "I'm no good at sneaking around and playing dead. We find our way to Donn's hearth, use the key to open the portal to Faerie, and find whatever clues my father left behind. With any luck, we'll find a way to control my powers, or a lead on where to find my father. Who knows, maybe he even left a 'how to train a wisp princess' manual behind."

"You know it will not be that simple," he said.

I shook my head, and sighed.

"No, it never is," I said.

CHAPTER 17

Ceff's color was back to normal, and he was once again moving with his usual grace, when we reached Torn. It wasn't hard to find the cat sidhe. We just followed the red glow of flames, and the growls and snarls of a creature I never thought I'd see outside of Kaye's occult books.

"A baphomet," Torn said, face rapt.

"I thought they were fiction, something the inquisition came up with to accuse witches of worshiping," I said, stopping mid-stride and giving the creature a double take.

"Oh, they're real all right," he said. "And this one's been eating human hearts like they're gummy bears."

Bile rose in my throat, and I swore never to eat another gummy bear as long as I lived—which may not be all that long since I didn't plan on letting some demon continue ripping hearts from people's chests.

As I watched, a middle-aged man appeared at the demon's feet. He barely had time to look confused before the baphomet reached down, plucked out his heart, and ate it. I started to shake, fury making my skin begin to glow.

"We can't let that thing get away with murdering innocent people," I said, bile rising in my throat.

"It is not murder if they are already dead," a woman's disembodied voice said.

"What the...?" Torn muttered, taking a step back.

Light began to flicker beside me, coalescing into the shape of a woman. Judging from her blood soaked dress, she had probably died in the Victorian era. The high neck trimmed in lace and the bustle of the skirt would have been the height of fashion in the 1800's. Well, except for the blood and brain matter.

If being bedecked in gore hadn't been a clue, the axe in the woman's hand would have tipped me off that this woman hadn't been a saint in life. I didn't know if my blades would be effective against a ghost, but I palmed my throwing knives, just in case.

"Come for the show?" I asked, nodding toward the guardian beast.

The woman turned her head toward me, eyes dark, empty pits in her pale face.

"I have come to aid new souls," she said. "It is my penance."

"And you are?" Torn asked, eyebrow raised.

"Cora," she said with a twitch of her lips.

"Penance...is this Hell?" I asked.

Tech Duinn was supposed to be where the Dark One, Donn, the Celtic lord of the dead resided. I'd expected a castle straight out of Transylvania, the kind of thing Dracula would find cozy. Instead, we'd walked into a wasteland of ash and smoke. With the demonic creature in front of us, eating the hearts of the dead, I had to reevaluate, and I wondered if this was, in fact, one of the many planes of Hell. If so, I didn't like our chances.

"No, this is Purgatory," she said, her translucent hand tightening its grip on the axe. "At least in Hell one belongs to a side. Here we wander until the balance of our souls has shifted. Until then, we are nothing."

As if to confirm Cora's words, the baphomet swallowed the heart, and a circle of bright light appeared above the man staggering around with a hole in his chest. With a pulse of light that brought tears to my eyes, the man was sucked up into the portal, a rapt look on his face. I'd heard of people who've had near-death experiences seeing a bright light—heck, I was one of them—but this was too much.

"Purgatory?" I asked, clearing my throat.

"Yes," she said.

A woman appeared, and the cycle was once again repeated, but this time when the baphoment swallowed the woman's heart, her body burned to ash. I gasped as a ghost rose from the ashes. With a shudder, the ghost began moving away from the baphomet, toward the ghost at my side.

"The souls of good men travel on to the Fortunate Isles, and the souls of the damned either remain here in the Underworld, or are sent on to Hell," Cora said.

I frowned, but Ceff nodded.

"Tech Duinn is where the newly dead must travel," he said. "A crossroads where the Dark One sorts the dead based on the deeds of their mortal lives."

I swallowed hard, mouth going dry.

"Purgatory—wait until I tell the cats back home about this," Torn said. "They'd give at least one of their lives for a glimpse of this place."

I shook my head, and sighed. The man was incorrigible. I don't know what could be fascinating about a barren plain of ash, and a creature munching on a steady supply of human hearts. Aside from the perverse curiosity of wondering if the souls would get sent to the bright light, the fiery pit, or reappear in spectral form to wander this place, there was nothing much to see.

"And what's up with the baphomet eating their hearts?" I asked.

It was possible that the creature was just an opportunist who enjoyed eating human organs like they were bonbons, but there was something about the men and women thrust at the baphomet's feet that stunk of ritual sacrifice.

"The guardian of Tech Duinn must eat the hearts of the newly dead in order to measure the weight of their souls," she said.

"That's disgusting," I said, nose wrinkling at the thought of someone tasting my sin, rolling my soul along his tongue like a sommelier savoring a fine wine.

"Some pantheons measure the heart against the weight of a feather, others use the skill of sin eaters," Torn said with a shrug. "So long as your soul ends up in your version of paradise, who cares?"

He was already starting to look bored, a potentially dangerous emotional state for a cat sidhe, but I had one more question for Cora before she left us to fulfill her duty to teach the ghost who was approaching with a shy smile on her translucent lips.

"What determines if a soul remains in the Underworld, or gets shipped to Hell?" I asked.

If Cora had some insight, I was all ears. The latter was one hand basket we all wanted to avoid.

"It's complicated…your friend Forneus could tell you more, but simply put, it depends on the weight of their evil deeds, and if they sold their soul to a demon," she said.

I narrowed my eyes at the ghost, and took a step closer.

"How do you know who my friends are?" I asked.

Not that Forneus was a friend exactly, we were more like reluctant allies, but we both cared about Jinx. And if this ghost knew about Forneus, she likely knew about my human friend. I resisted a shudder as icy tendrils ran up and down my spine.

"It is my job to know," she said, lifting her chin to look down her nose at me. "The baphomet tastes your sin, but I must sift through your memories. Have you ever tried to escort a terrified stranger? Mark my words, it is much easier if you know something about them."

"You're psychic?" I asked.

"Not as gifted as the Dark One, but yes," she said, flickering as a new soul appeared beneath the guardian beast.

I didn't want to share anything in common with this woman, but a pang of sympathy ran through me. If my options were to touch every new soul who came to this place so that I might someday make my way to Heaven, or do nothing and stay here, or worse end up shipping off to Hell, I'd have to get used to the smell of ash, or sulfur, because that was one job I would quit before I started.

"Now I must return to my duties," she said, gesturing to the ghost who was shifting from foot to foot. "And your souls must be measured."

She pointed to the baphomet who was licking his lips and eyeing us like we were coated in honey and sprinkled with chocolate.

"Oh Hell no," Torn said. "I still have one life left, lady, and while I am tasty and oh so lickable, I am not on that thing's menu."

"You don't miss a chance to be a pompous pervert, do you?" I muttered.

"Now why would I do that?" he asked. "Women everywhere would lose all reason to live. Keeping my lascivious thoughts to myself would be a travesty of epic proportions."

Ceff ground his teeth, a vein throbbing on his temple, but he didn't say anything. That was good. I needed a minute to figure a way out of our current predicament.

I pinched the bridge of my nose, and squeezed my eyes shut. As much as Torn deserved being taken down a notch, snarling at each other wouldn't help me think.

I took a deep breath, opened my eyes, and turned back to Cora. She was lifting the hand that held the axe, perhaps in an effort to shepherd us to the baphomet. Either that or she was ready to put a permanent stop to Torn's narcissistic comments.

"If you're psychic, then you know that we're not souls of the newly dead," I said. "We're just passing through."

She tilted her head, flickering as she examined each of us in turn.

"You are not dead," she said.

"That's what we've been trying to tell you, Love," Torn said.

"You do not belong here," she said.

Her nostrils flared, and she raised her axe above her head, her body becoming larger and more solid by the second.

"We seek passage to Donn's hearth," Ceff said, a sharp edge to his voice. "Will you not show us such remedial hospitality?"

Cora stiffened, spine going rigid. Way to go, Ceff. Nothing like insulting the crazy powerful ghost lady.

"I will show you the way," she said.

Wow, that was easy.

"Lead on," I said, eager to get this crazy train moving.

The ghost behind Cora nodded rapidly, and shuffled her feet, obviously eager to leave behind the place where her heart had been ripped from her chest and eaten. Her face clearly said she was ready to hightail it out of here. I agreed with the ghost.

"But first, you must defeat the baphomet," Cora said.

"Wait...what?" I asked.

"Defeat the baphomet, and I will be your guide," she said. "If not, I will gather those who dwell in Tech Duinn and together we will make sure that your souls are weighed."

"But we aren't dead," I said, body tensing.

"If you don't fight the baphomet, you will be," she said, baring her teeth in a vicious grin.

Of course, it wouldn't as easy as asking for help. Nothing was ever simple in the Otherworld. I rolled my shoulders, and tested the weight of my blades.

It was time to take down the Dark One's pet guardian beast.

CHAPTER 18

"Are you sure that this is how you wish to proceed?" Ceff whispered, his lips close to my ear.

His nearness sent tingles along my neck where his breath caressed my skin.

"Yes," I said.

He nodded once, and moved to my left, giving me room to fight. He drew his trident, the wicked points of his weapon gleaming with the reflection of the fire that licked the ground where the baphomet stood.

The guardian creature ran a tongue along his bloody lips, and tossed a woman's body over his shoulder. The lifeless corpse turned to ash, falling like gray snow to blanket the otherwise barren plain.

A memory surfaced just as the woman reappeared as a ghost. Perhaps it was the endless plain of ash and flame licked shadow, but I recalled a passage in one of Kaye's books mentioning that the baphomet was a creature born from Hell. If that was true, then the baphomet might have the same weaknesses as other demons I'd encountered.

"Wait," I said.

I shifted my blades into one hand, and reached inside my jacket. I pulled out vials of holy water, tossing one to each of my friends.

"If this thing is demonic, holy water might give us an edge," I said.

I sprinkled holy water onto my weapons, tilting each throwing knife so that the water ran along the full length of the blade. After coating the tip of my dagger, and the long cutting edge of my machete, I rolled my shoulders and returned the throwing knives to my hands.

I grinned, showing a line of small, white teeth. I didn't need fangs, not with silver and iron blades coated in the magic equivalent of venomous acid.

"Time to dance," Torn said, lunging forward with catlike grace.

I shifted my weight onto my back foot and lifted my right hand, the tip of a throwing knife pinched between my index finger and thumb. Torn ducked beneath the baphomet's pitchfork, and raked his holy water dipped claws across the creature's stomach. I aimed higher, shifting my weight forward and releasing my blade to turn end over end until it lodged itself in the baphomet's eye.

The creature roared, kicking up ash as he flailed. I covered my face with one arm, and tried not to suck in a lungful of ash. I squinted, trying to locate Ceff on the battlefield. Where the hell was he?

A cry rang out, and Ceff thrust his trident into the baphomet's flank. While Torn and I had kept the creature busy, Ceff had circled in from behind, getting inside the baphomet's impressive defenses.

Our enemy was a mass of rippling muscle. As if that wasn't terrifying enough, rams horns grew from the sides of his skull, small, pointed horns ringed his bald head like a crown, leathery, bat-like wings sprouted from his naked torso, his fingers were tipped with evil-looking claws, his mouth was filled with sharp, pointy teeth—all the better to devour our hearts with—and he held an enormous pitchfork that gleamed blood red from the flames that flickered where his cloven hooves touched the earth. By Mab, he was one badass son of a bitch.

I was particularly wary of that pitchfork. With the baphomet's size, and the length of his weapon, his reach was far superior. No "size doesn't matter" jokes here. It was amazing that none of us were shish kebabed.

Then again those claws were nothing to sneeze at.

I held my breath as the baphomet thrust a clawed hand toward my boyfriend's heart. Ceff had his feet braced, and was tugging at his trident, trying to dislodge his weapon from the creature's side. Being too close for the pitchfork to be effective didn't make him safe.

"Ceff, look out!" I screamed.

Torn appeared through the growing fog of ash, once more raking his claws across the beast's stomach. It wasn't enough. The baphomet was intent on Ceff.

I slowed my breathing, and with a fluid motion I raised my arm, swung my hand down, and released my second blade. The knife punched through muscle and bone, skewering the baphomet's hand to his chest. It was a temporary fix, but it gave Ceff the time he needed to make it clear.

My heart raced as he twisted, narrowly missing the baphomet's stymied attack. I was already reaching for my machete, a blade long enough to qualify as a sword, when he yanked his trident free, and ran. The baphomet turned to follow Ceff, and I rushed in.

I blinked against the ash that the baphomet's wings churned into the air. I could barely see where the creature was going. Thankfully, the Dark One had the forethought to chain the baphomet to a pillar of stone that rose up like a skeletal finger from the ashen plain.

With his massive leathery wings, there was no way we could keep up if the beast was free to fly. Fighting a tethered baphomet was challenge enough. Blood pounding in my ears, I dove toward calves the size of tree trunks. I needed to slow the beast down before he got close enough to eat my friends.

I sliced across the back of the baphomet's leg, severing the Achilles tendon. I rolled as the creature crashed down to one knee, the damaged leg no longer holding his monstrous weight. I hurried back to our rally point, a shaky laugh escaping my lips as I saw that Ceff and Torn were both safe.

I smiled, and flashed my friends a thumbs up. We'd wounded the baphomet, and made it out of his reach. With a continued pattern of strikes and retreats, we just might win this fight.

The sound of crashing stone and shrieking metal cut my celebration short. I spun, keeping my machete out in front of me as I watched the baphomet thrash against his restraints.

"Those chains aren't going to hold him much longer, Princess," Torn said.

Torn was right. The baphomet was already using his wings to make up for his injured leg, and the pain from the wounds we'd inflicted only served to fuel the creature's rage.

"Thoughts?" I asked.

Torn and Ceff were immortal fae. They'd been doing this kind of thing a lot longer than I had. If they had any tactical advice, I was open to suggestions.

"Do you have any more holy water?" Ceff asked.

I nodded, retrieving the remaining vials from the utility belt slung across my hips. Those reinforced nylon mesh pouches came in damn handy.

"Yes, though I'm not sure if it works on this thing," I said.

"Oh, it works, Princess," Torn said, holding up one of his clawed hands. "I dipped these claws in holy water and smoke rose from the wounds. Not so with this hand."

He waggled the fingers of his other hand, which was covered in blood up to his wrist. I'd seen Torn rake his claws across the baphomet's stomach on two separate attacks. The first made the creature scream, the second was brushed off like Torn was no more irritating than a gnat.

"Okay, I'll try for his other eye," I said.

It wouldn't be easy, not with the baphomet thrashing around. I'd be lucky get a clear shot past his wings, and I'm pretty sure I used up all my luck for this fight. In fact, hitting my target on the first try had been a total fluke. Fate was probably scheming ways to bite me in the ass, but that wouldn't keep me from trying.

"I have a better idea," Ceff said. He turned to Torn, eyebrow raised. "How good are you at climbing?"

"Why?" he asked.

"Because we need someone to upend one of these vials into the creature's ear," Ceff said.

Torn eyed the thrashing baphomet, licked his lips, and smiled.

"I'm your man," he said.

Yep, he'd just confirmed it. Torn was a psychopath. Thankfully, he was on our side.

"What's the plan for you and me?" I asked.

"We're the distraction," Ceff said.

Oh goody.

I handed over several vials of holy water, which Torn secured in the many pockets and leather pouches strapped to his body. If I didn't know better, I'd think that the cat sidhe had come along with the intent to steal his weight in valuables. I shook my head. Actually, that was a distinct possibility.

"If we survive this, you're going to tell me the real reason you tagged along for this trip," I said.

Torn flashed me a grin, batting his eyelashes.

"Can't an ally come along just to help?" he said.

"Not when that ally is you," I said.

"This is no time for discussion," Ceff said.

I nodded, took one last deep breath, and ran toward the baphomet, yelling and waving my arms. The creature turned his one remaining hungry eye my way, saliva dripping from razor sharp teeth. If Torn didn't follow through with the plan, I was likely to lose my heart real soon.

Leaving my heart in Tech Duinn was not an option. I was not going to end up the title of a country western song.

Ceff ran toward the baphomet in the opposite direction, and the creature spun, red eye glowing with rage. Apparently, we hadn't been forgiven for the injuries we'd recently inflicted. That was great for drawing the beast's focus. Now if only Torn would take advantage of the situation.

It's all fun and games until someone loses a heart.

The baphomet's claws were mere inches away from my chest when I ducked and rolled between his legs. I kept my eyes open, terrified of touching the thing's tail and risking a vision. Sadly, a vision was not the only thing risking my sanity. His tail was not the only thing hanging between the baphomet's legs.

Forneus always claimed that demons were well endowed. I thought he'd been bragging. Maybe if I'd believed him, I could have avoided getting an up close and personal look at the baphomet's junk. The fact that the thing was barbed made me glad the creature only wanted to eat our hearts.

"You have only seen him hungry," Cora said, her spectral form appearing to my right. "When he is sated, he plays with his food."

Damn the psychic ghost.

"Not helping," I said through clenched teeth.

With a shudder, I rolled to my feet. Cora had disappeared, but her words rang through my ears, twisting my gut. We needed to take this thing down before it got any ideas.

Once on my feet, I dodged left and right, not wanting to provide a stationary target for the baphomet to focus his rage. Bile rose in my throat as I circled the creature, eyes straining to locate Ceff and Torn in the choking cloud of ash.

A scream had me sprinting past the baphomet. Heart racing, I ducked beneath a leathery wing. *Please, please, please let Ceff be okay.* In that moment, I swore that if Torn had run off and left us to die, I'd drag his furry ass to Hell with me.

I imagined the worst until I caught sight of Ceff screaming and waving his trident. I smiled as it quickly became apparent that Ceff was only yelling curses, not screaming in pain as I'd feared, in an effort to hold the creature's attention.

He pointed to something climbing onto the baphomet's shoulder, and I gasped. The cat sidhe hadn't abandoned us, after all. Torn had managed to climb up the baphomet's back, his progress previously hidden from me by large, leathery wings.

"Hey, big guy," I yelled. "Over here!"

I grabbed a glass vial of holy water and lobbed it at the baphomet. It hit below the belt, not that the demon was wearing one, and from the shrieking, I guessed that the vial had released its contents on a particularly sensitive part of the baphomet's anatomy.

Now it was up to Torn. If broken glass and acid burns between the legs didn't keep the creature distracted, nothing would.

I held my breath, bracing for a shit storm of retaliation, when Torn popped the cap off a vial with his teeth, and shoved it in the baphomet's ear. He punched the vial, jamming it further into the ear canal, and launched himself to the ground. He landed on his feet, a feral grin tugging at his lips.

Torn was one scary dude when he wasn't trying to screw anything that moved. Thankfully, that wasn't often. If I didn't see that look on his face again, it would be too soon.

The baphomet thrashed, stretching his chains as he clawed at his head, and I heard the distinct sound of snapping metal. Torn's smile slipped, and a cold knot of fear gripped my insides.

"Run!" Ceff screamed, grabbing my arm.

I didn't even try to push him away, or chastise him for touching me. Visions from Ceff's past were the least of my worries with an enraged baphomet hot on our tail. In fact, we were blasted by heat as wings fanned the flames rising from beneath the creature's feet.

The flames weren't the only things rising.

Cloven feet no longer touched the ground as the baphomet's wings took advantage of his newfound freedom. I stumbled, watching wide-eyed over my shoulder as we ran.

"Ivy?" Ceff asked, examining me for injury while on the move.

"I'm out of holy water," I said.

I blinked up at him, tears making his face blur. The fog of ash was so thick that I could barely see him shake his head.

"We must run," he said, tugging on my sleeve.

I hurried to keep pace with him, but he was pureblood fae, not a half-breed like me. He also wasn't searching the gloom for our friend.

"Torn?" I asked.

"I do not know," he said, lips in a hard line.

Bile rose once again, and I had to swallow hard to keep from puking. A blast of wind and heat had me looking upward, adding to the urge.

The baphomet, who'd clawed his head so viciously that the bone lay bare on one side, came racing toward us. Now that it was free and its focus was once again on us, there was little hope of escape.

"Don't stop now, Princess," Torn said.

Eyes with slit pupils and a lopsided grin appeared a few feet away. I smiled, never so happy to see the cat sidhe, but a frenzied shriek had me following his advice.

We ran, but instead of having our hearts carved from our chests, the hot wind at my back ceased. I glanced to the sky, mouth going dry as realization set in. The baphomet's wings had stopped beating, and its face was frozen in a rictus of pain.

The holy water had finally reached the creature's brain, but I wasn't celebrating. Not when a massive demon was about to plummet to the ground, and we were standing squarely in its drop zone.

"Run!" I screamed.

"Thought that's what we were already doing, Princess," Torn said, but he lost his smug look when he realized our predicament.

We ran, muscles burning against the strain, until the ground heaved, knocking us off our feet. The world spun, confusing my sense of up and down until I ended up hitting the ground face first.

I lifted my head and wiped an arm across my face, squinting as my eyes darted back and forth searching for Ceff and Torn. An enormous claw-tipped finger was jammed into the ground a few feet from my head, and I scrambled away on my hands and knees. Mab's bloody bones, that had been close. But had my friends also been so lucky?

"Ceff?" I asked.

My voice squeaked, turning quickly to a ragged cough. I told myself that the tears running down my cheeks were also due to having a face full of ash, but I knew better. I hadn't been looking for love when I met Ceffyl Dwr. I never dared to imagine a life with someone else to share it with. But now that we were together, and Ceff had popped the question, I couldn't bear the thought of going on without him.

"Ivy?" Ceff asked. "Are you hurt?"

I spun, a different kind of tears falling from my eyes, as I fell on my butt, grinning like an idiot.

"I think she hit her head," Torn said. "She looks deranged."

"Look who's talking," I said.

And then I started to laugh hysterically, holding my sides when the laughter turned into a coughing fit. Maybe that fall really did break my brain.

"Ivy?" Ceff asked again, approaching me slowly.

"I'm okay," I said. "Just give me a moment."

The laughing subsided, making me fully aware of every bruise and aching muscle. I also couldn't ignore the ash that had managed to get into parts of me I didn't even know existed.

I ran a tongue over the grit coating my teeth and grimaced. I was thankful that it wasn't triggering visions, but there's nothing pleasant about having the ashes of dead people in your mouth.

"Oberon's eyes," I groaned.

I spit, tamping down the anxiety that battled to take over. Now that the adrenaline was wearing off, I became aware of just how close I'd come to losing myself to an avalanche of visions. If the ashes of dead people covered my skin, and coated the inside of my ears, eyes, and mouth, while I was anywhere but Tech Duinn, I'd be buried by those visions right now.

I placed a hand on my stomach, and took slow, steadying breaths.

"Where the Hell is Cora?" I asked.

I was dimly aware that if the ghost didn't stick to our bargain, we'd gone through all of this for nothing. Since that was too depressing to think about, I focused on what we needed to do next.

A woman's form stepped through the baphomet's body, trailing a few wide-eyed newly dead. Those two had picked a bad day to end up in Tech Duinn. Not that it's ever a good day to die.

"I imagine you require the location of the Dark One," Cora said.

I leveled Cora with a cold stare, and nodded. She waved a hand, and ash swirled, making me blink. When I opened my eyes, a castle had emerged, drawbridge covered moat and all.

Torn whistled, and I swore.

"Follow these three into Donn's lair, and then wait for the Dark One in the main hall," she said to the other ghosts.

"You aren't coming with us?" I asked, eyebrows raised. "I thought that was your job."

Cora smiled, and gestured to the baphomet's corpse. A slithering sensation worked its way up my spine, and I shivered. Were her teeth always that sharp?

"Not anymore," she said.

The ghost thrust a hand through the baphomet's chest, and though her body was spectral, her hand held an enormous heart when she removed it. Cora's smile widened showing off her very pointy teeth, then unhinged her jaw. I knew what was coming next, but I couldn't look away.

Cora ate the baphomet's heart, and licked blood from her now solid looking fingers. As she preened, she flexed her hand, and tossed the axe she'd been holding to the ground.

"I no longer need that," she said in response to Torn's questioning look.

She eyed him up and down, as if considering the new possibilities open to her now that she was flesh and blood. Before the two of them acted out any fantasies, I stepped between them.

"We have to get going," I said. "Duty calls."

A man appeared to my left, and Cora smiled.

"Yes," she said, licking her lips. "Yes, it does."

CHAPTER 19

"Can't believe Cora just bargained her way into the baphomet's job," Torn said with admiration.

The ghost chick had balls all right. Although now that she'd been promoted to Donn's guardian, I wasn't so sure what she was anymore. Ghosts aren't flesh and blood. Just ask the ones trailing us like lost lambs.

I just hope I wasn't unwittingly leading them to the slaughter.

Kaye's books hadn't said much about Donn, other than the fact that he was the Celtic god of the dead and he often went by the name, Dark One. I half expected a skeletally thin white guy holding a scythe in one hand and wearing a black, hooded cloak. If so, he'd fit the castle that now stood before us.

I'd been right about that at least. The castle loomed from a mountain peak that I could have sworn hadn't been there when we arrived in Tech Duinn. The place was made of dark stone, though it may have just looked that way due to the ash that coated everything in this godforsaken place. As if to add to the overall dreariness, someone had strung bodies from a gibbet that hung in front of the drawbridge, and carrion birds pecked at something impaled on a pike that rose from one of the castle's turrets. Dracula certainly would have felt at home here.

I'd have laughed if I didn't still have a lungful of corpse ash. Instead, I let out a wheezing snort. Ceff raised an eyebrow, and I waved him off.

"Nothing," I said. "It's just so...predictable."

"Since when is the belly of a whale predictable?" he asked.

"Wait...is that what you see?" I asked.

"Of course," he said, eyebrows drawing together as he studied my face.

"Look, I'm not crazy," I said. "I just don't see a whale. I think we see whatever we expect to see."

"That explains the harem," Torn said. "I thought it was too good to be true."

Ceff's lip twitched, and I shook my head. I guess we all had different expectations for a death god's lifestyle. Hopefully, seeing different versions of Donn's home wouldn't impede our search for the portal to Faerie.

"At least a castle is likely to have a hearth," I said. "Come on."

I started toward the bridge, but stopped when I realized Ceff and Torn weren't with me. I turned to see them both staring wide-eyed over my shoulder.

"Well I'll be…that's just freaky," Torn said.

"For once, I agree with you," Ceff said.

"What's freaky?" I asked, hoping the castle hadn't sprouted teeth and claws.

"As soon as you said castle, that's what it became," Torn said.

"It still smells like whale," Ceff said, wrinkling his nose.

Okay, that was freaky.

"So long as we're all seeing the same thing," I said, rubbing the back of my neck as I turned to examine the castle. "Does it look like something out of a bad horror movie?"

"If bad horror movie castles are shrouded in shadow, decorated with decaying body parts, and perched dramatically on a mountain peak, then yes," Ceff said.

"I much preferred the harem," Torn muttered.

We made it onto the drawbridge, up the winding path, and to Donn's doorstep without incident. I'd have preferred a fight. My shoulders had crawled up to my ears, my hands hurt from the stranglehold I had on my weapons, and if I didn't relax soon, I'd likely grind my teeth to dust.

No one can accuse me of being an optimist.

I'd expected some kind of guardian beast to rise up out of the moat. When we made it safely across the bridge without so much as a burble from the inky water, I'd become convinced that the crows would descend to tear at our flesh and peck out our eyes. Even the entrance had taken on an ominous gleam.

That might have had something to do with the gargantuan portcullis. The metal had sharp, pointy tips, not that it needed them. The heavy gate itself could crush our bodies into exploding tubes of meat jelly.

To say I didn't want to step under that portcullis was an understatement.

"I smell brownies," Torn said.

"If that's some kind of euphemism, I might just kill you," I said through clenched teeth.

"I smell them too," Ceff said.

"Do you mean brownies, as in fae?" I asked.

"No," they said in unison.

I frowned, not overly eager to suck in a lung full of corpse ash, but inhaled deeply. My sense of smell wasn't as good as a pureblood fae, but I had better olfactory skills than a human. I dragged the air across my tongue, and started to salivate.

"Definitely brownies," I said. "Anyone else thinking trap?"

Only a very sick individual would try to lure us into his lair with evil brownies. Sadly, we didn't have much choice. We needed to get inside, find Donn's hearth, and get the hell out of Dodge.

"Do we care?" Torn asked, eyebrows lifting.

"No, I guess we don't," I said.

I eyed the portcullis, gripped my blades, and ran. I let out a shaky breath when I made it into the adjoining courtyard without being crushed to death, impaled, or magically vaporized.

Ceff and Torn were close behind, but the ghosts who'd followed us so far, hesitated on the threshold.

"Can we, um, cross over?" one of the women asked.

The other woman bit her lip, stifling a nervous giggle. Yeah, I'm pretty sure they'd already done some crossing over today. Not that I envied their afterlife. I also had no idea what would happen to them when they entered Donn's castle.

"Maybe you should wait for an invitation from the Dark One himself," I said.

"That's good advice."

The voice came from behind me, and I whirled to see a portly man with rosy cheeks and a white beard. His eyes twinkled, and his lips twitched. If he wasn't emanating so much power, I'd have suspected he was a life-sized garden gnome, or a department store Santa Claus.

Now that was a terrifying thought.

I, for one, didn't want the Celtic god of the dead coming down my chimney on Christmas Eve. I shivered, suddenly glad our loft didn't have a fireplace. But speaking of fireplaces...

"Donn?" I asked.

He nodded, and I swallowed hard.

"We've helped to deliver these newly dead souls to your door," I said. "In return, we'd like a look at your hearth."

Torn snorted, and I resisted the urge to stomp on his foot.

"Then come in," Donn said, his belly rising up and down as he chuckled. The man was way too jolly for a death god. "You too, newlings."

Donn waved his hand, and the ghosts shuffled their feet. Ducking their heads, they entered the Dark One's house single-file. We all followed Donn through an archway that led from the courtyard into a cavernous room that must have been the castle's Great Hall.

"Go to the kitchen, children, and tell Cook that we'll be taking our tea in the library," he said.

Donn pointed to a corridor to our right, and the ghosts hurried off, chattering and gesturing at the castle's interior. The place was impressive, without a speck of ash marring its gleaming surfaces. After the gloomy plain and shadowy mountainside, I'd expected flickering candlelight, groaning coffins, and cobwebs.

I shook my head. I'd been spending too much time with vampires.

"Wait until you taste the brownies," Donn said.

I just hoped he meant the chocolate pastries we could smell baking in some remote corner of the castle. When you're talking to a death god who looks like Santa Claus, but has a guardian who weighs sin by eating people's hearts, you never can be too sure.

CHAPTER 20

Donn was a surprisingly gracious host. He led us past an armory that would have made Jenna salivate, and into the castle's library where we were greeted with spectral servants bearing tea and brownies.

I don't know how ghosts could carry trays of refreshments. Perhaps it was a quirk of Tech Duinn. And while nearly a dozen souls of the dead flit about like servants, others poked their heads in for a peek at their master's guests—literally. Heads protruded from book-lined walls, and more than one ghost stared down from the ceiling. Even the taxidermied creatures interspersed amongst the books lining Donn's shelves seemed to take notice of us.

"Come, this way," Donn said, gesturing to an arrangement of chairs and small couches.

We'd stepped around a painted screen and, though the conversation nook was void of monsters, I froze.

"Ah, yes, the hearth," he said. "You will have to tell me why you're so interested in my hearth. Or have you come to visit Skilly?"

"Skilly?" I asked, brow furrowing.

I looked to my friends, but Ceff gave a minuscule shake of the head and Torn lifted a shoulder in a one-armed shrug.

"Our resident hearth brownie," Donn said. "But no, I suppose not. You are faeries, but I don't think you've come to visit with Skilly."

"Um, no, but now that you mention it, I'd like to leave Skilly a gift," I said, belatedly remembering my manners. I did not want to get pranked by a strange hearth brownie I'd never met before. "May I?"

"Yes, of course," Donn said. He hooked his thumbs into the suspenders that held up his red trousers, eyebrows raised to his hairline. "I dare say our Skilly hasn't received a gift in some time.

"Why?" I asked.

Now it was my turn to look surprised. A person would have to be a fool not to provide a gift to a hearth brownie. Hob was my friend and he'd still pix me six ways to Sunday if I ever forgot.

"We don't get many visitors here who are able to bear gifts," Donn said. "The dead do not bring their physical wealth when they enter this world."

No, I suppose they didn't. I winced, glad I wasn't one of the dozens of spirits living here in the castle. They may be incorporeal, but I was sure Skilly would find a way to exact his revenge. Hearth brownies were as clever as they were stubborn.

"Well, thankfully, we're not dead," I said.

I retrieved a small packet of glitter from my pocket, and set it gently on the mantle, careful not to step so much as one toe on the hearthstone. I needed to get a better look at the hearth, but first I needed to appease the hearth brownie and this castle's master.

I held a breath, but there was no sign of Skilly. After a moment, I turned and took a seat beside Ceff. I sat on the edge of the hard sofa, and met Donn's steady gaze.

"Yes," he said, as if there'd been no pause in our conversation. "I noticed that."

Shadows coalesced around Donn, and he no longer resembled a jolly old man. The gleam in his eye was but one star in a galaxy so vast, it made my heart ache. Round cheeks became sharp as a razor, and the red and white of his suspendered pants resembled a mortal wound so deep it exposed the bone.

I came to my feet, nearly knocking over the table that held our tea, but the darkness was gone. I blinked, and the benign man with rosy cheeks was back. The only clue that I wasn't going a crazy was a crow perched on his shoulder.

"Morrigan, my love, come for a brownie?" he asked.

His words were spoken to the bird, but his eyes never left my face. A smile tugged at his lips, and I fought to keep my hands from shaking.

He'd made his point. Donn was a powerful badass, a god. He might not appear as terrifying as the baphomet, but he was a much larger threat. They didn't call him the Dark One for nothing.

And if he wasn't just toying with us, the bird on his shoulder was no less powerful. Kaye's occult library had been sparing when it came to details on Donn, but there were plenty of entries about the Morrigan. The goddess of war had left a mark on the human world, much like the blood and scorch marks of the battlefields over which she presided.

"Morrigan?" Torn asked, leaning forward. He squinted at the bird, and smiled. "It's been a while. I didn't recognize you."

Torn knew the Morrigan? That was news to me. Then again, I shouldn't be surprised. Cat sidhe hoard secrets like dragons hoard gold.

The bird shot upward, and spun. I lifted an arm against the winds unleashed by a magic tornado, wondering if maybe Torn and the Morrigan weren't on such good terms after all. One of my throwing knives hit my palm, and I stood, ready to strike if it came to that. I swallowed hard as a woman wearing gunmetal gray armor and a cloak of black feathers strode from the spinning vortex.

The Morrigan's prominent nose and pointed chin were not classically beautiful and, like Torn, her face was crisscrossed with scars. But there was something magnetic about her confident stance, muscular body, tanned skin, and black, short-cropped hair. This was a woman who men would follow into battle, a goddess many had voluntarily given the ultimate sacrifice. Some women were born for the stage, but the Morrigan was at home in the theater of war.

Mab's bones, if this woman touched me, I'd never regain my sanity.

How many dying men had seen those jet black eyes on the battlefield? How much blood had been spilled at her command? My knees weakened, but I held my stance. It helped that Ceff had also come to his feet to stand beside me. We were a united front.

Torn may be a pain in the ass, but I'd claimed him as an ally and he'd accepted. We'd come here together, and I would not leave him behind. And Ceff would never leave me behind. I wasn't sure if that made us brave or certifiable. Considering the Morrigan's idea of a good time was being on the front lines of a combat zone, I was going with the latter.

I reached inside my jacket pocket, rubbing gloved fingers over my father's key. If only we could make it out of here without a fight. I flicked my eyes to the hearth, but there was no obvious keyhole. If we made a run for the portal, I had no idea how long it would take to open it. I clenched my jaw, and focused on the Morrigan.

"You dare draw your weapons against me?" she asked, head tilted to the side as her eyes slid to my blade and Ceff's trident.

"Don't worry about these two jokers," Torn said. He waved a hand at us, and gave a quick jerk of his head, but he kept his eyes on Morrigan as he smiled. "They'd never really try to attack the goddess of war. They wouldn't be that stupid."

I got Torn's message loud and clear. We slid our weapons away, and I forced a smile on my face.

"Sorry, force of habit," I said. "Nothing personal."

"We are pleased to make your acquaintance," Ceff said. "I have heard much about you, but have never been blessed with your company. You honor us with your presence."

Ceff was pouring it on thick, but it seemed to be working. We'd ruffled the Morrigan's feathers, but she seemed willing to overlook our bad manners, for now. Rather than draw her weapons, she stroked the pommel of her sword with one gauntlet clad fingertip.

"Well, I do understand the instinct," she said.

She smiled, and an oily sensation slid through my gut. The Morrigan might be giving us a pass for drawing our weapons, but I had a feeling she'd never forget it.

"You are beautiful as ever," Torn said. "Been working out?"

Donn narrowed his eyes, and I prayed that Torn would stop hitting on the war goddess. Was that too much to ask? I thought about my experiences with Torn over the past year, and winced. He was pathological in his flirtations.

Oberon save us all.

"So, um, how did you two meet?" I asked.

I winced, hoping that it hadn't been at some mass orgy. There's only so many things my brain could take, and stories of Torn's sexual exploits was not one of them. Plus, I had a feeling that Donn wouldn't appreciate reminders of Morrigan's past romantic entanglements.

"It was at the siege of Carthage, wasn't it?" Torn asked.

"Now that was a good battle," Donn said.

"It was a thief's paradise," Torn said, a faraway look on his face. "And the secrets humans were willing to bargain for freedom...those were the days."

"I remember that siege like it was yesterday," Morrigan said with a smile. "The screams, the clash of weapons..."

"Death," Donn said, slipping an arm around her waist.

"Oh yes, there was quite a lot of death," she said, licking her lips.

Donn's hand most definitely slid lower to cup the Morrigan's ass, and I tried to think of something, anything, to change the subject. Ceff cleared his throat.

"A memorable day indeed," he said. "But perhaps we can once again focus on the present."

Right, now it was my turn. Maybe I could take advantage of Donn's present good mood, and grill him for answers about his hearth.

"Yes, as much as we'd, um, love to stay and chat, our mission is time sensitive," I said.

"A mission?" Morrigan asked. "What is your objective?"

"To find the portal hidden inside your hearth," I said.

"Finding the portal will do you no good," Donn said. "Only someone with a key can open that door."

"Then I guess it's a good thing I brought this," I said, pulling the key from my pocket.

I held the key out so that they could get a good look at it, but I didn't hand it over. My fingers ached from gripping the key so tightly.

Donn's eyes widened, and he let out a bellowing laugh.

"You are full of surprises!" he said. He squinted at me, and nodded. "I should have known you were Will's spawn. He's one of the few living souls ever to pass through this place."

"You knew my father?" I asked, heart racing.

That was something I hadn't anticipated.

"For a time," he said. "He hightailed it out of Faerie like a horde of demons were hot on his heels."

"Did he ever disclose the reason for his rapid departure?" Ceff asked.

It was a good question, and I was relieved that at least one of us was still thinking straight. I was still reeling from the realization that we were retracing my father's footsteps. I'd been searching months for clues, any possible hint, about my father. I held my breath, waiting for Donn to respond.

"Something to do with the Unseelie Queen," he said. "This was before the kings and queens left Faerie, of course, and Mab was on a rampage. Someone had stolen something from her, and Mab and her minions left no stone unturned in her search for the traitor and her prized possession."

"Some say that is why Mab left Faerie," Ceff said. "To find that which was lost."

"Why haven't I ever heard this before?" I asked, frowning. "And if that was true, why would Oberon and Titania also leave Faerie?"

"Balance," Morrigan said. "The plains of the Otherworld are all quite different—Faerie, Tech Duinn, Mag Mell—but they have one thing in common. The darkness must always be balanced by the light."

"It is true," Donn said, nodding and stroking his beard. "Even here, there must be an equal number of souls that head into the light as there are that fall into the pit. When Mab left Faerie, she tipped the scales in favor of the Seelie Court. Oberon had no choice but to leave."

"And Titania?" I asked. "If that's true, shouldn't she have stayed? One Seelie King for one Unseelie Queen?"

"You're assuming Oberon and Mab are equals," Torn said.

"Well, aren't they?" I asked.

"Not even close," he said. "It's like the difference between a grenade and an atomic bomb. So when Mab left, Titania had to join Oberon to make up for the shift in power."

"And now they're in the human world," I said.

My friends were in the human world. Jinx, Jenna, Kaye, Marvin, Hob, Sparky, Galliel…I'd left them behind, believing that they were safer staying at home. But the faerie equivalent of nuclear weapons were back home, and who knew when those bombs would go off. I bit the inside of my cheek to keep from screaming.

"Do not worry," Ceff said. "No one has seen Mab in over a hundred years. It is possible that the rumors are true, and the king and queens of Faerie are sleeping through the centuries of human technology."

"To answer your earlier question, Princess, no one really knows why they left or when they'll return," Torn said. "No sense losing sleep over it."

He had a point. Worrying over the possibilities was as useful as a cat chasing its tail.

"Did my father mention anything else about his escape from Faerie?" I asked. "Was he protecting the person who stole from Mab? Or maybe he was just trying to get out before the roads between the worlds were closed?"

Before leaving Faerie, Oberon, Titania, and Mab had sealed the pathways to and from Faerie. As king of the wisps, perhaps my father had received word of the closing borders and wanted to leave Faerie before that happened, although I couldn't think of a reason why he'd want to leave his court behind. Maybe he didn't believe the borders would remain closed for so long. He couldn't have been motivated by his love for my mother. Two hundred years ago, they hadn't even met. She, a human, hadn't even been born.

"He was protecting someone, a child," Donn said. "Though whether she was the kin of the one who betrayed Mab, or some other faerie babe, I do not know."

"Where was this child you say was under his protection?" Ceff asked. "Was he carrying her with him when he passed through this place?"

"Yes, of course, it's one of the reasons I let him leave Tech Duinn with his soul intact," Donn said.

"You were going to steal his soul?" I asked.

That also begged the question whether Donn was planning the same fate for us. For all his tea and brownies and rosy-cheeked smiles, he was the god of death. Collecting and sorting souls was his job, and we'd barged into his workplace.

"Don't worry," he said, waving a hand. "Things were different then. I hadn't learned to delegate yet, which meant I had to personally weigh the sins of every new soul that entered this realm."

I grimaced, imagining Donn doing that job day in and day out. It was like picturing Santa Claus tearing into the chest of every newly dead person to cross over to Tech Duinn, pulling out their heart, and eating it to see if they had been naughty or nice. I inched further away from the death god, stomach churning, happy that I hadn't accepted any of the tea and brownies.

"He was grouchy, and stubborn," Morrigan said, rolling her eyes. "It took him centuries to finally hire a guardian beast."

A guardian beast that we'd killed. I probably owed Cora a fruit basket for taking over that job.

"I was overtired and overworked, so my first instinct was to take his soul regardless of how strange it looked," he said.

"But he convinced you to let him live because of a child," I said.

"Yes, the babe began to wail, and I finally snapped out of it," he said. "I went from running on autopilot to really listening to what Will had to say."

"Autopilot?" Ceff asked.

"Donn is a huge fan of modern aviation," Morrigan said.

"I do love anything with wings," Donn said, raking her with his eyes.

"So, um, what did my father say?" I asked, trying to bring Donn back to our original subject.

"He pleaded for me to spare the child's life, promising never to pass through this way again," he said.

"Did he give any indication of who the child was, or why he was taking the babe from Faerie?" Ceff asked.

"Only that the child must be hidden at all cost," Donn said.

"And you say that the child was a faerie baby, not a human...you're sure?" Torn asked.

"Yes, I'm sure," Donn said. "I read her soul. It was one of the reasons why I let them go. Pureblooded faerie children are rare. So few are born, and even less survive until adulthood."

"I wonder who she was," I said.

"I never saw Willem with any child but you," Torn said. "She must have been sent into hiding as soon as he reached the human world."

"Perhaps his task was solely to aid in her escape," Ceff said. "It would not have been difficult to find a fae family to foster her, not with how rare our children are."

He stared down at his hands, and impulsively I reached over, squeezing his hand with my gloved one, a rare public gesture due to my psychic affliction. Thanks to that same psychic gift, I knew firsthand just how much Ceff had suffered when Melusine murdered their children. It had been centuries since his sons' deaths, but the grief was always swimming just beneath the surface.

I also knew just how much it hurt to lose a parent.

"I wonder if she has any living family," I said.

"If they were the traitors who screwed over Mab, they better hope they're dead," Torn said. "There are much worse fates than death, Princess."

Torn was right, but the hurt little girl I'd been still yearned for the father she'd lost. I swore that if I discovered anything during the search for my father that would reunite that other girl with her family, I would do my best to bring them together. In a way, it would be like continuing my father's work. He'd obviously cared enough about the child to risk the perils of Tech Duinn, not to mention Mab's wrath.

I smiled, eager to find a way to feel closer to the man I'd loved so completely before a magic geis stole my childhood memories. While so many of those memories had returned over the past few months, I still longed for more.

I stood, eager to be on our way. What secrets had my father left for me at the wisp court? Would I discover the name of the child he'd taken to the human world? Were her parents members of his court?

I shifted on my feet, and flashed Donn my most gracious smile.

"Thank you for the tea," I said, even though I hadn't touched a drop.

"This was fun, but we do need to be going," Torn said, coming to his feet.

Ceff nodded and stood on my left, using his body to shield me from the Morrigan who was watching me intently.

"Perhaps, Donn, you could show us the hearth," Ceff said.

"Of course," Donn said.

"We need to find the portal," I said, inching toward the hearth.

"That won't be a problem," he said. Thank Mab, I thought, something easy for a change. "Finding the lock that fits your key is another story."

He waved me closer, and I bent down to see that what I'd assumed was decorative stonework lacing the interior of the hearth was, in fact, a series of locks. There were hundreds of them.

"We don't have time for this," I groaned.

I ran a hand through my hair, eyes searching the hearth for clues. It was then that I noticed that the glitter I'd left on the mantel was now gone, giving me an idea.

"Perhaps the hearth brownie can help us," I said.

"That won't be necessary," Donn said. "Plus, Skilly is shy. It's unlikely he'll come if you call out to him, since we've been sitting close to the hearth all this time and he hasn't yet joined us."

"So how do I find the lock?" I asked.

"The answer is in the prophecy," Donn said.

Starlight flashed in his eyes, and I was once again reminded of his power.

"Donn is right," Ceff said.

I remembered the druid Bechuille's prophecy, trying to find a clue in her words.

Inside Donn's hearth bend your knee, close your eyes and turn the key.

I guess the trick was getting down on my knees and closing my eyes while holding my father's key. Since we were dealing with a magic portal to Faerie, it wasn't all that crazy of a concept.

"I guess now we just need to put the fire out," I said. "Are you sure we shouldn't consult with Skilly?"

"That won't be necessary," he said. "Allow me."

He snapped his fingers and the flames of the fire winked out, leaving only a small pile of smoking ash. It reminded me of the ash that coated the inside of my mouth, and I wished silently for a toothbrush.

With another snap of Donn's fingers, the pile of ash disappeared.

"Well, it was nice meeting you both," I said, forcing myself to smile.

It had actually been terrifying and somewhat disturbing, but I figured it was wise to be polite to the god of death and the goddess of war.

"Until next time," Torn said with a wink.

"I will see you soon enough," Morrigan said, lips lifting in a grin.

Ceff stiffened beside me, and I let the full meaning of her words sink in.

"So Jenna was right," I said. "War really is coming."

"Yes," Morrigan said, tilting her head back and letting out a hearty laugh.

I flinched as her laughter soon became a croaking caw as she shifted into a crow. The bird snatched a brownie, and flew up to one of the room's many bookshelves, ghostly heads making a rapid retreat at her approach. Crumbs rained down as she pecked at the brownie, and Donn smiled.

"She has such a sweet tooth," he said. "Not that she'd ever admit it."

"I'll remember that next time we meet," I said.

"Safe travels," he said.

I took a deep breath, ducked my head, and knelt inside the hearth. I was careful not to brush my head against the tapering rear wall of the fireplace. The last thing I needed was a psychic vision, or a pissed off hearth brownie.

I closed my eyes, and held the key in both hands like a dowsing rod. Kaye had taught me a thing or two about dowsing, for which I was grateful. When the key rotated to the right, I let my arms follow the movement.

With a gasp, my hands were jerked forward, and it was all I could do not to pull back. The key shot into the lock as if drawn by a powerful magnet. The key clicked in the lock, and someone whistled.

"Wow, Princess," Torn said. "Looks like you found the right lock, all right."

I cracked an eye open, half expecting to be surrounded by needles protruding from the hearth walls. Instead, I faced an ornate lock that glowed faintly with a bluish light.

"Now what?" I asked.

"I'm guessing you turn the key," Torn said with a shrug.

"Wait," Ceff said, leaning in for a better look. "We don't know how the portal functions. Perhaps we should all be touching when it opens, just in case. We do not want to be separated."

It was true that I hadn't come all this way to be separated from Ceff and Torn because of some magical technicality, but I hesitated, sucking in air through my teeth. Touching hadn't been part of the plan.

"Don't worry, Princess," Torn said. He gestured at his body, and smiled. "I know you can't handle all this, not many women can, so I'm sure holding onto your jacket will be enough to keep us together."

Ceff narrowed his eyes at Torn, but nodded.

"Okay, fine," I said. "Make it quick."

The faster we got this over with, the better. I bit the inside of my cheek to keep from snarling, as Ceff and Torn each grabbed one of my biceps.

"Ready," Ceff said.

I breathed in through my nose, and turned the key once. Donn's castle disappeared, leaving only the hearth suspended in empty space. We were no longer in Tech Duinn, but I doubted this was Faerie.

"Well," Torn said, a grin stretching from ear to ear. "That wasn't boring."

Only Torn would think battling a baphomet, and having tea with both the god of the dead and the goddess of war was fun.

"You are the king of understatement," I muttered.

I turned the key a second time, but nothing else happened. Smoke from the doused fire tickled my nose. *Third time's the charm.*

I bit my lip, and turned the key. My stomach suddenly became acquainted with my throat, and I gasped.

The void was gone, replaced with someplace alien, yet beautiful—a world that both repelled me, and sang like sweet music to the blood within my veins.

"Faerie."

CHAPTER 21

The smoke from Donn's fire had been replaced by mist. A land of thick, shapeless fog now stood at our backs. The hearth we'd traveled through was gone, feasibly returning to Tech Duinn once it finished transporting the three of us to Faerie.

Faerie. We'd actually made it. I was so close to answers about my father, I could almost taste it. But before I could get the answers that I so desperately needed, we had a new challenge to face.

My chest tightened at the realization that the portal hadn't led us somewhere convenient, like a secret chamber containing all of my father's secrets. The land before me was a riot of vivid colors and textures, every inch a new wonder to behold, but the fact remained that rather than arriving within the walls of the wisp court, we'd stumbled onto a crossroads.

"Welcome to Faerie, Princess," Torn said.

I blinked, and tried to force a smile. We'd made it. Now I just had to figure out a way into my father's court.

"Any idea which way leads to the wisp court?" I asked.

I spun in a circle, frowning at the two obvious choices. Aside from the veil of claustrophobia-inducing fog, there was a living wall of vines in front of us, and a shimmering path to our left.

I crouched down to get a better look at the path, mouth falling open when I realized that the glittering surface was ice. Frost created a delicate tracery of lines that resembled lace, or the web of a particularly poisonous spider.

I jerked my head up, squinting to make out the structure that wavered like an illusion on the horizon. I gasped, my breath fogging, as I realized what lay at the end of the icy path. I backed away, earning a hiss from one of the carnivorous plants as I moved closer to the wall of vines.

"Certainly not that way, Princess," Torn said. "Not unless you want to get dead."

"Is that really what I think it is?" I asked, pointing a gloved finger.

"Mab's palace," Ceff said. "Her royal seat of power, and the location of the Unseelie Court."

I shivered, and I was pretty sure it wasn't from the cold emanating from the icy path. Mab may not currently be in residence, but that didn't make her palace any less formidable.

The Unseelie Court was the same group of powerful fae who'd ordered my execution at the hands of the Moordenaar. While my dealings with the assassins had been in the human world, I had no illusions that Mab hadn't set up some way for the members of her court to communicate between the realms. No, the ones who'd decided that I was a traitor to our kind would be found within those walls.

If the Unseelie Court realized that I was alive, they'd finish what the Moordenaar started. Until I could demonstrate control over my wisp powers and create a glamour to protect our secret from humans, I'd be labeled a traitor—a crime punishable by death.

As if that wasn't reason enough to avoid the Unseelie throne, there were also the warnings that Kaye had given me before leaving Harborsmouth. Reaching Mab's castle would require a trip through the Forest of Torment, and that was one stroll through the woods I'd rather avoid.

Fog rose from the glistening path, once again obscuring the ice palace. I shook my head, pushing away thoughts of the Unseelie queen and her court. We weren't taking that path, so there was no sense worrying about Mab and her minions.

"If my father was fleeing Mab's wrath, I doubt he would have wanted me to give her palace a visit," I said. "I think we can scratch that path off our list."

That left the living wall of vines in front of us. The plants hissed and snapped, writhing like thorn covered snakes in their attempts to cannibalize one another.

"Looks like we have some gardening to do," Torn said, lips lifting in a grin.

"I would not be so certain," Ceff said, pointing to a camouflaged gap in the wall.

I squinted at the wall, eyes finally finding the outline of an opening, and sighed.

The only visible entrance through the vicious plants was blocked by a creature that resembled an enormous toad. Unless we wanted to take up Torn's idea of cutting our way through, we'd need to get the creature to move out of our way.

A plant resembling a Venus fly trap lashed out, snatching a bird that had flown too close to the wall, and I swallowed hard. Hacking our way through that wall of vines was becoming less and less appealing.

Giant toad it is then.

"Is that really a giant toad?" I asked.

The thing was the size of a Volkswagen Beetle, and covered in leathery skin that was a greenish hue, which matched the surrounding vines, and mottled with warts. Some of those warts were bigger than a grapefruit.

Torn shrugged.

"You're the one with second sight," he said. "You tell me."

I turned my head from side to side, trying to catch a glimpse of glamour, but the thing continued to look like a huge, sleeping toad.

"Maybe it'll move if we toss a rock over there, or poke it with a stick?" I asked.

"Poke it with a stick? Are ye daft, lass?"

I spun around, blades hitting the palms of my gloves. Ceff let out a warning snort, his eyes going black as he took up position at my side. Torn sauntered to my other side, looking bored, but I knew better. The stocky fellow at our feet had caught the cat sidhe's interest, and he was looking at it the same way a cat watches a tasty mouse.

"Who are you?" Ceff asked, voice hard.

"Ye not earned me name, an ye know it," the man said.

There was something familiar about the hairy, little man. He was short, with knobby hands and stubby legs, and beneath his thick eyebrows gleamed intelligent, mischievous eyes that were probably quick to anger. His hair was black, not white, but his resemblance to Hob was uncanny.

I slid my knives away in their sheath and lifted my hands, palm up.

"He meant no offense," I said.

"Well, I do," Torn said, shifting his weight to the balls of his feet as if to pounce. "I don't trust anyone who can sneak up on a cat sidhe."

Good point.

"I think what my friend meant to ask is why you're following us," I said, keeping my voice slow and even. I knew better than to piss off a hearth brownie. My friends did too. I'd just have to point out who our diminutive guest was. "You had such a clean and beautiful hearth to tend back in Tech Duinn. I'm surprised you'd leave it to follow us here."

"He's a hearth brownie?" Torn asked.

He hissed, and took a step back. Smart kitty. Even the lord of the cat sidhe wasn't immune to being pixed by a vengeful hearth brownie.

"Didna get dis treasure for me looks," he said, showing us a handful of glitter and cubic zirconia jewels, and flashing me a gap-toothed smile.

I nodded.

"He's a hearth brownie," I said. I cocked my head, and rubbed my chin, studying the brownie. "Now what shall we call you?"

He shrugged.

"How about George?" asked Ceff.

"Pfft!" The brownie sputtered, and stomped his feet.

"Or Lucille," Torn said, eyes glinting. "I like Lucille. Such a pretty name."

"I'm no George, and I aint no lassy!" he said, face going red.

I stifled a giggle, and nodded solemnly. If we actually laughed at the brownie, we'd be pixed for sure.

"Yes, we need a better name for you," I said. "But what?"

"Skillywidden!" he yelled.

"Ah, a fine name," Ceff said.

I nodded. It matched the nickname, Skilly, that Donn had used for his hearth brownie. While I was glad to solve that mystery, I still had no idea why Skillywidden had left Tech Duinn.

"Welcome, Skillywidden," I said. "So why did you follow us here?"

"You had a perfectly nice hearth back in Tech Duinn," Torn said, eyeing the brownie like he might sprout fangs any minute. "Why leave?"

"It was too bloody perfect," Skillywidden grumbled, kicking at a rock. "The dead dinnae leave messes, and Donn is a god. He dinnae even leave ash in the grate for Skilly to clean. I right gone sodding doololly when you lot showed up with your magic key."

"So you followed us out of Tech Duinn," I said.

"Always did want to ken where that portal went ta," he said with a shrug.

"Okay," I said, rubbing a hand over my face. "You can tag along if you like, but stay back if there's trouble. I can't guarantee your safety."

I wasn't sure how we were getting back to Harborsmouth now that the hearth with its magic portal was gone, but maybe if we could find our way here again, we'd be able to uncover the portal on our way out.

"Wouldna mind a bit o' danger," he said.

"Well, I do mind," I said. "Look, we need an exit strategy. Can you keep track of the way back to this spot? Eventually, we'll need to make our way through the portal again."

"Aye, I can see the hearth right there," he said. "I'd have to be blind not to find me way back."

The little brownie could still see Donn's hearth? He was already worth his weight in cubic zirconia. If we ever made it back to Harborsmouth, I'd make sure to send him his own bejeweling kit. Donn wouldn't know what hit him.

"Good," I said. "Keeping track of our location, and remembering the way back to the hearth, will be your job. It's an important job. We'll be counting on you."

"Think you can do all that?" Torn asked.

"Course I can," Skillywidden said. "I can do it while cleanin' Tech Duinn's ash from your hair, and shinin' your boots."

It was ironic that the very cleanliness that drove Skillywidden from Donn's hearth hadn't been true outside the doors of the death god's home. Corpse ash covered our hair and clothing, with streaks of ash and blood like war paint on both Ceff and Torn's faces. Skillywidden's eyes gleamed and his hands twitched, but I shook my head.

"If you're coming with us, you have to agree not to touch me," I said. "Ceff and Torn might be glad of your services, but I'm a different matter."

"But ye be filthy!" he said, waving his hands.

"I know," said with a sigh. "I'll try to fix that, but I need your promise."

"Just ye boots?" he asked, eyebrows raised.

"No," I said. "Now do we have a bargain?"

Skillywidden blew out a heavy sigh, but nodded.

"Aye, we have a bargain," he said.

If I hadn't experienced my share of bargains, I would have missed the sheen of sweat that broke out along his forehead, and the tightening of his lips. Faerie bargains hold power over the fae, especially purebloods. Even as a half-blood, the act of making a bargain usually stole my breath away.

I nodded, satisfied that Skillywidden would keep his word. Once made, there was no way to break a faerie bargain—not without dying and coming back from the dead. Been there, done that, and I don't plan on trying it again. Resurrection is highly overrated.

"As much as I'd love to be free of this filth," Ceff said, brushing ash from his shoulder. "I suggest we formulate a plan on how to move the creature that's barring our way inside the barrier."

"I say we fight," Torn said, a gleam in his eye as his claws extended.

"Fools," Skillywidden muttered.

"Got a better idea?" Torn asked, raising an eyebrow at the grumbling brownie.

"I do," I said.

"So how do you propose we get rid of our giant toad problem?" Torn asked.

"With a distraction," I said. "And I know just the thing."

CHAPTER 22

"I can't believe I'm doing this," I said through clenched teeth.

"It was your idea, Princess," Torn said. "Not our fault you drew the shortest stake."

I glared at Torn, and groaned. Damn the man, but he was right. This was my bright idea. The thing was, when I dreamed up this plan, I hadn't expected to play the role of bait. I also hadn't thought about how humiliating it would be to pretend to be toad food.

I turned to the toad, and grimaced. I lifted my arms, trying to remember if flies waved their wings up and down. I hadn't given the annoying insects much thought until now.

"Less groaning, more buzzing," he said.

Ceff choked on a laugh, and I folded my arms. He struggled to keep a straight face, and nodded.

"Torn is right," Ceff said. "It could have been any one of us."

"I bet Torn cheated," I said.

"Stop being a sore loser, and go be our distraction before I get bored with our plan and take matters into my own hands," Torn said, faking a yawn and waggling his claws in the air.

"Fine," I said.

I sighed, and scowled one last time at my friends. Torn was sporting a Cheshire cat grin; Ceff's lip continued to twitch as he wiped tears from his eyes; and Skillywidden stood off to the side, arms crossed over his chest. The brownie's scowl matched my own, though for different reasons.

Skillywidden had tried to add his two cents to our plan, but every time he started to speak, Torn cut him off. I'd talk to Torn about it later, but, for now, I had to focus on getting us past the giant toad, and inside the wisp court.

Frowning, I lifted my arms and started "flying" toward the toad faerie. When the creature didn't so much as twitch, I started to make a buzzing sound through clenched teeth. I blushed, keeping my eyes on the creature.

The plan was for me to lead the toad away from the wall, allowing my friends to slip through the gap. Once inside, they'd give me a signal, and I would run to join them. The toad was too large to fit through the wall, so we'd be safe once we were out of its reach.

At least, that was the plan. I should have known luring a giant faerie toad wouldn't be that easy.

The toad lurched toward me, and I flinched. There was something strange about its movements, and it never opened its eyes. In fact, from what I could see, its face hadn't moved a muscle.

Buzzing and flapping my arms, I sprinted away from the wall, trying to give my friends the opening they needed. I was so focused on my role as bait that I almost missed the first real clue that we weren't dealing with a toad, or any other kind of amphibian.

The creature straightened, unfurling from its shell. That was no toad. A beetle-like creature came to its feet, waving a multitude of barbed, segmented arms and legs, and snapping dripping mandibles in the direction of my friends.

I'd foolishly mistaken the designs on the creature's carapace for the face of a giant toad. No wonder the creature hadn't so much as blinked. I might have felt relieved that my fly charade was over, if it wasn't for my friends' predicament. Instead of slipping in behind a distracted giant toad, they now faced the business end of a pissed off beetle creature—one that looked capable of cutting them in half with its mandibles.

"Look out!" I screamed.

I lunged toward the beetle, all pretense of being a harmless fly gone. I was no juicy meal, and neither were my friends. The thick exoskeleton of the creature's shell deflected my first strike, but I'd expected as much. My goal was to try to distract the beetle fae long enough to get in position to defend Ceff and Torn. Together we might just have a chance against this thing.

I ran around the side of the creature, calves straining as I pushed myself to move faster. Heart racing, I searched for my friends, relieved when I caught sight of Skillywidden ducking inside the wall. With any luck, we could scare the creature off long enough to all slip through the opening.

I started to smile, but my relief was short-lived. The diminutive brownie was the only one of my friends to have escaped. Ceff and Torn hadn't been so lucky. They danced within reach of the creature's barbed limbs and dripping mandibles, fighting for their lives.

I needed to help them, and I needed to do it yesterday. As I came into range, I planted my feet as best I could in the spongy, mossy ground. But before I could set up a proper throw, one of the creature's limbs came at me like a black, barbed two by four. I spun, twisting out of its reach.

Damn, that thing was fast.

Blood pounding in my ears, I gave up on my throwing knives, and drew my machete. My blades wouldn't do much against the creature's hard exoskeleton, but its spindly limbs looked more vulnerable than its shell. I might be able to keep it from whipping those barbed arms and legs around, permanently.

I took a deep breath, and leapt. The spongy ground worked against me, but I still managed a decent jump. Thank Mab for enhanced speed and agility. Holding the handle in a flexible pinch grip, I swung the machete in an arc, my body spinning slightly with the movement. I grit my teeth as the blade cut through the outer layers of chitin and sank through the softer meat of the leg. The machete pulled at my wrist, but I tightened my grip as the blade came out the other side. The leg fell twitching at my feet.

I spun, allowing my momentum to carry me closer to an arm that was crashing toward me, and proceeded to hack off another one of the creature's multi-segmented limbs. Ivy-2, Beetle-0.

I caught Ceff's smile, and nodded as we danced past each other. My lips lifted in a grin, and I pushed myself to move faster. Maybe this wouldn't be so tough after all.

A strange chirp-like whirring sound drew my attention, and I realized why the loss of limbs wasn't causing the beetle to lose its balance. It was vibrating wings that had until now remained hidden on its back, beneath the outer carapace. Those wings were helping to keep the beetle on its feet, not that it needed to keep its balance for long.

The grin slid from my lips as a pale grey, wormlike protuberance emerged from one of the wounds, quickly forming into a new leg. Eyes wide, I watched as a second limb did the same. The damn thing could regenerate. Within seconds, the limbs were fully formed and had grown layers of black protective chitin.

We needed to change our strategy. There was no way we could wear this creature down, or scare it off. Instead, it could continue fighting until we grew tired and sloppy. With what we'd already faced in Tech Duinn, and the vines sneaking out from the wall to grab at our feet, that probably wouldn't take too long.

I jabbed between the legs, dancing in and out of the beetle fae's reach, hoping to find a weak spot. My blade repeatedly scraped across armored exoskeleton with the telltale clack of metal against chitin, until finally, the edge of my machete sliced into flesh. Too bad I didn't have time to do more damage.

The minor cut infuriated the beetle fae, eliciting a series of high-pitched, brain numbing shrieks. Its limbs flailed, and one of the arms struck a lucky blow, knocking me off my feet. I flew through the air, eyes wide, but managed to keep hold of my weapon, even when I hit the ground hard. The moss that had made for difficult footing while fighting, now managed to break my fall enough to keep from breaking bones, but sadly it wasn't soft enough to prevent getting the wind knocked out of me.

As soon as I could catch my breath, I waved my arms and yelled, "Go for the abdomen!"

I pulled myself to my feet, but Torn was already darting in, and Ceff hacked away at limbs, keeping the creature busy. Torn raked his claws across the creature's soft, unprotected belly, and I gasped.

Flowers sprang from the creature's abdomen in a bright riot of color. With one final screech, the beetle fae's wings stilled, and it toppled onto its back. Flowers continued to sprout from the bloody wound, reaching up toward the wall where plants were already sending out the tips of leaves and the curling ends of vines to give the newcomers a tentative prodding.

"I guess you really are what you eat," Torn said, wiping his claws on the mossy ground. I groaned, and he raised an eyebrow. "What? Too soon?"

Not wanting to find out how the local flora would respond to the flowers spiraling up from the beetle fae's guts, I shook my head and ducked through the gap in the wall. Ceff and Torn followed close behind.

Skillywidden stood waiting for us, his hands on his hips. I nearly turned back the way we'd come. I'd rather face carnivorous plants than a pissed off brownie any day of the week.

CHAPTER 23

"I tried to warn ye, but ye wouldna listen," Skillywidden said.

I shook my head, remembering the brownie's frustration during our planning session. Now I knew why he'd been so angry with Torn. He'd been trying to explain that the giant toad was, in fact, a beetle fae. If only we'd listened.

"You knew it wasn't a toad?" Torn asked with a hiss. "Why the Hell didn't you tell us that in the first place?"

"He tried, Torn, but you kept cutting him off," I said.

I rubbed a hand over my face, grimacing at the corpse ash, sweat, and who knew what else I smudged across my skin.

"Now quit sulking and let Skillywidden clean you off," I said, flashing Torn my teeth in a smile.

"And you, Princess?" he asked. "You going to stay looking like a character from The Walking Dead?"

"No," I said, face warming. "I have other ideas. Ceff?"

"It would be my pleasure," he said.

As Ceff used his water magic to draw moisture from the air, I closed my eyes and tried not to think about some of the more creative ways he'd used that power. Ceff could do amazing things with his water magic, but right now, I just needed a simple rinsing off. Water flowed over my skin, washing away the thick layer of ash.

"I am done," Ceff said. "And so, it appears, is Skillywidden."

I opened my eyes to see Ceff and Skillywidden grinning from ear to ear. Torn, on the other hand, was glaring at the brownie, claws retracting and extending as he flexed his hands. Someone wasn't pleased with their bath.

"Problem?" I asked, cocking an eyebrow at Torn.

"He...he...the little bastard scrubbed off all my skin!" he said.

"Ye was dirty," Skillywidden said, thumbs hooked in his suspenders as he rocked back on his heels.

"Stop whining, Torn," I said. "You still have plenty of skin."

"Easy for you to say, Princess," he muttered. "It's not like you had a brownie scour all the skin off your arse. I won't be able to sit for a week."

My lip twitched, and I turned away from the cat sidhe and the wall of writhing vines. We'd made it through Tech Duinn and into Faerie, but we still had a long way to go. My father's key had led us to the edge of his domain. Now it was up to us to survive long enough to get the answers we'd come here for.

I just hoped we didn't kill each other first.

"Come on," I said. "It looks like we've reached Nithsdale. There's a swamp over there."

I ignored Torn's grumbling, and stalked toward the swamp until the ground became too wet to walk easily. The mossy ground had become progressively spongier until finally, we were calf deep in water. That was when I noticed that the shifting, low-lying fog ahead of us had taken on a greenish tinge.

"Kaye said that my father's court is surrounded by a bog that belches poisonous gas," I said, grimacing at a whiff of sulfur that burned my nose.

"She share anything else about this bog?" Torn asked.

"Yeah, it swallows men whole," I said. Torn waggled his eyebrows suggestively, and I frowned. "Her words, not mine. Anyway, we need to find a way across."

"Word of advice?" Torn offered. "Don't follow the wisps."

"Torn is right," Ceff said. "Ignore any lights you see in the bog. They will try to lead you astray. Don't let them."

"You think my wisp cousins will try to kill me?" I asked.

"It is in their nature," he said with a nod. "Plus, they may not recognize you as one of their own, let alone the daughter of Will-o'-the-Wisp."

"It's not like you're a little ball of sunshine, Princess," Torn said. "Odds are, they'll try to kill us first, and ask questions later."

"Well damn, I guess they won't be getting solstice gifts this year," I said.

I forced a brittle smile. I could make light of the fact the wisps might try to kill me, but I was far from okay with having homicidal branches on my family tree.

I also didn't like the parallels between what I was doing, and what was typical wisp behavior. I was leading my friends into a deadly swamp—I just hoped that it wasn't to their deaths.

"Stayin' outta the bog won't do ye any good if ye can't breathe," Skillywidden muttered.

He had a point.

"Ceff?" I asked. "Do you think you can use your water magic to create a bubble around our heads? One that will keep the poisonous gas out?"

"Yes," he said with a nod. "But once the water is in place, we will have to move fast. The amount of clean air in each bubble will be limited."

"Okay," I said as Ceff's magic tingled along my skin.

Right, move fast and risk getting sucked into a deadly sinkhole, or suffocate. I didn't like either of those alternatives. I looked around as we started to run, searching for a way to increase our chances of survival.

I tried not to breathe too heavy, but I was already seeing spots, the first signs of oxygen deprivation. At this rate, we'd never make it out of the bog. I shook my head, and took a slow breath, but the spots of light didn't go away.

Wisps.

Even with the water surrounding my head muffling the sound, I could hear a humming ring through the air. It was different from the discordant sounds the sickly wisps had made back in the junkyard. These wisps were healthy, strong, and on their home turf. I should have been afraid, but instead, I smiled.

The wisp song was the same tone that my father's key had made when I used it to unlock the portal to Faerie. What if that same tone would help us navigate the bog? I'd thought of a dowsing rod when I used the key to find the lock inside Donn's hearth, but maybe it was more like a magical sonar.

With nothing to lose, I unzipped the pocket where I'd stashed the key, and held it out in front of my body. Immediately, the key pulled to the right. My body jerked, just as my left foot began to sink into the ground. My stumble yanked the foot free with a sucking sound, and my eyes widened.

It worked, and just in time. I waved to my friends, and took the lead, holding the key in front of me as I ran. Wisps streamed alongside us, a cavalcade of deadly fireflies lighting our way.

CHAPTER 24

Wisps buzzed through the air, their musical humming rising in pitch as they darted in for a closer look. I sat on the mossy embankment and smiled, watching the playful wisps.

With my father's key helping to guide us, we'd left the deadly bog and its poisonous gas behind. I breathed deeply, and let out a happy sigh.

"I don't know what you're so happy about," Torn said, shaking water from his hair. "We're covered in mud and smell like troll farts."

It was true. The sulfurous swamp gasses did smell an awful lot like something that would come out of Marvin after he ate an entire cauldron of Kaye's chili, but I didn't care. We were alive. And so far, my wisp brethren weren't trying to kill me.

I'm not sure what it said about my life that the lack of fratricide upon my homecoming made me feel all warm and fuzzy inside. Probably best not to think too much about it, and just enjoy the moment.

I shrugged, and kept on smiling.

"Well don't get too comfortable, Fish Breath is on his way over with his pensive face on," Torn said.

He stalked off to sit on a rock a few paces away, but I shrugged again and closed my eyes, turning my face to the moon and stars above us. I wasn't going to let Torn ruin this moment.

"Are you feeling well?" Ceff asked, settling on the mossy ground beside me.

I cracked an eye open, grinning from ear to ear.

"I feel great, never better," I said. In fact, I felt a bit dizzy and my lips tingled, like I'd had too much to drink. Only I would get buzzed off the buzzing of wisps. "Just buzzed off the buzzing."

I hiccupped, and giggled, the laugh coming out in an undignified snort that startled the nearest wisps.

"Are you sure that you are not angry, or afraid?" he asked.

I forced myself to look up into Ceff's face. His head was tilted to the side, as if listening for something, but his attention was focused solely on me.

"I'm fiiine, really," I said, waving a hand. My eyes widened, and I let out another giggle. "I'm glowing."

"Which is probably what has his highness' panties in a bunch," Torn said, coming over to tower above me, arms crossed. "There is something weird about seeing you smile like that, especially when you're glowing."

"What?" I asked. "I smile."

"Almost never, and when you do, it's usually because you're killing something," he said. "Not that I'm judging. I'm just saying Fish Breath has a point. You're different."

"She is high on power," Ceff said, eyes going tight. "I should have recognized the signs sooner, but I was focused on our flight through the bog, and then with releasing the water magic that held our masks together."

"You think it's the wisps?" Torn asked.

"That would be my guess," Ceff said, rubbing his jaw.

"This didn't happen after our run in with those wisps in Ocean Overlook cemetery, did it?" Torn asked.

"No," Ceff said. "Not that we noticed. But Ivy was badly wounded that night, and took days to recover consciousness. And...I...I was not at my most attentive."

That was the night that I'd killed his ex-wife. Melusine may have been the raging psychotic bitch who'd murdered his children, and tried to kill us as well, but that didn't mean her death had been easy on Ceff.

The memory of Ceff's grief flooded me, pushing the giddiness away.

"I think...I think I'm back to normal now," I said. I yawned, covering my mouth with the back of my gloved hand. Ignoring the encroaching bone-deep fatigue, I tried to pull myself to my feet, but sank back down when a wave of dizziness nearly toppled me over. "I just need a minute."

"You are exhausted," Ceff said, brow wrinkling. "Rest here. I will keep first watch."

"But my father's court..." I said, but my words were cut short by another yawn.

"Will still be there tomorrow," Torn said.

"Plus, I can scout ahead while you sleep," Ceff said. "We will make better progress if we are rested and certain of the path ahead."

"Fine," I said, eyes fluttering closed. "But just a quick nap."

The last thing I saw, before losing myself to the darkness of sleep, was a cloud of wisps hovering over me, lending me their warmth...and their power.

CHAPTER 25

"What the...?" I asked with a grunt.

The white hot pain returned, and I lost the ability to speak. I was reduced to the primal drives of fight or flight—and to remove whatever was sending burning spikes of pain on either side of my spine.

I clawed at my back, trying to dislodge whatever sharp object I'd been pierced with, but my gloved hands met only the smooth surface of my leather jacket.

"Princess?" Torn asked, moving into my field of vision. His face swam before me, and for a split second, I wondered if I might puke on his boots. It would serve him right for staring at me like I was a cat toy on a string. "You don't look so good."

"You think?" I snapped, struggling to find the source of the pain and only managing to contort my arms painfully behind my back. "How about a little help here?"

"And what, pray tell, would I be helping with?" he asked, flashing me a look that said he clearly thought I was deranged. That was rich, coming from the lord of the cat sidhe.

I struggled to make sense of the situation. We'd made camp shortly after crossing the poisonous bog. Ceff had gone off to scout ahead, and to guard the perimeter, while Torn had stayed here with me. I'd fallen into a coma-like sleep, but woke feeling refreshed. Heck, I was better than refreshed, my body tingled with energy.

I was pacing the mossy embankment like a caffeinated pookah when I'd been stabbed in the back. But that didn't make sense. I hadn't seen or heard my attacker, and obviously, neither had Torn, judging by his smirk.

"If this is a ruse to get me to rub your back, we can skip the theatrics," he said, crossing his arms. "We both know what you really want."

Oberon's eyes, Torn thought I was asking for a back rub, with all that that implied.

"What I want is for you to..." I said, through clenched teeth.

I gasped at another jolt of pain. Sweat broke out on my forehead, immediately running into my eyes. I blinked, and when I opened my eyes again, I was on my knees. I continued to claw at my back, but I couldn't find the source of the pain, not with my gloves on.

Torn slid onto all fours, making the pose appear both graceful and sensual as he brought his face once again close to mine. I was guessing that unlike me, he wasn't suffering from bruised kneecaps.

"Ah, Princess," he said, a slow smile building on his lips. "Panting and on your knees...have you finally succumbed to my charm? It did take you an awfully long time, but I'm willing to forgive you—after a good spanking or two."

"Torn, you arrogant...bastard...help me remove whatever's stabbing...me...in...the...back," I said.

I gave up trying to reach my back, and placed my gloved hands flat on the ground, leveling my most terrifying glare at Torn. It was a look that said, "When this is done, I will kill you," and not, "Hey, baby, I'm in the mood for cat sidhe sexy times."

Torn tilted his head to the side, and slunk around me with feline grace. I had to fight to remain still, especially when his leather clad ass was positioned inches from my face for what seemed an eternity, but eventually, he completed his circuit and came to a stop in front of me, sitting on his haunches.

"There's nothing sticking out of your back, Princess," he said, eyebrow raised. "Are you sure this isn't some twisted sort of trick to get me to check out your butt?" His slit pupils widened, almost appearing human, as he leaned closer. "I like twisted."

"I'm going...to skin...you alive...and turn...you into...slippers," I said.

"I'd like to see..."

The rest of Torn's witty rejoinder was cut off as his head slammed into the ground, six feet away. I blinked, my brain trying to catch up with this turn of events. I took a deep breath, struggling to grab my blades and fight—had my attacker returned?—but I froze as I recognized my boyfriend's profile.

"What did you do to Ivy?" Ceff asked, slamming Torn's head against the ground one more time before stepping away.

Ceff's fists opened and closed as his chest heaved, nostrils flaring. Veins protruded from his neck, and his eyes had gone black as a stormy night.

"Nothing, Fish Breath, though the night is young," Torn said, dusting himself off. He flashed me a wink, and I sighed.

"Ceff," I said. "Don't let Torn get to you. He's not worth it."

I slid my knives back into their wrist sheaths, but when I tried to stand, I was once again wracked with a wave of pain.

"Mab's bloody bones on a god's damned stick," I hissed.

"Where are you hurt?" Ceff asked.

"My back," I said. "Either side of my thoracic spine. Both shoulder blades."

He ran his fingers over my leather jacket, and I let out a low moan. My hands fisted in the bog moss, and I clamped my jaw shut against a scream.

"I see nothing," he said.

"Um, Princess?" Torn asked. "I have an idea, but you're not going to like it."

"Spit it out, Torn," I said.

"Take your jacket and shirt off," he said.

"Bite me," I hissed through clenched teeth.

"Back off, cat," Ceff said, moving between me and Torn at lightning speed.

"Think, Ivy," Torn said, ignoring my overprotective boyfriend, and maneuvering back into my line of sight. "What do you know about wisps?"

I tried to think, but it was impossible to focus through the pain.

"If you know something, say it now," Ceff said.

I took a shaky breath, watching Torn shrug as Ceff's trident suddenly appeared inches from his face. The cat sidhe pushed the weapon away with the tips of his fingers, but kept his eyes on mine.

I swallowed hard, a rush of heat making my skin burn.

"Wisps glow," I said, breath ragged.

"Yes, and?" Torn asked.

"Wisps...fly," I said.

He nodded, watching me like I was a tasty mouse.

"And how do you suppose they fly?" he asked.

"Wisps...wisps..." I said, voice breaking off in a strangled cry.

"Wisps have wings," Ceff said.

He took a step back, face going pale.

"Wondered when you two would figure it out," Torn said. "Now take off that jacket before I have to cut it off."

I growled at Torn, partly over the threat to my clurichaun crafted jacket, and partly due to the pain that was coming now in near constant waves.

"Ceff?" I asked.

But when I looked up, expecting his strong hands to help me, he hadn't moved. He stood with eyes wide, as if rooted to the spot. *Wisps have wings.*

A familiar fear crept to the surface, one that I'd stifled over the past few months. Doubt gnawed at old insecurities, taking advantage of my pain and confusion. My hands fisted in the moss as I fought to quiet the tiny voice inside my skull that whispered that it was no wonder my father had abandoned me, my mother and stepfather avoided me, my schoolmates taunted me. I was unworthy of love.

I was a monster.

My cheeks burned, and I wished that I could run away, be alone. I didn't want my friends to see this ugly side of me, the part of me that I'd always feared would one day take over. Even before I knew about my fae blood, I'd known that I was different.

I'd come here hoping for answers that would bring me closer to my father, closer to having the family that I'd lost. I'd come here looking for a way to control my wisp powers, so that I could create a glamour and hide my otherness from the world. I'd wanted to play at being a happy, normal human.

I'd been a fool.

"Get out of the way you imbeciles!"

A man appeared at the top of the embankment. I don't know how long he'd been standing there. I wasn't exactly at my best.

But I should have noticed such a force of raw power. The man stood tall and slender, all lean muscle beneath his calfskin boots and flowing robes. Pale, pointed ears poked through long, straight hair the shade of burning cities. He was at once familiar, and yet I had never met him before. That made his next words all the more shocking.

"Unhand my niece."

CHAPTER 26

I *have an uncle.* The thought danced through my head, ebbing and flowing with the increasingly frequent waves of pain, but managing through it all to stay afloat. Beyond the pain, I could think of nothing else.

I should have noticed the family resemblance as soon as I set eyes on the man, but in my defense, I felt like goblins had climbed inside my skin and proceeded to poke me with burning brands from the inside out. I wiped tears and sweat from my eyes, squinting at the man in a rare moment of respite.

With the pale skin and flame red hair, it would have been easy to mistake my uncle for my father at first glance, but where my father had kind eyes, my uncle seemed impervious to emotion. I'd met stones that were less stoic than this man.

"I bet he'd make a mint at poker," Torn whispered.

I tried to picture this elegant man in his white knee breeches and flowing spider silk robes sitting at a card table playing Texas hold'em, and snickered. At least, I snickered inwardly. To everyone else, it came out like a whimper.

"This is Ivy Granger, daughter of Will-o'-the-Wisp, princess to the wisp court, and my consort," Ceff said.

"Yes, I know that she is the lost princess," my uncle said. "I would recognize that face anywhere. She bears an uncanny resemblance to her parents, and, of course, she has my brother's eyes."

Eyes that were currently glowing like the sun.

"Then can you help her?" Ceff asked.

He'd moved in to protect me, with one hand on my shoulder, and the other on the handle of his trident.

"Of course, but the cat sidhe is right," my uncle said. "You must strip her of her garments, or they will impede the transformation."

"No one is stripping me of anything," I said, biting out the words.

I shook off Ceff's protective hand, bit the inside of my cheek, and pulled off my leather jacket, one arm at a time.

"She does'na like to be touched," Skilly said, shaking his head.

"Interesting," my uncle said, his auburn brows lifting toward the slender crown that banded his forehead.

Panting with the effort, I struggled to remove the stretchy black shirts that clung to my sweaty skin like a wet bathing suit. I left the sports bra where it was. No matter what was going on, there was no way I was getting naked in front of Torn.

Head spinning, my hand went to the utility belt at my waist that held most of my charms. I'd kept my wrist sheaths on, which meant I still had my throwing knives handy, and a dagger in each boot, but being without my charms would make me vulnerable, which was saying a lot considering that I was shirtless and on my knees wracked with pain.

I narrowed my eyes at the man who so resembled my father. He was watching with the intensity of a raptor, prepared to strike at any moment. This man may look familiar, but if he'd resided in Faerie all these years, I didn't doubt that he had the equivalent of a razor-sharp beak and claws—and knew how to use them.

"How do I know that you're my uncle?" I asked. "I don't even know your name."

His lips pressed into a hard line, but he waved his hand.

"We don't have time for this," he said.

As if to prove the validity of his claim, my shoulders contorted, the muscles in my back writhing beneath the skin. A tear escaped to fall onto the mossy ground.

I'd been prepared to face monsters. Not once had I suspected that my own body would betray me.

"Tell her your name," Ceff said.

He used the tone he normally reserved for dealing with petulant subjects who'd brought their quarrels before him at court. Ceff was a king, and when he put that edge of power into his voice, he expected to be obeyed. My uncle frowned, glancing away from me to give Ceff a closer look.

"I have many names, but you can call me Kade," he said. "Now stop wasting time, and grab one of those knives. If I am to believe that this is truly her first transformation, then she will need assistance. Someone will need to cut through the skin about a hand's width from either side of the spine."

"No," I snarled, sweat rolling down my face.

"You are wing bound," he said. "Do you know what that means?"

"No...and I don't care," I said.

"You will care when your wings carve a reverse path through your chest cavity, slicing your heart and lungs to bloody ribbons," he said. "Now stop acting like a child."

"I'm not a child," I said petulantly, stomach clenching.

My blades had drawn a lot of blood. If they touched my skin, I'd be in for more than surgery at the hands of my friends. I'd be sucked into a round of violent visions that I didn't know if I could pull myself out of.

"Obviously, though I do have to wonder how you have managed to reach maturity without ever having completed the change," he said, head tilted to the side. "Why has no one ever taught you these things? And physically...how are you so...stunted? Developmentally, you are no more advanced than an infant."

Gee, thanks, uncle. Nothing like kicking a girl when she's down.

"She was raised in the human world," Ceff said.

"Being raised in the human world explains some things," Kade said, his eyes on me. "For one, that you are still alive. Someone with your lack of skills would never have survived this long in Faerie. But what I truly do not understand is why your father never taught you any of this."

"He left me," I said.

I gasped, my chest tightening.

"Fine, we will continue this discussion later," he said. "Now, who will cut her, or do I need to do it?"

He grimaced, and I could tell that family connection or not, my uncle did not want to touch the lowly half-breed. I waited for Ceff to come forward, but he'd backed away again. He stood watching me, face an impenetrable mask.

"I'll do it," Torn said.

My eyes widened, but I shook my head.

"You are not touching me," I said.

"I won't use the blades," he said. "I don't think you can handle a vision right now. For that reason, I'll be careful not to touch skin to skin—though for the record, you're missing out."

"What'll you use then?" I asked.

"These," he said, extending razor sharp claws. "My body builds a new layer of keratin every time they retract. It helps to keep them sharp and strong. It also means that touching you with them shouldn't induce a vision."

Normally, I'd be intrigued by Torn revealing the inner workings of cat sidhe claw physiology, but not today. All I cared about was that he'd considered the risk of visions, and deemed his claws to be my best bet. My eyes widened as I realized that was good enough for me.

"Do it," I said with a nod.

"Ivy," Ceff said. "Bite down on that."

He was pointing to one of the wooden stakes thrust through my utility belt. I'd carved and sanded them myself, and they'd never been used. I reached for my belt, grabbed the stake with shaking hands, and bit down.

"You ready, Princess?" Torn asked.

I nodded. Ready as I'll ever be. Two lines of heat welled on either side of my spine as Torn raked his claws down my back.

"Now what?" Torn asked.

"Now she must complete the transformation, or die," Kade said.

My gloved hands fisted in the moss as I tried to focus on pushing wings through the cuts Torn had opened in my back. I'm pretty sure that all I did was give myself heartburn. I shook my head, and moaned.

"She's dying," Ceff said. "Help her."

"We've done what we can—now she must help herself," Kade said.

"But she doesn't know how," Torn hissed.

"It is not that complicated," Kade said with a sigh. My uncle's face came into view as he crouched before me. "Listen, you must focus on releasing your wings. It is like breathing, or stretching your arms. You are a wisp, so be a wisp."

Oh yeah, that was helpful.

"Come on, lass," Skillywidden said. "Ye can do this with yer hands tied. It's just like ridin' a cat."

The thought of Skilly riding around on Torn's back was enough to distract me momentarily from my pain. But that was all I needed. My body relaxed, allowing the muscles in my upper back and neck to ease, and I focused on my breathing.

Come on, Ivy. Skilly's right. You can do this.

"Yes, draw your power inside with each breath," Kade said. "On the exhale, release your wings."

I did as he said. I breathed in through my nose, drawing power from Faerie and the nearby wisps as I inhaled, and felt the stirring of something in my chest. I focused on my upper back, sending the heat of my power there. Teeth digging into the wooden stake, I let out a primal scream.

Pain exploded inside my ribs, nearly knocking me out, but I held on. I forced my magic to pour through the openings in my back, and, to my surprise, it did. A strange, new part of me reached to the sky, and unfurled. Blood, my blood, rained down on my back and the side of my face, and I sighed.

The muscles in my back and neck throbbed as the final spasms wracked my body, but the worst of the pain was gone, replaced by a dizzying euphoria. I spit the wooden stake from my mouth, and took a steadying breath.

"Is it over?" I asked.

"Yes," Kade said.

"You have wings," Ceff said.

I bit my lip, and my heart started to race. I couldn't tell from Ceff's voice what he was thinking, and from where he was standing, I couldn't read his face.

"Are they…hideous?" I asked.

"They're a bit like a damselfly's wings," Torn said.

"Aye, they're shimmery, and kinda skinny," Skillywidden said.

I swallowed hard. Don't panic. It could be worse. They could be leathery like a bat's wings. Insect wings weren't all that bad.

"They are beautiful," my uncle said. "You are beautiful, and you are one of us. Welcome to Faerie, Ivy. Welcome home."

CHAPTER 27

A buzzing filled my ears, and soon dozens of voices were roaring in my head. I put my gloved hands to my temples and moaned.

"What is it, Princess?" Torn asked.

"Ah, she is unprepared for the psychic connection she now has to the wisps here," Kade said.

"Psychic connection?" Ceff asked.

"Yes, until she can control it, the voices will be overwhelming," Kade said. "Our wings act like an antenna, amplifying the thoughts and voices of wisps in close proximity."

"How do I make it stop?" I asked, squeezing my eyes shut tight.

It didn't help. My back teeth were vibrating with the voices screaming in my head.

"I can help with this, but it will take training," he said. "Until you are more skilled, I suggest you retract your wings."

"And how do I do that?" I asked.

"The process is similar to releasing your wings, but do not worry, it will not hurt like before," he said.

I focused on my back, but nothing happened. I opened my eyes, and shook my head.

"Come," he said, gesturing toward the nearby water's edge. "It will be easier if you can see your wings, at least until you become accustomed to them. It is easier to visualize what you have seen."

"Makes sense," Torn said with a shrug. "As kits, we look at our paws when we practice extending and retracting our claws. Same general concept, I suppose."

I struggled to my feet, and raised an eyebrow at Ceff.

"I am sorry, I cannot relate to this," he said. "My transformation is very different."

I suppose he was right, though his words set my stomach churning. This was just one more difference for us to overcome. I'd known from the beginning that we were different from one another, but I had no idea that I was some winged wonder with voices in her head. I winced. I was pretty sure that bug wings and hearing voices weren't attractive qualities.

I turned, and followed my uncle to the pool of water. My eyes widened at the woman I met there. Her hair was matted with sweat, and her luminescent skin was pale and dotted with drops of blood, but she wasn't ugly. She wasn't hideous. She wasn't a monster.

With the glowing skin and translucent wings, she looked almost fragile. I suppose in a way that was true. I survived my first transformation, and it had changed me. For all intents and purposes, I was a newborn faerie.

I took a deep breath, and turned to get a better look at the wings that sprouted from my back. Skilly was right. They were slenderer than a dragonfly's wings, but with a similar shimmering quality, like an oil slick on water.

My wings twitched, attracting a handful of wisps. Glowing orbs appeared in the mirror surface of the puddle, and I started to smile. If you ignored the blood and sweat, it was nearly a fairytale scene from a children's book. But fairytales rarely have happy endings.

A cacophony of voices joined the buzzing in my head, and I gasped.

"Mab's bones, make it stop," I said.

"Open your eyes, and look at your wings in the reflection," Kade said. "Ignore the voices, and focus on the wings."

I blushed, heat rising to my cheeks, and I opened my eyes, staring at my reflection. I hadn't even realized that I'd squeezed my eyes shut.

"Okay," I said.

Ignoring the voices was easier said than done. Thankfully, I was no stranger to pain. I'd been experiencing skull crushing headaches for years as a result of my psychic abilities. Now those years of suffering might just pay off.

I grit my teeth, and pushed the voices and my emotions into an icy cage. I focused on my wings, twitching in time with the beating of my heart.

"Good, now imagine your wings slowly curling from the tips inward," Kade said.

I did as he said, and my jaw dropped as my wings began to curl behind my back. I sighed as the muscles in my shoulders relaxed.

"Now draw your wings inside your body," Kade said.

I swayed, listening to the musical quality of my uncle's voice, but I couldn't recall the words. My body was light, and the air caressed my fevered skin. If it wasn't for a distant humming, I could have closed my eyes and fallen asleep on my feet.

"Ivy?" Ceff asked.

"Hmmm?"

"She looks drunk," Torn said.

"Aye, drunk as a clurichaun on payday," Skillywidden said.

"It is what happens to our children when they are learning to use their magic," Kade said. "I believe she is intoxicated by the power running through her veins. She will become accustomed to it, in time."

"This is not her first time using her wisp powers," Ceff said.

"I do not know what my brother did to her, but it is obvious that her magic has been shackled," Kade said. "When she arrived in Faerie, she was barely fae. Now she is closer to her true self."

"It hasn't had an effect on any of us," Torn said. "Is it because she's half human? Is Faerie stripping her of her humanity?"

I wanted to tell Ceff and Torn to stop worrying. The pain was gone, and except for a heaviness between my shoulder blades, I felt great, better than normal. Heck, maybe being human was overrated.

"I do not have all the answers," Kade said. "I do not know what sorcery my brother used. All I can say is that she is evolving into the faerie she was always meant to be."

"So we must wait and see," Ceff said.

"Yes, but first she must complete this," Kade said. "Ivy?"

"Mmm?"

"You have done very well," Kade said. I smiled. My uncle thought I'd done well. "But there is one more thing you must do before you can rest."

I frowned, and tried to focus on his swimming face.

"What now?" I asked.

My lips felt rubbery, but the words came out clearly. No slurring.

"Your wings are curled, now you must pull them inside," he said. "Can you do that for me?"

"Mmm hmm," I said.

I took a breath, and pulled. I frowned when they got stuck partway, but I didn't give up. I wanted this over with, wanted to rest...and to please my uncle. I knew that latching onto my uncle, a total stranger, was probably unhealthy, but I didn't care. I'd had a gaping hole in my heart my entire life, and if he could help to fill that emptiness, then I would do everything to make him proud of me.

I raised my arms, rotating my shoulder blades until the wings finally fit. With a grunt, the wings were gone. If everyone hadn't already been staring at me, I might have thought it was all a dream.

"Better?" Kade asked.

I nodded, a tentative smile on my lips. I was more fae than I'd been when I woke up this morning. I now had wings, a new psychic connection with wisps, and an uncle I hadn't known existed. I wasn't sure what to make of the situation, but I was in Faerie and I was alive.

Better didn't cover the half of it.

CHAPTER 28

I wouldn't let them carry me. I hadn't experienced a vision since stepping foot in Faerie, and I didn't plan on starting now. So I chugged a Red Bull that had somehow managed to remain in Ceff's satchel unscathed, and followed Kade into a nearby cave that he claimed was the entrance to Tearlach, home of the wisp court.

I may have daddy issues and a desire to be loved by my uncle, but that didn't mean I was a fool. I kept my eyes open, weapons handy, weight on the balls of my feet, and forced my body to stay alert.

I gripped my blades as I entered the stygian darkness. These tunnels might lead to the wisp court and answers to my father's whereabouts, or certain death. Either way, it was best to be prepared for the worst.

"How...far?" I asked, voice still shaky from the wing ordeal.

The euphoria-inducing endorphins that had flooded my bloodstream were dissipating, slamming me with fatigue and a plethora of body aches.

I stifled a yawn, blinking rapidly, struggling to stay on my feet. Steel-toe boots had saved me from crippling my toes, but stumbling over rocks was likely to pitch me face first into Torn, who was walking ahead of me, and that was one round of visions I did not need.

"If you are too tired to walk..." Kade said.

"No, no, I'm fine," I said, waving a hand. "Lead on. I just wish I could call up enough anger to light the way."

I hadn't realized that I said that last part until Kade came to a halt, nearly causing me to collide with Torn after all.

"Why would you need anger to light the way?" he asked. "Is this a colloquialism? Except for indirect communication through the Unseelie Court, I have long been out of contact with the human world."

"Her anger fuels her wisp magic," Ceff said. "With...unpredictable results."

That was putting it mildly.

"Is this true, Ivy?" Kade asked.

"Um, yes, it's not like I've had any training," I said. "My father took off when I was just a kid, going so far as to lock away my memories of his existence, and it's not like I can ask the other wisps."

"Why not?" he asked.

"Because," I said with a weighty sigh. "Until their voices flooded my skull today, I've never been able to communicate with other wisps. Not that I've had much practice at that either. Like I said, I didn't know I was half wisp until a few months ago. And I've only run into wisps twice since then."

From the memories of my childhood that had begun to return in fragments, I could piece together memories of wisps floating around me protectively like tiny fairy godparents. But if I'd been able to communicate with wisps as a child, I'd lost the ability along with my memories.

I'd encountered wisps at the cemetery who seemed to understand me, but we'd only been able to communicate through rudimentary yes and no gestures. And after the Danse Macabre, they hadn't stuck around. My only other exposure to wisps before entering Faerie was facing the iron sick wisps at Jinx's father's junkyard—and that hadn't gone well.

In fact, that was another reason why I was here. There was so much I needed to learn about my powers.

"Interesting," he said. "Perhaps your non-wisp blood is more powerful. It is not unusual for fae to have a dominant side."

"Great," I said. "If my human side is more dominant, that would explain why my night vision sucks compared to the rest of you."

"Do you truly require light?" Kade asked.

"It would be helpful, sure," I said.

He let out a musical chirp, and my eyes widened as the tunnel filled with glowing wisps. Now that was a handy talent.

We started walking, and this time I was able to keep up. Even my fatigue was soon forgotten as my eyes traced the details of Tearlach. We were entering the heart of my father's realm. Hopefully, this place would soon reveal his secrets. As it was, I'd learned more about wisps in one day with my uncle than I'd found in all of the books in Kaye's library.

"Can you teach me that trick you did, with the wisps?" I asked, hurrying to reach my uncle's side.

He was much taller and slenderer than me, which gave him a speed advantage. I'd never thought of being human as a deficiency before now, but walking at my uncle's side, I suddenly wished that I'd been born with more of his natural grace and agility.

He arched an eyebrow, but continued to stride along silently, as if dancing above the rock-strewn floor. When I finally thought that I'd offended him into silence, he tilted his head, focusing his amber eyes on my matching ones. I'd never met someone else with amber eyes before, and it sparked even more questions, but I held my tongue. I wasn't going to become that annoying student who nagged the teacher incessantly with questions.

"It was no trick," he said. "All wisps can speak with one another, though it takes practice when communicating between wisps in different forms."

"You mean we have different forms?" I asked.

Okay, so much for not badgering Kade with questions.

"Of course," he said. "At least, those of us with adequate power can shift between our larger and more diminutive forms. The smaller wisp form is invaluable for stealth and scouting..."

"He means spying," Torn said.

"But it leaves us vulnerable to attack," he said, ignoring Torn. "Never underestimate the danger from a hungry bird when in that form."

He pointed to one of the wisps floating ahead of us, and I swallowed hard.

"So can I become small like that?" I asked.

"I do not know," he said. "You were born with the power to do many things, but that was before your father's meddling."

"Can all of these wisps become full size?" Torn asked, pausing to examine the wisps that darted around our heads like excited fireflies.

"No, not all," Kade said. "In fact, it is very rare. But the ability has always passed along the royal line. Being able to communicate between both forms is a necessary part of ruling the wisp court." He stopped and shook his head. "I am...sorry, Ivy. That was insensitive of me. I am sure that you came here with expectations."

"What, me?" I asked. "I don't want to rule. If being able to shift forms is a prerequisite, then I'm glad that I don't have the ability."

"Then why did you come here to Tearlach?" he asked.

"I came here for answers about my father, and about my powers," I said.

"Ah, I was afraid you would say that," he said.

Kade turned away, and led us farther down the tunnel, leaving me pondering his words. My uncle hadn't so much as blinked when I'd entered his realm with a kelpie, a brownie, and a cat sidhe, or when I'd sprouted wings and started hearing voices in my head, but when I told him that I'd come here for answers, he looked like he'd swallowed a pixie.

What could be so terrible about the truth?

CHAPTER 29

I blinked, eyes adjusting to the sudden bright light, as the low stone ceiling of the tunnel opened up into a large cavern. Moonlight shone from high above, the moonbeams captured and transmitted through a dome made up of a clear, amber-hued crystalline substance that grew from the stone like a latticework of tetragonal fungus. Below the amber crystals, alcoves dotted the walls. Some of these openings were so small that only the smallest wisps could float through, while others were large enough for two mountain orcs to march side by side.

Tiers of benches that were carved into the stone ringed the room on one side. Opposite the stadium-like seating rose a platform on which stood two ornate thrones. A small pool of water sprouting cattails, lilies, and lotus flowers marked the center of the moss-covered cavern floor.

"Nice digs, Princess," Torn said.

"It has its charm, I guess," I said with a shrug.

I swallowed hard, and tried to push away thoughts of Jinx and Sparky. Coming to this place only made me miss my friends worse than ever. But I couldn't return home yet. I might long for my drafty, old loft apartment, but I'd come here for answers, and I wasn't going to leave without them.

Too bad the place was crawling with wisps.

Wisps filled the cavern, some flying through the room on their way to other areas of Tearlach, while many floated in from the darkened alcoves to crowd the rows of carved seats, or to hover near the pool of water.

Ordinarily, I'd have found the scene pretty, maybe even awe-inspiring. My family had helped to build this place. My father had ruled here for centuries. But I couldn't forget the effect that the wisps in the bog had on my awakening powers—and I was in no mood for a repeat performance. My neck and shoulders tightened, and my back ached at the thought of sprouting wings again so soon.

I grit my teeth, and stepped into the cavern, following my uncle down stone stairs worn smooth by the fae who'd

walked these steps before me. I was so focused on holding my
power in check, and putting one foot in front of the other, that
it took me a few minutes to realize that the cavern had gone
silent. All I could hear was the sound of our footsteps—notably
the clop-clop of my clumsy half human feet, since Ceff, Torn,
Skilly, and Kade were all adept at moving silently—and the
trickle of water below us.

I lifted my chin to survey the room for threats, and
froze. The wisps had gone silent, but not because of the threat
of a predator in their midst. No, the cavern pulsed with light
that matched the familiar cadence of my heartbeat. The entire
wisp court was responding to my presence, their bodies glowing
in time with the beating of my heart.

When Kade noticed the growing space between us, he
looked up at me, eyebrow raised.

"Are you fatigued?" he asked. "Do you require one of us
to carry you, after all?"

"No, no, I'm fine," I said, trying to ignore the increasing
speed at which the surrounding wisps glowed and dimmed.

"Are you sure?" he asked. "You are welcome to take my
arm."

My chest swelled, a part of me warming at his offer.
He'd been so reluctant to touch me during my transformation.
I'd thought his reaction was born of revulsion for his half-
breed, country bumpkin of a niece, but perhaps my human
blood wasn't as large a barrier as I'd first thought. But as kind
as my uncle's offer, there was no way I'd take him up on it. I
wasn't touching him now, or ever.

Plus, fatigue was the least of my worries.

"No," I said, unable to fully stifle a full-body shudder.
"Thank you. It's just…the glowing…will I change again?"

His eyes widened, understanding smoothing the lines of
concern.

"Ah, our people have long awaited your return," he said,
waving a hand. "Many will want to see their princess, and they
would gladly lend you their power, much as the ones in the bog
did before, but I took the liberty of sending word ahead that
they are to look only. I assumed that you would require rest
after your journey, and that you would prefer to wait before
attempting to use your powers again."

"Yes, thank you, Uncle," I said.

"Please, call me Kade," he said, leaning forward.

"Lord Kade," Ceff said, stepping between us. "Perhaps we can impose on your hospitality and be provided accommodations for the night. Ivy is obviously quite tired."

My uncle blinked, and took a step back, putting him further down the stairs. Ceff towered over him, bristling with rage.

"Of course, this way," Kade said, turning and continuing down the stairs. "I can point out a few things on the way to your quarters, though it would honor me, Ivy, if I could give you a more thorough tour when you are well rested."

"Sure," I mumbled.

I looked back and forth between Ceff and Kade, but I couldn't divine much from watching them from behind. Something had gotten under Ceff's skin, I could tell that much from the rigid way he held his neck and shoulders, but I was too tired to make a guess at what was troubling him. Maybe he'd be willing to share once we were safely inside our room.

Either Torn or Skilly muttered something about horses in heat, but when I spun around to glare at them, they both batted their eyes innocently. The two of them continued to keep quiet until my uncle stopped to point at a nearby alcove.

"That is where we keep the stone, once said to be the heart of our people," Kade said.

We poked our heads inside the large, ornate room, and Torn let out a low whistle.

"Now that be a worthy hearth," Skillywidden said.

"Who the Hell is looking at the hearth?" Torn asked, walking past us to get a closer look at the glowing stone in the center of the room. "Is that an adder stone?"

"Yes, a piece of the Glain Neidr of Tír na nÓg," Kade said, puffing up his chest, and shifting his weight onto his heels. "They are very rare..."

"And very valuable," Torn said, licking his lips. "I'm surprised you don't keep it locked up."

"As I said before, the stone represents the heart of our people, and this..." he said, gesturing at the room lined with shelves of books and jars. "This room is a repository of history, a treasure trove of knowledge, open to all of our people."

"It would be a crime to lock such a room away," Ceff said with a grudging nod.

Five seconds in that room and I was already salivating at the thought of searching those shelves for knowledge of my father, reading through those books, and perhaps finding some of his personal possessions. This room truly did contain treasure, but not the glowing stone or ornate hearth that Torn and Skillywidden coveted.

I would have stood there for hours, slack-jawed with my boots rooted to the floor, but a yawn broke the spell. This room might contain the answers that I'd come here for, but I was in no shape for research. I could barely stand up without listing to the side.

"Come," Kade said. "We have kept Ivy waiting long enough."

He spun on his heel, and led us back out into the corridor. After more twists and turns than I could keep track of, he stopped in front of a door decorated with delicate flowers that seemed to grow straight out of the smooth wooden surface. There were no windows or skylights, and I knew that we were far below the earth, so the flowers were either magic or extremely realistic fakes. I was guessing magic.

That was confirmed when the flowers rustled and danced until they spelled out my name. My uncle must have sent more than one wisp ahead to prepare for our arrival. Kade licked his lips, and held out a hand.

"My dear, I have waited long for this day," he said, hand shaking slightly as he opened the door. "I hope your room is to your liking."

I stepped inside, and gasped. The room was fit for a queen. The high ceiling was a deep indigo and decorated with fey lanterns that were arranged to mimic constellations. A huge bed was positioned in the center of the room, beneath the starry sky. It was piled high with pillows, and the sides were draped with swaths of sheer fabric that gave the illusion of privacy, and hung from posts made of ornately carved quartz that rose from the floor to arch over the bed. The overall effect was like a bed within a palatial gazebo of ice that rested beneath the stars.

"It's beautiful," I said. "But I'm fine with sharing a room with my friends. I don't need something this fancy."

"Don't be silly," Kade said. "This room has never been slept in. With your sensitivity to touch, I would think this the perfect place for you to stay."

I bit my lip, trying to decide if the reduced risk of visions was worth splitting up. I didn't like the thought of staying somewhere separate from Ceff and the others. Obviously, Ceff had the same concerns.

"I will stay and stand guard while she sleeps," Ceff said.

"You have already invoked the rules of hospitality," Kade said, hands fisting at his sides. "Do you intend to insult my ability to keep the princess safe from harm?"

"Good going, Fish Breath," Torn muttered. "Nothing like pissing off our host."

"What's going on?" I asked, keeping my voice low.

I didn't want to interrupt Ceff and Kade's pissing contest, but I was pretty sure I was missing something, and I was too tired to try to smooth things over. Diplomacy wasn't one of my strengths, even when I was at my best.

"It sounds like when Ceff got pushy earlier about wanting to get a move on and find you a room, Kade took that as Ceff invoking the rules of hospitality," Torn whispered back. "Fae take the rules of hospitality very seriously, and your uncle is no exception. Think of it as requesting asylum, which is how the rules came about in the first place. Allies, no matter how much they may despise each other, could invoke hospitality and the host would be required to protect the guest from outside harm."

"So, Ceff insulted my uncle when he implied that the wisps couldn't keep me safe," I said, a tendril of cold twisting my gut. "What about internal threats?"

"The bargain doesn't provide protection from the inside, but to say you need a guard implies that either Kade and his people can't defend you, or that we perceive them as a threat," Torn said.

So by offering to stay and guard me in my room, Ceff had managed to doubly offend my uncle. That was just great. As much as I wanted to talk to Ceff about the day's events, we couldn't risk going to war with my uncle. I needed to patch things up. Oh goody.

"We don't doubt your skill at arms," I said, stepping forward and facing my uncle. "I'm sure my friends will be comfortable in whatever guest quarters you've prepared for them."

"So you do like the room?" Kade asked, blinking slowly and pulling his gaze from Ceff's icy glare.

Up close, I was surprised to see that my uncle's otherwise flawless skin was marred by dark circles around his eyes. Who knew what kind of hardships he'd faced since my father had fled Faerie. He'd obviously taken on the daunting task of keeping the wisp court running. That must have been difficult without his brother's help, difficult and lonely.

"It's perfect," I said, trying to force enthusiasm and managing to yawn.

"I am so glad," he said. He held open the door, and fixed Ceff with a cold stare. "Now let us leave the princess. She requires sleep, and I need to return soon to my court. If you would follow me, I can show you to your rooms along the way."

"Do ye have an empty hearth?" Skillywidden asked. "Perhaps the one in the treasury?"

"Not that one...not yet," Kade said, hesitating. "But there is a hearth in the kitchen, if you would prefer a hearth over a guest room. If you do well with the kitchen hearth, there's a chance of a promotion to the treasury in the future."

Skilly rubbed his hands together and smiled, but Ceff stood rigid.

"I do not like this," he said.

"Go on," I said. "I'll be fine. These are my people."

I turned my hand, allowing him to see the blade in my palm as if to say, "And I'm not unarmed. I can defend myself if needed." He frowned, but nodded and handed me one of the satchels he wore slung across his back.

I didn't like this turn of events either. There was so much I needed to discuss with Ceff. Today, I'd grown wings, amongst other things, and I still hadn't had a moment alone with Ceff to talk about it. I wanted to know how he felt about my transformation, and what it meant to our relationship.

"I'll be fine," I said again, but I wondered who I was trying to convince.

CHAPTER 30

"I thought you said that Ceff and Torn were on their way," I said around a mouthful of pancakes.

Actually, I wasn't sure if the pastries were technically pancakes, but the less I scrutinized the food, the better. My fae blood meant that I could ignore the prohibition against humans to eating and drinking while visiting Faerie—a fact I'd badgered Kaye about for weeks leading up to this excursion—but that didn't mean I was cool with eating worms or butterfly wings. So far, I'd stuck with the food that didn't move.

"I sent some of my staff to let your friends know that breakfast was ready in the Great Hall," he said. The Great Hall was apparently what they called the cavern. It also doubled as the throne room, but for now, they'd set a banquet table beside the pool of water at the center of the cavern floor. It was like being on an extravagant picnic. "But as I said before, your transformation yesterday is likely to make you ravenous. There is no reason to suffer while you wait for your friends to arrive."

"Yes, hunger is not an attractive quality in a princess," Flavio said.

I rolled my eyes, and growled around another bite of pancake. Flavio was the captain of the guard, and one of only three human-sized wisps that I'd seen since arriving here in Tearlach, aside from my uncle. He was also pricklier than a porcupine.

"Flavio, why don't you go check on our guests," Kade said. "Tell them that the princess requires their presence."

"I didn't mean..." I said.

"Let the guard fetch them," Skillywidden said, putting something that wriggled on his plate, and licking his lips. "It wouldna do to let this feast go to waste."

While I wasn't as enthusiastic about some of the food on the table, it was true that we shouldn't let the food go to waste. The wisps must have been up all night working in the kitchens, not that I was sure anymore what was night and what was day. What I did know was that missing breakfast would be rude.

Ceff was a king whose job required diplomacy. He knew better than to turn down an invitation to breakfast. And while Torn may not care as much for what my uncle thought of his actions, I'd never known the cat sidhe lord to miss a free meal. Where the heck were they?

I was working through my third pancake, which I'd smothered in what I hoped were elderberries, when I got my answer.

Flavio strode into the room, making a beeline for my uncle. I kept my eyes on Flavio and Kade, as I shoveled food into my mouth. It probably wasn't behavior befitting a princess, but my uncle was right—I was starving. I'd also give anything for a cup of coffee. My body had expended a huge amount of energy yesterday that even a solid night of sleep hadn't replenished.

Kade frowned, and his eyes flicked to mine before sharing a look with his guard captain. With a stiff nod, Flavio took a step back to resume his guard position behind my uncle's chair—a smaller version of the throne that sat on the dais at his back. As if responding to an unknown signal, the wisps that had been flitting about the banquet table shot into the surrounding cattails and tufts of marsh grass.

My uncle cleared his throat, fixing me with a stare void of emotion. I recognized that look. It was the same one I gave clients when I had to tell them bad news. I slowly set down my fork, a quiver in my stomach replacing the hunger that had overwhelmed me only seconds before.

"I have regrettable news," he said, a frown beginning to mar the otherwise impenetrable mask. "Your friends appear to be…missing."

"Missing?" I asked.

"When they repeatedly did not answer our summons, Flavio forced their doors open," he said. "He was…understandably concerned."

I flicked my eyes to Flavio, and my breath caught in my throat. His nostrils flared as he watched me with a fevered stare, a vein on his temple throbbing in time with my rapidly beating heart. The look of devotion that he'd shown my uncle was now replaced by raw hatred.

"Beware that one," Skillywidden whispered.

I didn't need the hearth brownie's warning. I had a nagging suspicion that Flavio had been more concerned with his job position than with my friends' welfare. I narrowed my eyes at Flavio before turning back to my uncle.

"What did he find?" I asked.

"Their rooms were empty," Kade said. "Your friends and their belongings were gone. The beds had not been slept in."

That meant that Ceff and Torn had been missing for well over six hours. My uncle had told me that I'd slept for nearly eight hours. If this was a kidnapping, their attackers could be long gone by now.

"Was there any sign of a struggle?" I asked.

I tamped down my emotions, locking them deep inside so that I could focus on the facts of the case. There would be plenty of time for tears and raging later, but right now, I had to focus. I'd worked missing person cases. The first twenty-four hours were crucial.

I held onto the rules of the job, the familiar steps in solving a case. We'd handle this carefully, methodically. I'd brought home people who'd been missing longer than twenty-four hours. Then again we were in Faerie. When even the local plant life was more than happy to unburden you of your blood, you had to make every second count.

"There was no sign of struggle," Flavio said.

"Forced entry?" I asked.

"No," he said.

"I need to see their rooms," I said, my chair scraping the floor as I pushed away from the table.

"The rooms have been examined," he said, face flushing red.

"No offense, but I'd like to see for myself," I said.

Flavio started to growl low in this throat, but Kade raised a hand, cutting off Flavio's protest.

"Come, I am sure there is a reasonable explanation for all of this," he said.

Kade started to sooth Flavio's ego by bragging about how reliable his guards were, and how he was sure that his captain had conducted a thorough search. He was about to start on me, but his words and placating gestures were cut off as another guard came running into the Great Hall.

"Lord Kade!" the guard shouted. I think his name was Marcus, and he, like Flavio, was human size. And at the moment, his eyes were wide, and he held a sword in a white-knuckled grip. "The adder stone..."

He gulped in air, gasping for breath.

"Yes?" Kade asked, eyebrow raised.

"The adder stone, My Lord, it's gone."

CHAPTER 31

I didn't need my P.I. training to recognize the implications of Ceff and Torn's mysterious departure and the missing adder stone. Things didn't look good, not good at all.

Flavio took a threatening step toward me, hand on his sword, and my throwing knives hit my palms.

"Halt!" Kade ordered.

Flavio stopped, but his lips remained pulled back in a sneer. Kade might have his guard captain on a short leash for now, but I didn't doubt that Flavio would strike down anyone he perceived as a threat to my uncle. Ceff and Torn were likely on that list, with me and Skilly firmly in the maybe column. I needed to diffuse the situation, but to do that, I needed facts.

At least I had an idea on how I could buy us some time.

"Ceff invoked the rules of hospitality, and you accepted your role as our host," I said, keeping my voice slow and a steady, and my eyes locked on Kade. "You swore to keep us safe, and now my friends are missing."

My uncle had taken over leadership of the wisps when my father fled Faerie. He was the one I had to convince of Ceff and Torn's innocence, not Flavio. We just had to stay alive long enough to prove our case. If invoking our rights as guests gave us temporary amnesty, I'd take it, even if my words did make my uncle look like he'd bitten into a sour lemon.

"My Lord, they came within our walls with a show of false friendship," Flavio said. "I do not trust them. We should imprison these two and continue our search for the others."

So much for amnesty.

"Flavio, there is no need to be hasty," Kade said. "The princess does have a point. We agreed to the rules of hospitality, therefore we must investigate further before assuming the worst. If an outside force has moved against our guests, I want to know how it happened."

"No one can breach the tunnels," Flavio said.

"Then you will not mind if I make inquiries about last night's security," Kade said.

"No, of course not, My Lord," he said, lowering his eyes.

"I wish to speak with the sentinels," Kade said.

A buzzing filled the cavern, and I had to grab the table to remain standing. Wisps came flying in from every direction, like glowing bullets shot from the dark tunnels above our heads.

Sweat beaded on my forehead, and I took a steadying breath. Now would be a really bad time to pass out. Flavio would probably take the opportunity to bundle me off to some sick room with bars conveniently placed at the doors.

"Do ye think they did it?" Skillywidden whispered.

I could barely hear him over the buzzing of the wisps. My uncle had unfurled his wings, and was nodding his head as the sentinels gave their report. His brow furrowed, and he looked like an avenging angel. I wished I could hear what was being said, but understanding wisps in their smaller form was one of many skills I had yet to learn.

"No, Skilly," I said. "It wasn't them."

"Well, I hope ye can convince your uncle of that," he said.

I nodded, and swallowed hard. I did too.

At a curt nod from my uncle, the wisp sentinels left the room. I took a steadying breath, and lifted my chin as he strode back to the table.

"Shall I arrest her, My Lord?" Flavio asked.

Oberon's eyes, that guy was as persistent as a pixie rash.

"Look, we didn't come here to orchestrate some elaborate gem heist," I said, letting out a heavy sigh. "My friends are victims here, not criminals."

"I would like to believe you, Ivy, but my sentinels inform me that your friends were overheard discussing their desire to leave this place," Kade said, lifting his hands up and letting them fall.

"That's impossible," I said. "They would never do something like this."

Well, I thought bleakly, Torn would do something like this. The cat sidhe loved a challenge, especially one that involved slinking through the shadows and a shiny reward, but I shook my head. No, Ceff would never have let Torn get away with it, and he certainly wouldn't have joined him in a hair brained heist that would jeopardize my chances of finding my father.

"They were also seen eyeing the adder stone," he said.

Crap, that much was true. Torn had looked at that stone like it was catnip. But that didn't mean he was guilty.

"With all due respect uncle, we all eyed your stone," I said. "You showed if off to us. What were we supposed to do, look away?"

"Aye," Skillywidden said. "She has a point."

"They had the motive, means, and opportunity," Kade said. "Why should I believe that they are innocent?"

"They would never leave me here," I said.

"Do not underestimate the lure of wealth and power—or of how far lust can motivate a man," he said.

There was something dangerous in his eyes, and I picked my words carefully.

"Have you ever loved someone so completely that you would do anything for them?" I asked.

I was taking a gamble. Many immortals fell out of touch with their emotions over the centuries. But I'd seen flashes of emotion from my uncle, and I hoped that he wasn't as cold-hearted as he'd like the rest of us to think.

His mask slipped, and an ache entered his amber eyes, etching his face with an old, familiar pain.

"I loved someone like that once, long ago," he said.

"Ceff and I share that kind of love," I said. He scowled, and I took a deep breath. "He would never do the things he's being accused of. He would never leave me here alone in potentially hostile territory."

"You are not alone," he said with a frown. "And I have no hostile intentions toward you."

"No imprisonment?" I asked.

"No," he said. "I do believe that you are innocent, but I can't say the same for your missing friends. There is too much evidence against them."

"But you can see why I can't give up on them, right?" I asked. "I won't stop looking."

"Yes, I understand," he said, letting out a heavy sigh. "The heart wants what the heart wants. But, Ivy? Do not waste your life pining over what you cannot have."

If Ceff was involved in the crime, then he'd stolen my heart, and the figurative heart of my people, in one fell swoop. I just couldn't believe that was true.

"I will find my friends, no matter how long it takes," I said. "A quest for truth, for love, that is never a waste."

Kade shook his head and muttered.

"Ah, the foolishness of youth."

CHAPTER 32

My uncle's words followed me down the maze of corridors. He thought that I was naïve and that my search for Ceff and Torn was foolish, because he believed that they'd betrayed me and left me here to rot. I took that as a sign of just how difficult his life had been over the centuries, rather than wise insight into the situation.

Sadly, my uncle was older and wiser about all things wisp, a fact that he never let me forget. Back in Harborsmouth, I'd proven myself. Heck, some even called me a hero. But from the moment my uncle and I met, he treated me like a child.

He wasn't about to listen to my opinions about what really happened to Ceff and Torn, because everything I said was tainted with what he saw as the blind foolishness of youth. It didn't help that he'd stumbled on my first physical transformation, a developmental milestone that most wisp children reached when they were toddlers.

I stomped away my frustration, marching up and down another series of windowless corridors. If I couldn't convince my uncle with words, then I would do so by providing cold, hard facts.

I needed to gather enough physical evidence and eyewitness statements to clear Ceff and Torn's names, and prove that my childish theories were correct. Only then would I gain my uncle's support, and find a way to rescue my friends from whoever had stolen them from their beds.

But first, I had to find those beds. I stopped and spun slowly on my heel, squinting at the stone walls and lichen covered doors. I sighed, and ran a gloved hand through my hair. I was pretty sure that I was lost.

Oberon's eyes, I was going to strangle Marcus. On my way out of the Great Hall, I'd asked Marcus for directions. He might not be all warm and fuzzy, but when the choice was between asking Marcus or Flavio, I'd pick the former in a heartbeat.

There was a chance that Marcus was just a guard following orders, but Flavio was another story. He radiated pure hatred, and perhaps a little jealousy. Flavio was my uncle's favorite, a man who'd climbed his way to the top ranks of the royal guard, but I was the long lost princess. I was family. And as far as the guard captain was concerned, I'd brought in two security threats who had scarpered off with his lord's covetous adder stone—and on his watch.

No wonder Flavio hated my guts.

I considered retracing my steps back to Marcus, but shook my head. I wouldn't find much help from the guard. Not while I was still an unknown variable. For all they knew, I was here to assassinate my uncle and take over the throne. The theft of the adder stone could just be a distraction. Damn, if I was in their position, I'd probably lock me in my fancy room and throw away the key.

Now that was a cheery thought.

I continued to the end of the corridor where the tunnels branched off in both directions. I dragged my knife against the corner to my right, scraping away an inch of lichen, and followed the right-hand tunnel. I passed eighteen doors before the corridor turned a corner that ended in a bench filled alcove. This way had been a dead end.

I sighed, and retraced my steps back to the intersection of tunnels, but when I reached the corner where I'd left my mark, the lichen was undisturbed. I kicked the wall, pain radiating up my leg. Sometimes pain helps me focus, gives me clarity, and allows me to push away distractions. But right now, it wasn't helping.

Ceff and Torn were gone, and instead of trying to help them, my uncle's men were on a manhunt that might result in their deaths. Up against elite guards who defended their home turf, I wasn't so sure if I wanted my friends to be found. I needed to know that they were safe, that they were alive, but if they were out there imprisoned or running from kidnappers, they'd be hemmed in on both sides and fighting on unfamiliar terrain. Terrain that itself could become the enemy.

I recalled the bog with its pitfalls and poisonous gasses, and traitorous tears filled my eyes.

"Please be okay," I whispered. "Please."

"Who ye be talkin' to?" Skillywidden asked.

I spun, knife in hand, to see the brownie a few yards away. He was standing in the corridor I'd come from a few minutes ago. I wiped an arm across my face, and sighed.

"Did you follow me?" I asked.

"Nothin' else to do in this place," he said with a shrug. "Kitchen hearth is clean, and they won't be cookin' again for hours."

Skillywidden had asked to man the hearth, rather than sleep in one of the guest rooms. It might be the only thing that had saved him from the same fate as our friends. I suppose I should be thankful that my uncle had put me up in the royal guest suite, but right now I'd rather be in a prison cell if it meant being reunited with Ceff.

"Any idea how to find the guest quarters?" I asked.

"Is me name Skillywidden?" he asked.

I didn't remind the brownie that we'd only recently met, and he could have given us the name of the brand of toothpaste he used. Pureblood fae couldn't tell a bald-faced lie, but they found creative ways to tell the truth. Then again, if his teeth were any indicator, Skillywidden probably wasn't the name of toothpaste.

"Lead the way," I said.

I followed the brownie down a maze of corridors, finally stepping into the tunnel that led to the guest quarters. Unfortunately, we weren't the only ones.

Two guards stood with their backs to a set of doors directly across from one another.

"Are those the rooms that Ceff and Torn stayed in?" I asked.

"Aye," Skillywidden said. "This is where I saw them last, before being led to the kitchens."

Both guards stood over six feet tall, wore amber armor, and golden swords hung on each hip. Judging from their rigid stance, they were there to guard the guest rooms. Could this get any worse?

One of the guards turned and glared at me, and I sighed. Oh yeah, it was worse. The guard blocking the room on the right was Flavio.

"Looks like they don't be wantin' anyone in those rooms," Skillywidden said.

"Think they'll make an exception for the princess?" I asked.

He shrugged, but his expression said, "Not bloody likely." I rolled my shoulders, forced a smile on my face, and strode down the hall.

*****

"What do you mean, I can't examine their rooms?" I asked, voice rising.

This wasn't the first time I'd asked the question, and my patience was wearing thin. The guard on the left continued to ignore me, keeping his amber eyes facing straight ahead. Finally, it was Flavio who broke the tension-filled silence.

"I recommended to my liege that we keep the guest quarters secured until we complete our investigation," he said with a sneer. "Lord Kade agreed."

He looked down his nose at me, eyes gleaming in amusement. My hands fisted at my sides—I'd had the foresight to put away my blades before antagonizing the royal guard—and I ground my teeth. It was all I could do to keep from wiping that smug expression off his face, but I knew I was beaten.

Flavio had Kade's approval. If I tried to force my way inside now, I'd face imprisonment or death. Judging from the way Flavio fondled his sword, he'd like nothing better than an excuse to stab me through the heart. My uncle might not like that, but Flavio would probably be forgiven in time—and time was something the immortal guard captain had in spades.

"Fine, but this isn't over," I said, biting out the words. "I am the princess. I am the daughter of Will-o'-the-Wisp. And I won't forget this."

The guard across from Flavio blanched. Good to know someone here understood the potential repercussions of pissing me off. I'd rejected the idea of being a member of royalty—I was no fragile flower—but if accepting my position helped me save my friends, then I'd become the best damn princess that Faerie had ever seen.

CHAPTER 33

"So, you wish to train with me?" Kade asked, a tentative smile on his lips. "Why?"

I'd had plenty of time to think over my answer on the long walk back to the Great Hall. Skillywidden had a better sense of direction than I did in this underground palace, but we'd taken a wrong turn at some point and I'd be damned if we backtracked past Flavio's smug face.

In addition to improving my position here within the wisp court by learning the ropes of acting like a princess, I also realized that I had an opportunity to learn to control my wisp powers. I'd nearly stumbled face first into a wall when the idea first hit me.

I'd been grumbling over the fact that the only members of the wisp court that I could question were the human size wisps. Unfortunately, that left my uncle, and a handful of his elite guards—guards who were led by Flavio. I didn't think I'd get much help there. That was when I remembered the cacophony of voices that had filled my head in the bog. My uncle had said that the psychic connection with my people was amplified through my wings, and that with training, I'd be able to control those voices in my head. He also said that the members of our royal family line could communicate with the smaller wisps; it was one of the things that made us fit to rule. It wasn't that much of a leap to assume that my uncle could provide that training, giving me the ability to question the rest of the court's staff about the night that Ceff and Torn disappeared.

Not to mention the fact that gaining control over my wisp powers would give me the chance to prove myself to the Unseelie Court. I'd been deemed a traitor back in the human world, because my lack of control threatened the secret of our existence. But if I learned how to control my powers, and how to create a glamour, I might finally get the sidhe assassins off my tail—and be able to return to my life in Harborsmouth.

There were a lot of ifs in my plan, but I had to start somewhere. First, I needed to convince my uncle to give me the training that I'd never received from my father.

"Like I said before, I don't have any interest in usurping your position, uncle," I said. "But while I am here, I'd like to make you proud. I keep making mistakes—blunders that a princess shouldn't make—because I was never taught our ways."

"You wish to stay with me?" he asked, leaning closer. "You do realize that training takes time."

"I understand," I said. "I have no intentions of leaving until I find my friends, and even then, it will be unsafe to return to the human world until I've learned to control my powers."

"Why would it be unsafe now?" he asked, tilting his head to the side. "You have survived this long in the human world, a land with fewer perils than this one."

"Because my powers continue to awaken, and because...I don't know how to create a glamour," I said. "I can't hide within the human world, and my magic isn't strong enough to survive long in Faerie on my own."

One of the guards standing behind my uncle's throne let out a gasp. There I go again, scandalizing the locals.

My uncle leaned forward, eyes glowing faintly in the moonlit cavern.

"If I agree to train you, then you must promise to practice your magic every day, no matter how difficult it becomes for you to do so," he said. "And mark my words, my dear, it will become very, very difficult. You have decades upon decades to make up for. Working fae magic will be like setting fire to your veins. It will change you, take back what your father's sorcery has stolen, and remake you into the woman you were meant to be at your birth. Are you prepared and willing to make this bargain?"

I nodded, and I fought the weight that settled on my shoulders and stole away my breath. I'd agreed to his bargain. Now it was time to learn some magic and save my friends.

"Bring it on."

CHAPTER 34

Pain seared my flesh, crawled beneath my skin, and crushed my bones to dust. Holding onto fae magic was like biting down on a live wire while skinny dipping.

I'd agreed to do this every day. What the hell was I thinking?

"If you wish to communicate with the members of our court, you will need to do better," Kade said through the roaring in my head. "You haven't followed any of the directives I spoke into your mind while in my other form, and you look like a constipated bugbear."

"Screw...you," I ground out through clenched teeth.

A familiar coppery taste filled my mouth, and I knew that either my nose was bleeding, or I'd bit my tongue. Again. Training with my uncle was grueling, painstaking work. But I'd never been one to shirk my duties. I'd promised to practice my magic daily. More importantly, I'd sworn to find answers to what happened to my friends.

It had been over two weeks and there was still no word from Ceff or Torn. Flavio and the royal guard had scoured the underground palace and the surrounding bog above, but had found no sign of my friends. The only positives were that they hadn't found any dead bodies, and Flavio was sweating not bringing in the men he believed were thieves.

I wasn't the only one who resembled a constipated bugbear.

"Now if only you would send your insults with your mind, I might be able to permit such language unbecoming of a princess," he said. "That will be an additional hour of history lessons. Would you like me to add more? I'm sure Marcus would be happy to trade guard duty for more time with his favorite student."

Marcus, a member of the guard and one of Flavio's lackeys, would probably rather pull out his own toenails than spend another hour with me. That fact almost made my history lessons bearable. Too bad Marcus had managed to drone on for hours without ever sharing anything useful about wisp history. I'd probably die of old age before he started talking about my father's reign, and that was saying a lot considering I was half fae. With immortal blood running through my veins, who knew how long I might live?

Kaye had guessed centuries, a fact that had been a relief to me and to Ceff. We'd had our entire long lives ahead of us, and now he was gone.

I dug gloved fingers into my temples, and focused on the buzzing that filled my head. Today, as soon as I'd managed the arduous process of unfurling my wings, my uncle had filled the room with wisps. He'd also shrunk down to a glowing ball of light, and set about giving me orders. But all I could hear was the constant buzzing in my skull and the rapid beating of my heart.

I was surprised that the wisp voices hadn't managed to shake all my teeth loose. Then again, I did have a mouthful of blood.

"Enough," Kade said. "Put your wings away, and attend to your other studies. We are done with magic for the day."

My stomach churned, but I lifted my chin.

"No," I said. I spit blood on the floor, and took a ragged breath. "Again."

"You remind me so much of her when you get like this," he said.

I'd become used to his odd comments. I was pretty sure that the mystery lady I reminded him of was his lost love, not that he'd ever open up and talk about her. It was just a feeling I got sometimes when he looked at me. In those moments, it was obvious he didn't see me as a niece. That was enough to make me want to run screaming, but I ground my teeth and growled at him instead.

"Again."

CHAPTER 35

I hung my head over the toilet, and vomited more blood. Today, after six weeks of training, I'd finally made a breakthrough. I'd been able to hear my uncle's voice in my head.

I hadn't been able to filter out the other voices when he'd brought the wisps into the room, but I knew that with more practice, I'd finally be able to question the wisps about the night Ceff and Torn disappeared.

Ceff. Oberon's eyes, I missed him. Still no word from Ceff or Torn, but no corpses either. So long as they remained unfound, there was still hope that they were alive.

I had brought them here, and I would fix this. I just needed to push myself harder. I could do that, as soon as I stopped puking.

"Are ye sure they really be out there, princess?" Skillywidden asked.

He'd become my post-training shadow. He fussed over me like a mother hen, bringing me food from the kitchen to make sure I didn't forget to eat—not that I could stomach much these days. It was like he was channeling Jinx.

A tear ran down my face, and I struggled to breathe. I hadn't told Jinx about where I was going, and I had no idea how much time had passed in the human world. I could only hope that Forneus had lived up to his end of the bargain, and was keeping her safe.

"They're out there, Skilly," I said. "And I won't give up on my friends, not any of them."

"But this magic," he said, wringing his hands. "It be killin' ye."

I vomited up more blood. Skillywidden had a point. But I'd rather die than fail my friends. And right now, fae magic was my best shot at fixing this mess.

"I need my magic to find Ceff and Torn," I said.

I sat back on my heels, and tilted my head toward the ceiling. I couldn't face Skillywidden's concerned face right now. If I did, I might crumble.

"Then will ye at least get some rest?" he asked. "Ye haven't slept for days."

I blinked at the fey lantern overhead.

"I'll rest when we've found our friends and proven their innocence," I said.

I pulled myself to my feet, and strode back into my room. I crossed the floor, and pulled open the door.

"Tell Kade I'm ready for more training," I said, barking out an order to the nearest guard.

"But, Princess," Skillywidden said.

I turned around to where the brownie stood in the center of the room, beneath the glowing ceiling of stars.

"I can't rest knowing that they might be out there somewhere, suffering," I said.

"If they be suffering, lass..." Skillywidden said, following at my heels.

I grabbed my things, and limped out into the corridor.

"...they're not the only ones."

CHAPTER 36

"You've made remarkable progress, my dear," Kade said.

He licked his lips as his eyes traveled over my chest, and I swallowed hard. He was in one of his odd moods, making frequent references to how I resembled some woman from his past, and looking at me like I was an ice cream cone. I wouldn't have liked the attention from any man, but the fact that he was my uncle made me want to gag.

"I am my father's daughter," I said, reminding him of our familial connection. "Magic seems to run strong in our family."

He blinked, and took a step away. I relaxed and let out the breath I'd been holding. My congenial uncle was back.

He'd been having these spells more often lately. I ran a jerky hand through my hair, casting a sideways glance at my uncle.

I'd seen this kind of behavior before in other long-lived fae. Melusine and her jealous preoccupation with Ceff. Leanansídhe and her twisted love for a man long dead. Manannán mac Lir and the centuries of self-inflicted torment over the guilt of his lost love. The common thread was a blind obsession with something, or someone, that they'd lost.

There was a price for immortality. For some fae, the cost was their sanity.

"Yes, our family's magic is indeed strong, but you have had much to overcome," he said. He licked his lips, an eager, feverish gleam returning to his eyes. "You are a fighter, just like her."

Damn, that didn't last long.

"I had to fight through *your brother's*, magic, true, but that just means I'm stubborn," I said.

I took a slow step away, sidestepping his hand as he reached for me. I kept my eyes on Kade, and tried to talk him down. I'd come to care for my uncle. We lived together, took our meals together, and he made time for me each day to teach me more about my wisp magic. In Ceff and Torn's continued absence, and with Jinx and my other friends back in Harborsmouth, I'd begun to rely more and more on both Skilly and Kade's solid presence. We'd grown to become more than friends—we were a family.

I just wished that Kade would stop looking at me like he wanted to get in my pants.

"My brother?" he asked, lips curling in a sneer. "You will always choose him over me, won't you? No matter how much I love you, it will always be him. It has always been Liam. Always. Always. Always!"

I grimaced, a bitter taste rising in my throat. I'd come to hate this dance, tiptoeing along the brink with a man I'd come to love and respect. I could leave, of course, but that would mean turning my back on more than my uncle. I'd be abandoning Ceff and Torn as well.

I'd dealt with enough abandonment in my life—my father walking away without a trace being a pivotal part of my childhood, even if it did take me years to unlock those painful memories—and I wasn't about to become the kind of person who left people behind just because things got difficult. No, I wasn't ready to leave, and I wasn't about to give up on my uncle. His mental instability was a symptom, not a reason to walk away, or to kill him like I had Melusine and Leanansídhe. Not yet.

There was also the nagging fear that these bouts of psychosis were partly my fault. My uncle had agreed to teach me wisp magic, but that continued use of power had its own price. I'd begun to see changes in me. Would it be such a stretch to imagine our training was fueling Kade's odd behavior?

"Let's go get something to eat, *uncle*," I said. "I'm sure the kitchen has dinner waiting for us by now."

"What?" he asked.

He stood there blinking, looking like a lost child. I wanted so badly to go to him, to put an arm around him and tell him that everything was okay now. But I had no idea if embracing him would spur another bout of crazy, and touching Kade was not an option. I never wanted to experience the loss of the woman he loved through his eyes. It was bad enough seeing the way it haunted him.

"We were discussing dinner," I said, forcing a smile.

"Were we?" he asked.

"I know I'm starving," I said.

"Yes, you are right," he said. "Enough magic for one day."

"Come on," I said. "We can see what the kitchen's cooked up. Maybe they'll have pancakes."

It had become a joke between me and Kade and Skillywidden. Apparently, my initial reaction to the palace's pancakes—smothering them in fruit and shoving them in my face two at a time—had inspired the cook to add them to the menu for every meal. Pancakes; it's what's for breakfast, and lunch, and dinner.

"I hunger for more than pancakes," he said.

A chill ran up my spine, and I swallowed hard, no longer in the mood for pancakes or any other food. I'd lost my appetite.

CHAPTER 37

"Let me inside," I said, looking down my nose at Flavio.

It wasn't easy. The man had at least four inches on me, and that wasn't counting the wings. I had wings too, of course, but they were safely tucked away. I'd made progress with my wisp powers, but I still hadn't mastered blocking out the voices of the wisps around me. I could handle a few at a time, but not a crowd.

And right now, we had an audience.

Kade had declared today was the day that his guards must unseal the guest chambers, and allow me to snoop around for clues. Their investigation had taken long enough. To say that Flavio was unhappy about that decision was an understatement.

But Flavio was loyal to Kade. He wouldn't go against his orders. That didn't mean he'd make this easy.

The corridor was filled with the floating glowing orbs of wisps hoping for a fight. Flavio wanted one too—I could see it in his eyes—which is why I wouldn't give him one.

"Lord Kade has ordered for these doors to be opened," I said. "Are you defying a direct order?"

"He ordered these rooms to be unsealed," Flavio said, lips curling in a sneer. "My Lord said nothing about opening the doors."

"Fine," I said. "I'll open them myself."

I pulled out one of my throwing knives, and Flavio licked his lips, his eyes beginning to glow. I rolled my eyes, and turned to the opposite door. I used the iron and silver blade to cut through the magic ward that crossed the door like police tape. I could almost hear Flavio's teeth grinding from across the narrow corridor.

My skin itched having him at my back, but I didn't keep a wary eye on him over my shoulder. I wouldn't give him the satisfaction. It's not like he could stab me in back with a corridor full of witnesses. He knew it and I knew it. His little stunt of orchestrating a public fight had backfired.

I smiled, and reached for the doorknob with gloved hands. I'd touch the knob, to check it for visions, later, once I'd searched the room for traps. I wouldn't put anything past Flavio and his lackeys. My smile slipped when the knob didn't turn.

"Having a problem, princess?" Flavio asked, a shit-eating grin on his face.

Bastard.

"Nope," I said, pulling a roll of fabric from the inside pocket of my leather jacket. "No problem at all."

My uncle had tried for weeks to get me to dress like a proper princess, but I'd argued that any clothing he gave me was likely to cause me painful visions, and he'd finally given up. I was especially glad of that now. My jacket and utility belt of tricks and weapons would have looked awfully silly worn over a spider silk dress.

I unrolled the fabric, spread it on the floor beneath the doorknob, and drew two lock picks.

"What are you doing?" Flavio asked, voice no longer so smug.

"My job," I said, inserting an L-shaped torsion wrench into the lock. "You'd be surprised how often I need to pick a lock in my line of work."

I applied tension to the lock cylinder, stopping when the cylinder turned a fraction of an inch counterclockwise. I applied gentle torque to the wrench, and held it in place with my left hand. With my right, I inserted a hook pick just above the torsion wrench. Working back to front, I pressed up with the pick, feeling each of the three pins. Starting with the pin which offered the most resistance, I pressed the pick upward setting the pin. I repeated the procedure, continuing with the final two pins. I removed the pick and turned the torsion wrench counterclockwise, holding my breath. The lock clicked, and I turned the knob. I was in.

This was it. I'd spent endless sleepless nights worrying about what I might find behind these doors. Would there be blood? Had Ceff or Torn left me some kind of message, a clue to point me in their direction, or the direction of their kidnappers?

With shaking hands, I packed away my lock picks. I took a ragged breath, stood, and pushed the door open.

It was a guest room, less opulent than the royal
quarters I'd been given, but nicer than your average hotel.
There was a queen size bed, a chest of drawers, and a standing
closet—an armoire I think they call them—but nothing overtly
out of place. No torn fabrics. No knocked over furniture. No
blood.

I was glad of the last, though blood would have given me
a clear connection to my friends. I'd just have to find another
way to exploit the memories in this room.

I spun in a slow circle, examining the layout of the
room, imagining where either Ceff or Torn might have stood. It
was then that I realized that none of their belongings were
here. I knew that the guard's initial reports stated that the
beds didn't appear slept in, but I'd assumed that my friends
had at least had time to drop their bags, strip off their outer
gear, perhaps even take off their boots.

I went to the nearest piece of furniture, the bureau, and
started opening drawers. I looked inside, even giving the
drawers a sideways glance that would pierce through glamour.
I ran my gloved hands along the top, bottom, and sides of each
drawer. I knocked on the wood, searching for hidden
compartments. Next, I got down on all fours, and searched
beneath both the bureau and the bed.

Nothing. Not a single rug fiber out of a place. Not one
damn clue.

"That's a good look for you, Princess," Flavio said, his
voice coming from outside the door. "You should spend more
time on your knees."

"Classy, Flavio," I said, leaning back to sit on my heels,
and shoot a glare over my shoulder. "I'll make sure to pass
your suggestion along to Kade."

That shut him up. Flavio's lips pressed together in a
hard line, and the vein on his forehead started to throb.

I turned back to the room, and sighed. I wasn't finding
any clues. It was time to get out the big guns.

I slid off my glove, took a shaky breath, and reached for
the top edge of the bureau. It was the type of spot a weary
traveler would rest their hands. Unfortunately for me, Ceff
and Torn weren't the wisp court's first guests. Hundreds if not
thousands of fae had passed through these rooms. It was likely
that I'd have to suffer through hours of visions just to find a
single one involving my friends.

Oh well, I was already on the floor. I wouldn't have far to fall if the visions were bad.

My fingers brushed the cool surface of the wood, and I closed my eyes. I was prepared for a psychic assault, but nothing happened. I frowned, and slid my hand further along the edge of the bureau. Once again there was nothing, not so much as a psychic whisper.

I opened my eyes, and tilted my head. Something wasn't right here. Had the bureau been a new acquisition just prior to our arrival? I rolled to my feet, and strode to the fey lantern beside the bed. I touched the purple orb, but again, nothing.

Next, I ran my hands across the bed, the comforter, and the stacks of silken pillows. Heart racing, I moved to the walls, the floor, every fixture. The world around me remained the same. Nothing happened. Not one psychic vision.

I bit the inside of my cheek, and tried to think. Either nothing extremely good or bad had ever happened here to warrant a psychic impression, or this entire room had been wiped clean.

The scope of that was overwhelming. It wasn't like scrubbing a room of fingerprints. The only way to remove psychic impressions was to remove the very surfaces of the room itself. If I was right, then Flavio and his men had taken these rooms apart piece by piece.

If that was true, I'd return the favor, starting with Flavio's pretty face.

CHAPTER 38

As I suspected, the second guest room was as devoid of clues as the first. Someone had gone to a lot of trouble to keep the truth of what happened to Ceff and Torn from me. I just had to prove who and why.

I figured my best chance of getting those answers was by questioning the other palace residents. I'd already interrogated the human size members of the palace guard. That left the rest of the guards, staff, and their families. It was a huge task, made more daunting by the fact that speaking to the tiny glowing balls of light required wisp magic that I was only beginning to control. It sapped my strength, made my nose bleed, and left me with one hell of a headache.

Good thing I wasn't a delicate little flower.

I methodically questioned every member of the palace staff. The sentinels were more difficult to track down, but eventually, I interrogated them as well. Head spinning, I returned to my room, and fell face first onto my bed.

"Ye look like ye should be pushin' up daisies," a voice said. "I take it ye didna find the answer ye were looking for?"

I couldn't roll over, or I'd crush my wings, and I was too tired to fold them away. Thankfully, I recognized the voice. It was Skillywidden, and the brownie posed a threat to nothing except my patience.

"No," I mumbled into the pillows. "Not yet."

"Maybe ye should accept that they be gone," he said.

"No," I said. "I can't do that."

"Do ye think they'd want this for ye?" he asked.

"I won't give up on them, Skilly," I said. "Just like they'd never give up on finding me. And...I know they're out there. I can feel it."

"I hope ye be right, lass," he said.

"Me too, Skilly," I said, too tired for tears. "Me too."

CHAPTER 39

"I need to leave the palace," I said.

"No," Kade said. "You are not ready."

"Then make me ready," I said.

"It is not that easy," he said. "Offensive magic will take time."

"I'm done waiting," I said, shaking my head. "I've scoured every inch of the palace for clues. I've searched every tunnel, and questioned every member of your staff. I need to expand my search."

"Please do not do this," he said. His shoulders drooped, and the powerful, majestic wisp lord evaporated, leaving a grief-stricken old man. "I cannot lose you, not when I've only just found you again."

I wasn't sure if he meant me—his niece—or the woman that he sometimes confused me with. Either way, I was going.

"I'll come back," I said. "But first, I need to do this."

I had no leads, no idea of where to start searching. We both knew this, but he nodded.

"Will you promise to return to me?" he asked.

His eyes had gone watery, and I looked away.

"I promise," I said.

"You'll come back and continue your training?" he asked.

"Yes," I said.

"Then go," he said.

"Thank you, uncle," I said.

"Safe travels, my dearest one," he said.

"Don't worry, uncle," I said, forcing a smile. "I'll be home for dinner."

CHAPTER 40

I kept my promise. I made it home for dinner, just not that day. Or the day after that.

Searching the bog lands was arduous work. I trudged through mud that threatened to swallow me whole, fought mosquitoes the size of pterodactyls, and escaped a horde of hobgoblins by the edge of my teeth.

And that was just a perimeter search. I couldn't push any deeper into the bog due to the low lying fog of poisonous gasses, and I still had no idea which route my friends' assailants had taken.

I came back covered in mud and sweat. I staggered into the Great Hall, unwrapped the fabric I'd wound around my face, and shed mud onto the gleaming floor beneath my uncle's throne.

He was sitting there, eyes wide, mouth moving, but making no sound. He'd been watching the wisps set the banquet table beside the pool of water where we ate our meals when I'd so rudely interrupted. I guess I looked as bad as I felt.

"Teach me how to use my wings," I said without preamble.

No sense letting my uncle regain his balance. I needed him to teach me to fly, and I wouldn't take no for an answer. It took Kade a minute to pull himself together, but eventually, his untouchable mask slid into place.

"Then you are ready to accept who you are?" he asked.

"No, not really, but I need to widen my search," I said.

"You wish to fly," he said.

"Yes, and I want you to teach me," I said.

"I will teach you," he said with a nod. "But first you must learn to control fire. It is the elemental power that all wisps must conquer."

"Why do I have to learn to control fire?" I asked. "I want to learn to fly."

"And what will be the first thing you do when you've mastered that ability?" he asked.

"I'll go looking for Ceff and Torn," I said. "I'll be able to fly above the poisonous fog."

It would also give me a strategic view of the land. That might help me unravel the secret of where the kidnappers had taken my friends. Oberon's eyes, I wanted to fly so bad I could taste it.

"Exactly," he said, looking satisfied. "You will take wing over Nithsdale, a dangerous place whether in the air or on the ground."

"Yes," I said.

"That is why I insist on teaching you the magic you will need to survive flying through the skies of Faerie," he said. "You will learn to control fire, an element that can be molded to our will as either offensive or defensive magic."

"Fine," I said. "When do we start?"

"Tomorrow," he said. "Now go eat your dinner."

I raised an eyebrow at him, causing even more mud to flake off and fall to the floor.

"Come," he said, stepping down from his throne, and walking toward the banquet table. "Cook made your favorite; pancakes with berry jam."

I shook my head, but followed my uncle to the table. For days, I'd been trudging through muck, living on rations of dried fruit and jerky. Who was I to argue with pancakes?

CHAPTER 41

Fire is a surprisingly diverse element. I tried to remind Skillywidden of that fact while he scowled at me and slapped embers from his pants.

"Ye nearly set me on fire!" he yelled.

"I was practicing using glamour," I said. "I guess I got distracted."

"Distracted?" he asked. "Do ye know how hard it is to set fire to a hearth brownie?"

Come to think of it, I'd never seen Hob with a burn, no matter how many times he flit in and out of the fire-laden hearth in Kaye's spell kitchen. My chest tightened at the thought of my friends back home, but I shook it off. I needed to focus. Daydreaming is what got me into this mess in the first place.

"I'm sorry, Skilly," I said. "My mind wasn't on practicing."

"Ye were thinkin' of them again, weren't ye?" he said, face softening.

"Yeah," I said, slouching on the bench where I sat. "Sometimes I get so frustrated. I know they're out there, but I can't find them. I just feel so helpless."

"Well, next time ye feelin' frustrated, don't practice on ol' Skillywidden," he said.

"Deal," I said.

"So what ye plannin' to do now?" he asked.

"Want to see my glamour?" I asked.

"Aye, if ye can do it without settin' yer hair on fire," he said.

"That was last week," I said. "I've been practicing."

"I can see that," he said sarcastically, casting a pointed look at his smoldering trousers.

"I'm better at fireballs," I said with a shrug.

"That ye are, lass," he said.

Not surprisingly, I was better at fireballs and blasts of heat than the more subtle use of my wisp magic. I'd taken to the larger offensive spells right away, but they tended to leave me weak and defenseless. That was why my uncle had insisted on also teaching me the more defensive side of fire magic.

Fireballs and glamour were all part of the same skill, at least that's what Kade said. I tried to recall my uncle's words as I prepared to work my glamour.

You know how the area above an open flame shimmers, distorting what you see beyond it? Take that and fold it around you. Use it to change what the world outside sees.

That was easy for him to say. My uncle had been using his wisp magic for centuries.

I breathed in through my nose, and exhaled slowly. I pulled my magic from deep inside of me, reaching for the fire that could burn or conceal. Today, I wanted it to conceal, which made the magic slippery. The fire slid through my fingers twice before I managed to grasp hold and bend it around my body.

"Sweet Maeve," Skillywidden said, sucking air through his teeth. "Why did ye pick that form?"

"What do you mean?" I asked. "It's human isn't it?"

The upside of learning to create a concealing glamour was that I'd be able to safely walk the streets when I returned to Harborsmouth—at least once I'd proven the skill to the Unseelie Court. But in Faerie, a human wasn't a good defensive glamour. Most of the fae in the Nithsdale bog would see a human and think I was dinner, so my uncle had insisted I learn to conceal myself as a frog.

That meant that I had to practice my human concealment on the side. Judging from Skilly's face, I hadn't done a very good job of it.

"Did I confuse them again?" I asked. "Am I a frog?"

"No, lass," he said, face pale. "Not a frog."

"Then what do I look like?" I asked.

"Like the Queen of Air and Darkness herself," he said.

"I look like Mab?" I squeaked, eyes darting around the room.

I knew she couldn't hear me. The faerie kings and queens had fled Faerie centuries ago. But Mab was the bogeyman in the closet, the monster hiding under your bed. She didn't exactly instill rational thought.

I dropped the glamour, and bit my lip.

"I guess I need to keep trying," I said.

"Aye," Skillywidden said, nodding slowly.

Heck, maybe I should stick with amphibians. A frog glamour was less likely to get me executed for impersonating the Unseelie queen.

Leave it to me to find a way to make safe, defensive magic potentially life threatening.

CHAPTER 42

Learning to fly wasn't as fun as I thought it would be. Considering that I was expecting long hours of agonizing pain—that was saying something.

Kade made me run drills of unfurling and retracting my wings for hours. When I was slick with cold, sickly sweat, he had me slowly draw enough energy inside my body to fry my brain, one synapse at a time. When I thought I'd burst like a flaming piñata, spilling charred organs and scorched bones, he told me to pour that power into my wings and take flight.

Power zipped into my wings, out through their tips, leaving me empty and weightless, until my face hit the stone floor. I woke up in a puddle of vomit, and I could taste blood. I'd managed to break my nose, again.

It was one of many breaks. I should have given up, thrown in the proverbial towel, but there was still no sign of Ceff or Torn. I badgered my uncle, and he continued my training.

After a week of practice, I'd broken six bones and bruised all of my ribs. My half fae body was more resilient than a human's, but even I couldn't push through that much pain. I dragged myself into the Great Hall, the one room of the underground palace large enough to practice flight, and sat on one of the steps leading up to my uncle's throne.

"What am I doing wrong?" I asked.

"You still believe that you are human," he said, eyes sad as they traced my injuries.

The black eyes from my broken nose were a spectacularly gruesome shade of purple today. I smiled, reopening a recently split lip.

"I am human, uncle," I said.

"And that way of thinking is why you fail," he said.

I licked my split lip, and spat blood onto the floor.

"Was there any chance I'd ever fly, or was this all a game to you?" I asked.

"I did not say it was impossible," he said. "I said that you have limitations because you believe that you have limitations, that you are human, that you cannot defy gravity, that you cannot fly."

"So what do I need to do?" I asked again, gloved hands fisting in my lap.

"Believe," he said.

"You make it sound simple," I said.

"It is simple," he said. "You have already done the hard part. Now all you must do is believe. Believe in your true self. Believe that you are fae, that you are magic, that you can fly."

I climbed up onto the dais, the room spinning as I stumbled up the steps. Concussion, I thought absently. Probably should stop falling on my head.

A giggle escaped my lips, and my uncle frowned.

"Do you think this is amusing?" he asked.

"Nope," I said.

I shrugged off my leather jacket, folded it, and laid it on the smaller throne that sat beside my uncle's. I never sat there, but it made a safe place to leave my belongings. None of the staff would dare touch it.

Torso stripped down to my sports bra, I unfurled my wings, letting them stretch to the moonlit cavern ceiling. A buzzing began to roar in my skull, the result of my mind touching the other wisps floating in and out of the Great Hall. It was evidence of what my uncle was saying. Kade was right—I am fae.

"You are a wisp, my dear," he said. "The gift of flight is yours if you are willing to believe. It is your birthright."

I cast aside my emotions, distancing myself from my humanity. I imagined my wings lifting me through the cavern. I believed that it was possible. I reminded myself that in Faerie anything was possible.

I reached for the magic that ran through Tearlach, through Nithsdale above, through all of Faerie. It burned through my veins, joined the roaring in my skull, making my bones vibrate and my wings hum.

I lifted my face to the moonlit ceiling, and smiled. Blood ran down my face, and I could feel a similar trail of warmth pour from my ear, but I lifted my arms and embraced Faerie. I am wisp. I am fae.

I can fly.

My body lifted, and I flew upward, raking the tips of my gloves against the glowing, crystalline ceiling. I rolled, spun, and shot through one of the alcoves. With a twist of my body, I returned to the cavern, spreading my wings wide, and glorying in the knowledge that I was free.

Wind rushed across my body, but I focused on one thing, a single thought that burned through the buzzing in my skull.

Hold on, Ceff. I'm coming for you, baby.

CHAPTER 43

I stood in front of the mirror and ran a hand over my wings, checking for damage. I'd flown further today than ever, but I had nothing to show for it except sore wings and a bruised knee. I suppose it was better than the broken bones I got when I'd started going out on these excursions.

My stomach growled, and Skillywidden snorted.

"I told ye to bring more food," he said.

He was perched on the side of the tub, swinging his stubby legs back and forth. No matter how long I left for, he was always here waiting for me when I got back—just like my uncle.

"I ate plenty," I said. "If I ate as much food as you shoved at me, I'd never be able to fly."

That probably wasn't true, but Skilly nodded and went back to swinging his feet. I'd learned that my ability to fly was only partially due to the strength of my wings. It was also fueled by magic. Magic that was having an effect on more than my ability to fly.

I stared at the woman in the mirror, and frowned. Aside from eyes the color of amber, there'd been nothing remarkable about my appearance before my wisp powers emerged. While in Harborsmouth, my eyes and skin had begun to show the truth of my fae blood by glowing brightly when my emotions ran hot. My inability to keep those signs of my inhuman nature hidden was why the Unseelie Court had ordered my assassination.

Oh if they could see me now.

I stared into the mirror, shocked by how much I'd changed since my arrival in Faerie. My cheekbones were higher, hands more slender, and there were now flecks of silver in those amber eyes that flashed like shards of ice beneath the moon.

My uncle was right. Using magic had changed me. My father had done something to me as a child, not only to block

my memories, but to bind my power. But with Kade's help, I'd
torn down those bindings piece by bloody piece.

I turned to the side, careful to keep my wings from
brushing the wall behind me. They'd grown since my first
transformation, now stretching over five feet from tip to
glistening tip.

I was certainly remarkable now. Lips the color of frozen
blackberries curved in a self-deprecating smile, and I shook my
head. The woman who stared back at me was a creature of
terrible, otherworldly beauty.

I may have a human mother, and have been raised in
the human world, but my fears had finally been realized.
Glowing skin had been a hint, but I'd tried to brush that off as
little more than a vestigial side effect of my father's blood.
Entering Faerie and coming to my father's domain had
triggered an awakening of that blood, an awakening that I'd
kindled further with the use of magic. I could no longer hide
from the truth.

I was fae. I was inhuman. I was other.

How could I return to my human life in Harborsmouth?

"Perhaps my uncle is right," I said. "This is where I
belong."

"Yer uncle is a man obsessed with the memory of a
woman long gone," Skillywidden said, shaking his head.

I couldn't argue with that.

"Have ye checked near the wall of vines?" Skillywidden
asked. "Perhaps Ceff and Torn be waitin' for ye there. I could
help ye find me hearth, if ye take me with ye. Let me help,
lass."

"No," I said, fighting tears. Moisture leaked down my
cheeks as I lost that battle, and I drew on my power, lashing at
my face with a whip of fire to rip the tears away. "I've searched
there, Skilly. I've searched our entire path over and over
again. On foot, by air...there's no sign of them. If Torn and C-
C-Ceff were there to be found, they would be."

Saying Ceff's name and knowing that I would never see
him again was torture. I'd survived the pain of healing my own
bones one by one. I'd flown until I tore the fibers of the muscles
and ligaments in my wings. But nothing was as painful as
hearing his name.

"I forbid you from speaking of them again, Skilly," I
said, pushing power into my voice.

"But, lass!" he exclaimed.

"No!" I yelled.

I spun to face the brownie, my skin glowing as I pointed a finger at his chest. When had I stopped wearing gloves? I shook my head. It didn't matter. What was important now was moving on.

"Ye no right to forbid me," he said, hands on his hips. "Ceff and Torn were ye friends. Ye do not give up on ye friends, and neither does Skilly."

"I forbid you to say their names to me," I said.

"Do not do this," he said, eyes going wide. "Ye do not know what ye be sayin'. Calm down and we can talk this through."

I'd talked this through so many times, it was tearing me apart. I was a P.I. and I knew the hard truth. The first twenty-four hours were the most crucial in any missing person case. Within the realm of Faerie, Ceff and Torn had been missing for twenty-four *months*. It was time to let go.

"I'm done talking, Skilly," I said. "I just...I can't do this anymore."

"Come now, lass," he said.

"I'm sorry, Skilly," I whispered. "I forbid you to say their names to me."

The geis hit me like an orc's fist to the gut. I'd given my order, the bidding of the wisp princess within the walls of her court, thrice. I couldn't breathe, and my head felt like it'd been stomped on by an angry troll, but nothing could compare to the pain in my heart.

I'd been a fool. Racing all over Faerie, trying to find two men who I believed were still alive. But friends don't abandon you. Friends don't leave you alone to face a new life. I'd entered a new world, one that I had been raging against, but I was done fighting the facts.

Either they'd left me, or they were dead. Talking about them, searching for them, saying their names wouldn't fix that. Once again I'd been abandoned. It was Fate, and I was done fighting with the bitch.

I'd foolishly held onto the hope that Ceff and I had a future together, but that was a lie. The sooner I accept that, the better. I had duties, responsibilities. What I needed right now was to focus on becoming the best wisp princess that Faerie had ever seen.

CHAPTER 44

Skillywidden wasn't waiting for me in my room when I rolled out of bed. I checked the corridor, and still no sign of him. The brownie was mad at me for forcing a geis on him, but I wouldn't take it back. I needed to move on, to heal, and I couldn't do that while being tortured each day hearing Ceff and Torn's names. The guilt and the pain over their loss were too much to bear.

So it was that I strode into the Great Hall on my own. It was strange walking to breakfast without Skilly, but I knew that I wouldn't have to eat alone. My uncle always made time to eat our meals together, no matter how busy he was with his other duties. I took comfort in that. I'd lost so much by coming to Faerie, but at least I'd gained part of the family I'd always longed for.

I took a seat across the banquet table from my uncle, and piled pancakes onto my plate. No matter how weird Faerie got to be, there were always pancakes. That bit of normalcy was something I could hold onto through all the pain and chaos.

"I am pleased with your progress, my dear," Kade said, lifting his lips in a rare grin. His entire face lit up. "I believe you are ready to begin your court training."

"Court training?" I asked, leaning forward.

That sure sounded more interesting than shooting fireballs at the same targets over and over again, day in and day out. My uncle had kept me sequestered away from the hustle and bustle of the wisp court, citing the importance of focus in my magical training. Since I'd been focused on finding my friends, and had risked so much coming here to learn control over my powers, I'd gone along with him.

But learning to control my wisp powers wasn't the only reason I'd come to Faerie. I'd also come to learn more about my father, a subject that my uncle patently refused to discuss. There was obviously some bad blood there, and though I burned with curiosity, I feared pushing my uncle to recall the reasons he disliked my father. I worried that if whatever my father had done was discussed, my uncle's hatred might spread to encompass his feelings for me.

I swallowed hard, and bit my lower lip. That was a risk I wasn't able to take, not now that my uncle and Skilly were all I had. But perhaps I could learn something while helping my uncle in court.

"It is time for you to take on your duties to our people," he said.

He lifted his chin, shoulders back, surveying me with a gleam in his eye. Was he...proud of me? A tiny spark of hope ignited in my chest, stealing my breath away. In that moment, I never wanted to please someone more.

It was a strange emotion for me. I didn't normally care what people thought of me. Even with my friends back home, I'd been gruff and stubborn, never going out of my way to make them like me. I hadn't sought out friendships, never expected them. Over the course of time, they'd just somehow happened.

Perhaps that's why those relationships failed.

I hadn't ever tried to make someone else happy, not really. I'd done everything in my power to protect my friends from harm, to keep them safe, but I hadn't changed who I was for them. I'd never done that for anyone, not even Ceff.

I bit the inside of my cheek, and forced a smile on my face. Court would be a distraction from the grief that threatened to swallow me whole, and I might even learn something about my father. I could do this.

I would please my uncle. He was taking the time to teach me, and I would honor him by obediently completing my duties. I was no stranger to weighty responsibilities. How hard could it be?

CHAPTER 45

I held my breath, and sat on the throne beside my uncle. I half expected to be struck by lightning. Will-o'-the-Wisp might be my father, but I was only half fae, and I didn't know the first thing about being a proper princess. I felt like an imposter.

I picked at the edge of my dress. My uncle had finally got me to dress like royalty. He'd had the dress specially made by a clurichaun. I'm not sure how much he'd had to pay to have the spider silk and amber beaded dress made, but anything clurichaun crafted was void of visions. The little faeries were never sober enough to leave psychic impressions. I flicked a gloved finger at one of the amber beads, feeling naked without my jeans and leather jacket.

I lifted my chin, surveying the room. Wisps lined the rows of seats that faced us, some sitting and others floating like beautiful fireflies. They'd come to hear my uncle, and to see their princess finally take the throne. I fidgeted on the edge of the stone seat, amber and wood rising from the back of the throne to twine together like a glowing crown above my head.

I'd come into the Great Hall day after day, taking my meals at the banquet table that often stood beside the cattails and lilies in the center of the room. My uncle had taught me how to fly in this cavern. I'd touched its glowing amber ceiling with the tips of my gloved fingers, and shed blood on its moss and marble floor. This room was a part of me, a part of my history, and I never felt that so much as in this moment.

My uncle turned, and nodded. I nodded back, and he smiled.

"I knew one day we would rule together, you and me, my dearest," he said.

A familiar feverish gleam was in his eyes, and I swallowed hard. This was temporary, I reminded myself. I could leave whenever I wanted to. I would make my uncle happy, learn all I could about my father, and return to Harborsmouth. Maybe. I wasn't sure about that last bit anymore. I'd wanted to go home, and I'd been telling myself that my friends there needed me, but now, after losing Ceff and Torn, I wasn't so sure.

Someone cleared their throat, and I blinked. Mab's bones, I needed to focus. I would grieve later. For now, I needed to make my uncle proud.

"Kill him," Kade said.

"W-w-what?" I asked, eyes darting from my uncle to the wisp who'd been brought before me. Flavio sneered at me, and my uncle frowned. I must have misheard him. I'd been so wrapped up in thoughts of my lost friends that...

"Kill him," Kade said.

He was serious.

"Yes, Princess, use one of those fireballs you're so fond of," Flavio said mockingly, keeping his voice low.

His back was to the assembled crowd, and my uncle wasn't paying him any attention. But I didn't have time for Flavio's cruel games. I had to find a way to save the wisp, and myself.

I stared wide-eyed at the young man kneeling on the hard marble floor of the throne room. Through the magnifying crystal mounted in front of me, I could see the wisp well enough to tell that he was little more than a boy.

"He's just a child," I said, one hand going to my stomach.

"He is a criminal and a traitor," my uncle said.

"That boy be no traitor," Skilly grumbled.

The brownie must have used his magic and stealth to sneak into the room. He now perched on the ornately carved back of the throne, whispering in my ear. I didn't know whether to be more shocked by Skillywidden's sudden presence, or by my uncle's expectation that I would execute a child.

"What crime is he accused of?" I asked.

"He stole vital supplies belonging to the crown," he said.

"Vital supplies, pfft!" Skilly said. "He stole a stale loaf o' bread to feed his mum and her wee barns."

"Was this a first offense?" I asked.

"What does it matter?" Kade asked. He shot to his feet, and began pacing back and forth in front of his throne. "Once a thief, always a thief. We mustn't tolerate thievery. Such crimes undermine our ability to rule."

"But it might just be a misunderstanding," I said. "What evidence do you have of this crime?"

"The stolen item was missing, and this man was the only one present," he said. "He must be the thief."

That sounded an awful lot like the logic that Flavio had used to accuse Ceff and Torn of stealing the adder stone. My hands fisted in my lap.

"So by your logic, if I was missing something, and you were the closest person to me when the item went missing, you must be the thief?" I asked.

I slipped the ash wand I'd been practicing with earlier out of my pocket and waved it behind my back. I just hoped that Skillywidden got the hint. If anyone had a chance of slipping it into my uncle's pocket, it would be Skilly.

"Well, y-y-yes, of course, but the very idea is preposterous," Kade said. "I would never..."

"Robe pocket, right-hand side," Skilly whispered in my ear.

I nodded slightly, careful not to look at the brownie. I didn't want to give my friend away.

"I am missing my wand," I said, raising my voice to echo through the Great Hall. "You are standing closest to me, uncle. I demand that you empty your pockets."

"How dare you," Flavio said, stepping forward, hand on his sword.

I lifted an eyebrow, palming one of my own blades. Thank Mab, this dress had sleeves.

"Are you really going to strike me down on my own throne, Flavio?" I asked.

"Captain!" Kade said. "Stand down, and guard the prisoner."

"Yes, my lord," he said.

"Uncle, your pockets?" I asked.

"I will humor you this once," he said, shaking his head in irritation.

His eyes widened as his hand closed on the object in his pocket. He pulled the wand out, narrowed his eyes at it, and frowned. He looked at me, lips pressed in a hard line.

"Are you going to admit your guilt, or the flaw in your logic?" I asked.

My heart raced, but I held his gaze. He could always go with option number three: turn Ivy into a smoking pile of ash.

I was hoping that his love for me, and the fancy throne I was seated in, would stay his hand, but there were no guarantees.

"Free him," he said through clenched teeth.

Flavio jerked his head back as if slapped, gaping at my uncle, but he followed orders, setting the wisp child free.

"You disappoint me, Ivy," Kade said. "I expected more from you."

I had expected more from him too. I'd had every intention of becoming the dutiful niece, helping my uncle with his court duties. After two grueling years, I'd made enough progress with my magic that he finally deemed me worthy of appearing at court.

And in one moment, I'd lost all of the progress I'd made toward earning my uncle's trust, and his heart. But I couldn't harm a starving boy whose only crime was taking some bread to feed his family. That wasn't who I am. It never would be.

"Return to your room," he said, eyes beginning to glow.

He could have forced me with his power, but he didn't need too. I looked away, blinking away tears, as I gathered the skirts of my dress and left the room.

What was I thinking playing the dutiful princess? I would never be this person. I hurried from the room, choking on a sob that threatened to bring back the tears that I'd vowed would never fall again. I'd lost Ceff, and now I was losing my uncle.

Was I incapable of being loved?

"Ye did good, lass," Skilly said as I closed the door to my room.

He'd followed me inside, and I hadn't had the energy to ask him to leave. If I had to be honest, I didn't want to be alone.

"I failed him," I said. *Just like I fail everyone. Like I failed Ceff.*

"And I couldna be prouder of ye," Skilly said.

I looked down at the brownie's wrinkled face, and let my tears fall.

CHAPTER 46

"I've decided to focus on my glamour," I told my uncle over breakfast. "I don't think I'm quite ready for court."

I needed to work on my glamour, it was true, but mostly I just wanted an excuse to be alone.

"I agree," he said, dabbing the corners of his mouth with a spider silk napkin. "Your performance yesterday...left much to be desired."

I looked down at the food I pushed around my plate, hoping he'd see shame, but what I really felt was anger. Thank Mab, he'd helped me put a leash on my wisp powers, or I'd be glowing like a Christmas tree.

While on some level I understood that he was an immortal who'd lived in Faerie for centuries, and thus had a different set of morals, I still couldn't get over what he'd asked of me. He'd wanted me to use my magic to strike down a child.

I put a hand to my stomach, and pushed my chair away from the table.

"May I be excused?" I asked. "I have a lot of work to do."

"Yes, of course," he said. "We should have spent more time on glamour during your magic instruction, but I knew how sensitive you were about the way you were treated in the human world. I was trying to be considerate of your feelings."

"Thank you," I said, forcing a smile.

On the one hand, he sounded sincere about his consideration for my feelings, and on the other hand, he'd asked me to murder that boy. It was like he was two different men, and I didn't want to think too much about that. He was still the only connection I had to my father, and the only friend I had here in Faerie other than Skilly.

Better to take a time out now rather than run the risk of strangling my uncle.

CHAPTER 47

I walked out of the Great Hall with no destination in mind. I let my feet carry me throughout the mostly empty palace. With my uncle preparing to hold court in the Great Hall, I barely saw a soul. After my humiliation yesterday, that was fine by me.

Lost in thought, I wandered the corridors for an hour before I realized that I was being followed.

"Come on out, Skilly," I said. "I know you're there."

"Who say I want to be speakin' with ye?" he asked.

He was still sore at me for putting a geis on him. We'd had a moment last night when he'd comforted me, but apparently, we were back to fighting. I was so tired, and everything was such a mess, that I wasn't even sure how I'd screwed things up so badly between us.

"Look," I said, running a hand through my hair. "I'm sorry. I was upset, and talking about them is really hard for me right now, but I shouldn't have forbidden you from saying their names."

"And?" he asked.

He tapped his foot, arms folded across his chest. Oberon's eyes, I wasn't going to get out of this easy. I'd have to break the geis. A geis wasn't a faerie bargain—Skilly had never agreed to the situation—but it was still a difficult thing to break. The only one who could do it cleanly was the caster, which happened to be me. I just hoped that breaking the geis wouldn't make me fall flat on my face. I was sick of bloody noses.

I looked at Skilly, and sighed.

"And I revoke my geis," I said. "I revoke my geis. I revoke my geis."

I gasped, the spell breaking around us.

Skillywidden shook his head, and clapped his hands together and stuck his tongue out at me.

"Ceff and Torn, Ceff and Torn, Ceff and Torn," he said.

"I suppose I deserve that," I said.

"Aye, now where are we off to?" he asked, looking up and down the corridor. "I don't remember comin' this way before."

Skillywidden was right. I'd scoured every inch of Tearlach looking for my friends, but I didn't recall ever coming down this corridor.

"If this was glamoured, it must have been done with powerful magic," I said. "I can usually see through glamour with my second sight."

"Well, ye did tell Kade you'd be workin' on glamour," he said with a wink.

"Yes, I did," I said. "I suppose we should see where this leads. Want to do some exploring?"

"I thought ye would never ask," he said.

The corridor wasn't as long as it looked, an illusion created by a trick of forced perspective rather than magic, and soon led to a nondescript door. It could lead to a custodian's closet, or certain death. I drew one of my blades. Monsters and attack brooms, here I come.

After a moment's hesitation, I pulled the door open, revealing an elaborately decorated room. The floor was carpeted in green moss and toadstools, and a bed rose from that floor as if it had grown there. Perhaps it had.

"This be your uncle's quarters," Skillywidden said.

Skilly was right. We'd found a side door to Kade's quarters, the one room in this palace I'd never entered. I'd only caught a brief glimpse once. There'd been a hungry, eager look in my uncle's eyes that day, and I'd avoided this wing of the palace ever since.

"Have you ever been inside?" I asked.

"No, never had the chance," he said.

"No time like the present," I said.

I pulled a wooden stake from my utility belt, glad I'd traded yesterday's dress for my trusty jeans, belt, and leather jacket, and tossed the stake onto the moss-covered floor. Nothing happened. No fireballs, flesh-eating beds, or raging, moss-covered beasts. I held my breath, and stepped into the room.

So far so good.

"You coming?" I asked, cocking a hip, and waving toward the room. "Kade should be busy awhile, trying to win points with the court after the stunt I pulled yesterday."

I winced, and looked away.

"Ye did good, lass," Skillywidden said, stepping into the room. "Ye did the right thing by that boy."

"So," I said, changing the subject. "Where should we start?"

I stepped to the side, revealing a huge fireplace, and Skillywidden's eyes widened. The thing was so large that three men could stand inside it without bumping their heads.

"I figured you'd call dibs on the hearth," I said.

"Aye," he said, eyes gleaming.

Skilly made a beeline for the hearth, and I went to a wall of books. I'd leafed through the books in the court's treasure room, but they'd been disappointingly boring. Maybe my uncle kept the good stuff here on his own personal bookshelves.

I reached toward one of the shelves when the entire room began to vibrate. A scraping sound came from behind me, and I spun on my heel in time to see the rear wall of the hearth slide away into a recess in the wall.

"Skilly?" I asked, eyes wide.

The brownie's head popped up from the opening, and I let out the breath I'd been holding.

"Look at this," he said, grinning from ear to ear.

I inched forward, arms loose at my side, weight shifted to the balls of my feet. When I reached the fireplace, I gasped. The rear wall had slid away to reveal a staircase lit sparingly with fey lanterns.

"The hearth's a fake," I said, gaping at the staircase.

Skillywidden nodded.

"Aye, no chimney," he said, knocking his knuckles on the stone above our heads.

"I guess we should see what's down there," I said, eyes darting to the dimly lit stairs.

Skilly rubbed his hands together, and nodded.

"Aye, lass, we should."

CHAPTER 48

I imagined a treasure hoard, or maybe a stash of faerie pornography. Instead, we found a dungeon.

"Is anyone down here?" I asked, my voice echoing down the hall.

"Ye think that's a good idea, lass?" Skillywidden asked. "Not sure we want to wake whatever needs cagin' in iron."

He was right about the iron. The place was full of it. Every cell had iron bars set into the stone floor and ceiling, broken only by support pillars and a gate made of more iron bars.

Skilly kept to the center of the tunnel, as far from the iron bars as he could manage. He already looked pale. Even with my human blood, I was already getting a headache. We'd have to speed up our search before Skilly passed out. Not that I wanted to linger. This place gave me the creeps.

A raspy, disembodied whisper floated down the tunnel, and I paused. I cocked my head to the side, and listened.

"Do you hear that?" I asked.

"Aye," Skillywidden said. "Though it be hard to believe any faerie could be down here for long."

"You stand watch," I said. "If anyone comes down those stairs, give me a signal, then hide."

It would be safer for Skillywidden if he stayed where he was. Plus, he could holler if he heard my uncle or any of his guards returning.

I hurried forward, but kept my eyes peeled. I'd met wisps with iron sickness in Jinx's father's junkyard, and it wasn't pretty. It was like the iron made them go feral. I reached for one of my blades. If there were fae down here, they might be violent.

I turned a corner, weapon raised in guard position, and stopped dead in my tracks. There were two men chained together in the cell to my left. I blinked, but it wasn't an illusion.

"Princess?" Torn asked, voice ragged.

His voice must have been the whisper we'd heard before.

"I...but..." I started, and then I was reaching for my lock picks.

"Took you long enough, Princess," Torn said.

My hands shook. I couldn't believe that Ceff and Torn were here within reach. What were they doing in my uncle's dungeon?

As soon as I picked the lock, I pulled open the metal grate and tore at the chains that bound my friends to the wall of their cell. I noted absently that the iron chains burned my hands, even through my gloves. I'd remarked recently to my uncle on how my blades, with a much lesser iron content than these chains apparently, had begun to make my wrists and hands ache. I still wore them, but I wondered how much longer I could keep that up. Faerie had changed me, and not all of those changes were for the best.

I hadn't used my blades much in recent weeks—or had it been months?—but I couldn't bring myself to discard them, not yet. I would have to dispose of them soon, but for now, they were a powerful weapon against the pureblood fae. Not that I needed mere weapons, not any longer. I was a walking weapon—my uncle had made sure of that.

Torn cleared his throat, putting a stop to my rambling thoughts.

"The lock, Princess," Torn said, pointing to where their chains were padlocked to a ring that was bolted to the wall above their heads. "Pick the lock."

I nodded, and fumbled with the lock, finally managing to open the padlock, and pulled the chains away. Ceff didn't move.

"Please tell me he's alive," I said. I grabbed Ceff by the shoulder, and shook him gently. "Ceff? Ceff? Can you hear me? It's me, Ivy." I turned wild eyes on Torn, my heart trying to beat its way out of my chest. "Is he alive?"

"Yes, he was alive last I checked," he said. "But he wouldn't have made it much longer. He's more sensitive to iron. Probably from being bound in iron chains by the *each uisge.*"

Torn was right. Ceff was strong, but he'd become more sensitive to iron after his torture at the hands of the *each uisge.* It was amazing that he'd survived this long.

"Help me get him up," I said, putting an arm under Ceff, and pulling him to his feet.

He was a dead weight, but I widened my stance and kept him upright. With the adrenaline coursing through me, I could probably carry both him and Torn out of here.

"Is there anythin' I can do to help?" Skillywidden asked from the corridor.

I left him standing watch, but he'd peeked inside the tunnel to see what all the fuss was about. Now he was standing wide-eyed, and wringing his hands.

"Is that the brownie?" Torn asked.

"Yes, he's a friend," I said.

"Probably the only one in this place," he said with a hiss.

I ignored Torn's grumbling. I'd need answers eventually, but I wasn't ready to start asking the tough questions. And Ceff was still out cold.

"Skilly, can you bring me that blanket?" I asked.

We wrapped the threadbare blanket around Ceff's naked torso, covering the worst of his wounds. Iron prevented healing, but I hoped that Ceff would recover once we got him out of this cell.

"Don't let it touch your skin," Torn said, gesturing toward the blanket.

"Why, visions?" I asked.

"It's made of horse hair," he said, nose wrinkling.

"They made him sleep with a horse hair blanket?" I asked.

"Better than my canteen," he said.

I glanced at the canteen, and swallowed bile.

"Is that cat skin?" I asked.

"Yes," he said.

"Why would anyone skin a cat?" I asked.

"To be cruel?" he asked. "Honestly, I don't care, so long as I get to return the favor."

There was a steely darkness in Torn's eyes, and I shivered. Ceff moaned, and I shifted his weight.

"Come on, let's get away from all this iron," I said.

We made it up the tunnel, but it was slow work. When we reached my uncle's room, I set Ceff on the edge of the bed. I started to pace the room, noticing for the first time how much it resembled a forest glade. Where my quarters appeared to capture ice and stars, Kade's room was made up of moss and wood.

My mind reeled, darting from object to object while trying to make sense of what had just happened. I'd been searching for Ceff and Torn for over two years. Had Flavio and the guards only just discovered them, and locked them in the dungeon. Or had they been imprisoned here all along?

The latter was too painful to accept.

"Did you steal the adder stone?" I asked, my skin awash in a spectral light.

"Don't be daft, lass," Skillywidden said, shaking his fist at me from a safe distance.

The brownie was brazen, but not a fool.

"We need to get out of here, Princess," Torn said.

"I'm not leaving, not until I get answers," I said. "Why were you in the dungeon? What have you done?"

"We haven't done anything wrong," Ceff croaked.

"Personally, I don't care if we take you out of here kicking and screaming," Torn said. "But His Horsiness over there might have a stroke if I toss you over my shoulder."

"You can try," I said, power flaring.

Magic rushed through my veins, coming to my aid. It rose faster now, my abilities growing with every cast spell, every use of my wisp heritage. I would burn my enemies from the world, leaving nothing but ash in my wake.

Wisps rushed into the room and gathered in the branches of the bedposts designed to resemble trees, like a deadly swarm of twinkle lights. I nodded, and gave my brethren a warm smile before turning cold eyes on the three men before me. No one was forcing me to go anywhere, not until I had some answers. Here, surrounded by my people, I was unstoppable.

"Ivy Granger, Princess of the Wisp Court, Consort and Betrothed to Ceffyl Dwr, King of the Kelpies," Ceff said. "You are pledged to me, as I to you, and you will grant me audience. Look at me and listen to my words."

His voice rang through the room, jerking my muscles to attention. There is power in a name, and Ceff had infused his voice with the melodic power of pureblood royalty. He also used the full strength of his claim on me, and of his rank as king, to make his demand.

I frowned, but nodded.

"Betrothed?" Torn mouthed, but I ignored him, my focus on Ceff.

"Fine," I said, showing small, white teeth. I didn't need fangs to subdue my prey. "I hear you Ceffyl Dwr, but you will also hear me. "If I find out that this was some half ass scheme to steal my uncle's treasure, I will kill you."

"Agreed," he said, stepping forward.

"I want the truth," I said, a tear slipping down my cheek.

I was shaking. When had I started shaking? I wasn't even cold.

"I love you," he said.

"You abandoned me," I said.

"No, I would never leave you of my free will," he said.

"Did you leave me for treasure?" I asked.

"Is that what your uncle claimed?" he asked. "Think, Ivy. He is pureblood fae. He cannot tell a direct lie, but he can twist the truth."

"He said you would hurt me, that loving you made me weak," I said. "Kade and Flavio and the rest of the guards claimed that you ran off with the adder stone. I didn't believe them. But I couldn't find you. I searched everywhere, and I couldn't find you. I thought you'd either left me, or that you were dead. You broke my heart."

"I did not steal anything, and I did not leave you—not by my own will," he said. "Your uncle set a trap, and imprisoned us in his dungeons."

"You...you didn't come back for so long..." I said. "I searched, and searched, and I couldn't find you."

"He drugged us and bound us with cold iron, Princess," Torn said. "Your uncle is a selfish prick, and a coward."

"I am sorry that we could not escape," Ceff said. "I am sorry that you were left alone."

Oberon's eyes, was he telling the truth? While I searched all of Nithsdale, had Ceff and Torn been languishing in the dungeons? My body tensed, muscles quivering. Two years bound by iron. If what Ceff said was true, it was a miracle that he survived.

I took a step toward Ceff, wanting so badly to believe what he was saying.

"He...he said that I was a fool to have loved you, to believe that I'd ever see you again," I said.

"He was wrong."

I ran into Ceff's arms, his body rushing up to meet my own. His lips were on mine, and then I was drowning in visions. I lived through all of the happiest and most painful moments of his life, and I knew firsthand that his love for me had never wavered.

I gasped as the visions ended, and then I was running my hands over his body, his face. His lips left a scorching trail up my neck and along my chin as he peppered me with kisses.

"You're really here," I whispered.

"Yes," he said, the words vibrating against my skin.

"You never stopped loving me," I said.

"Do the tides ever stop changing?" he asked. "I gave you my heart. It is yours for eternity."

"I love you," I said. "I never stopped loving you. B-b-but I searched and I searched and I couldn't find you and..."

My words were cut off as his mouth pressed against mine. I moaned as his tongue slid inside my mouth, and I might have taken him there on Kade's bed if Torn hadn't interrupted.

"Not that I mind the free show, but this might be a good time to get our asses out of here," he said.

Ceff groaned, but Torn was right. We weren't free, not yet. I ran a hand through my hair, and took a shaky breath.

"You're right," I said. "But before we leave, my uncle and I have some unfinished business."

CHAPTER 49

"So, betrothed eh?" Torn asked, shaking his head. "When were you two lovebirds going to fill me in?"

We hurried down the tunnel, heading steadily toward the Great Hall where my uncle was holding court. The wisps that I'd somehow drawn to me in my anger and confusion had confirmed that Kade had been busy flexing his political might by making examples of any other perceived traitors to the throne (ie, bread thieves). My little stunt yesterday had cost him. Considering that he may have taken part in Ceff and Torn's abduction, he had only begun to pay what he owed me.

"It's not like we've had time for an engagement party," I said. "I haven't even told Jinx."

"I want an invite," Torn said.

"What?" I asked.

I was only half listening, my mind trying to sort through every conversation I'd had with my uncle since arriving in Faerie.

"To your engagement party," Torn said. "I want an invitation, Princess. After this little excursion of yours, I think I've earned it."

My chest tightened. I owed Torn a heck of a lot more than an invitation to a party.

"You got it," I said.

"How are we going to handle this?" Ceff asked.

I'd been mulling that over, but I wasn't sure what my friends would think of my plan.

"I want answers, and then we're blowing this taco stand," I said.

"And if there's a fight?" Ceff asked.

"There will be a fight, Princess," Torn said, flexing his claws.

"I don't trust Flavio, the captain of the guard, and his lackey Marcus, but we don't know yet who is involved in this," I said.

"And if your uncle is behind our abduction?" Ceff asked.

"No one is punishing my uncle but me," I said.

Anger and grief waged a war inside my chest. It was like someone had carved a hole through my body, and I was spilling my guts on the floor. My uncle was my family. He'd taught me how to control my wisp magic, helped me to survive. But if I found out that he had imprisoned my friends, I might just kill him myself.

He'd seen me suffer with their loss every day. Could my uncle truly be that cold? And if so, what was his motivation? Why hurt my friends?

Flavio stepped around the corner, eyes going wide. Damn, we'd almost made it to the Great Hall without a fight.

"You!" Torn hissed.

"I take it you two have already met," I said, widening my stance.

Flavio drew his sword, and sneered.

"I told him we should have killed you," Flavio said, aiming his sword at me.

He'd dismissed my iron sick friends, and decided that I was the biggest threat. That was his second mistake. His first was torturing the king of the kelpies and the lord of cats for two years.

Torn and Ceff recognized Flavio all right, and they weren't in a forgiving mood. I can't say that I could blame them.

"You chained us in cold iron," Ceff said, eyes shifting to black.

"I could almost forgive the iron, but no one skins a cat and lives to tell about it," Torn said. "Not on my watch."

Oh yeah, Flavio had been a naughty boy and he deserved what was coming to him.

"Is it true that you chained my friends in the dungeon?" I asked, keeping Flavio busy.

I sent a fireball whizzing over his shoulder, and he smirked. He thought that was all I had. Flavio hadn't shared in my uncle's enthusiasm over my magic training. He had no idea how strong I'd become.

"I did, and I would do it again," he said, raising his sword.

"Why?" I asked.

"Because you are nothing, all of you are nothing," he said. "I am his captain. I am wisp. I am everything."

He ran at me, sword raised overhead, but he never stood a chance. Torn raked his claws across the backs of Flavio's calves, tearing through his boots. Hamstrung, he staggered one more step before taking Ceff's trident through his heart. I'd had my blades and my magic ready, but I wasn't in danger from Flavio. No one ever would be again.

I frowned, hands tightening on my blades. I should have been saddened by this man's death, or perhaps a little relieved, but my heart hadn't caught up with the events of the past hour. I was still processing the fact that Ceff and Torn were here with me, alive. I would do anything to keep it that way. I just wish I knew who my enemies were.

I shook my head, and started down the corridor.

"Come on," I said. "That's not going to go unnoticed. We need to reach my uncle before word of Flavio's death reaches the other guards."

I strode in the direction of the Great Hall, heart pounding in my chest.

"Your uncle wants us dead," Torn said.

"We don't know that," I said. "Flavio hated me. He was always looking for a chance to take me down. It doesn't mean that my uncle sanctioned this attack."

"You still don't think Kade orchestrated this whole thing?" Torn asked.

"I don't know," I said. "All I know is that my uncle cares about me, and it's hard to believe that he'd do this do me. Flavio being behind it all makes more sense."

"It be true," Skillywidden said. "Kade has a soft spot for the princess, though I dinnae think his affections be so innocent."

"He just gets confused," I said, frowning at Skillywidden. "That doesn't mean that he had my friends tossed in the dungeon, or that he wants us all killed."

"He looks at ye the same way yonder kelpie looks at ye," he said.

"Does he now?" Ceff asked, eyes shifting to black.

"Fine, Princess," Torn said, ignoring Ceff. "We'll do things your way, but if Kade attacks, I'm not holding back."

"Not before I get answers," I said.

"We will wait until you get your answers," Ceff said. "But Torn is right. If Kade is responsible for our imprisonment, we will not hold back."

After two years in iron chains, I didn't expect them to. But I still wasn't convinced that my uncle was behind their abduction.

"Just give me a chance to talk to him," I said. "Maybe this was all Flavio's idea. The guy was a creep."

"I agree that the guard was a creep, but that tunnel came out in your uncle's quarters," Torn said. "I find it hard to believe he had no idea that we were down in that dungeon."

"We will give Ivy her chance to talk," Ceff said.

"That's all I ask," I said.

"Fine, whatever," Torn said. "No sense arguing with the married couple."

I blushed, and led the way to the Great Hall. Married couple? I liked the sound of that.

CHAPTER 50

"If that is the last order of business..." Kade said.

He looked around the room, a serene expression on his face until he caught sight of me.

"My dear, what are you...?" he asked.

Ceff and Torn stepped into the Great Hall, cutting off the rest of his question, but I answered anyway.

"I'm here for answers, uncle," I said.

"Seize those men!" Kade shouted.

Marcus and two of the other guards broke away from the throne, and charged forward. I lifted a hand, eyes glowing, and sent a fireball at their feet.

"I don't think so," I said. "They're with me."

The guards hesitated, eyes darting to Kade for orders. My uncle's lips pulled back from his teeth.

"Is this your decision?" he asked. "Have you forsaken our bond? Have you come to stand against me?"

"I've come for answers, uncle," I said. "I deserve the truth."

Having seen my uncle's face when he caught sight of Ceff and Torn, I had a pretty good idea of what those answers would be, but I still wanted to hear his side of the story.

"What truth?" he asked. "That I wanted you for myself? That these men were no good for you? They are unworthy of your beauty. You must see that."

"So it's true then," I said. "You were behind their disappearance all along."

A buzzing hum filled the room as wisps started talking all at once, and I was glad that I hadn't tried to reach the Great Hall from one of the alcoves above. With my wings extended, the crowd of wisps would have been deafening.

"I did it for you, can't you see that?" he said. "I've done it all for you."

"How could you?" I asked. "They are my friends. Ceff is my betrothed. I love him."

"You would choose the kelpie over me," he spat. "Do you know what you are giving up?"

"Do you?" I asked.

"With my knowledge and your power, we could have ruled over all of Faerie," he said.

"I don't think Oberon and Mab would appreciate that," Ceff said.

"Oberon and Mab are gone!" Kade seethed, chest heaving. He turned back to me, a feverish gleam in his eyes. "Faerie is rife for the taking! It can be ours. Cast aside these fools, and join me. We can have it all."

"I never wanted power, uncle," I said. "All I wanted was a family."

"Sniveling brat," he sneered. "You're as bad as your father. He ruined everything when he left Faerie. He brought down Mab's wrath on our kingdom."

My chest tightened, and my vision blurred. I knew that there had been bad blood between the brothers, but I had no idea just how deep seated my uncle's hatred was for my father.

"He did it to protect a child," I said.

"You don't even know, do you?" he sneered. "He claimed that he did it for the love of the child, but what of my feelings? All those years, all I wanted was one thing, one woman, and he stole her from me."

"What are you talking about?" I asked.

I knew that there was a tragic love story in my uncle's past. He'd confused me often enough for his lost love. I wanted to know more about her, why he'd come out of that relationship so broken, but I dreaded hearing anything that might mar my father's memory. Then again, I'd come here for the truth.

"Who was she?" I asked.

"The most beautiful woman in all of Faerie," he said. "And she would have been mine. She'd sent for each of us, your father and I, but he went first, he always went first. It was his birthright, and now I wish he'd never been born. He had her first, and so she sent me back to our court without giving me a chance, and kept him there in the palace. But she should have wanted me. Don't you see? It should have been me."

"You've lost it, old man," Torn said. "You're not even making sense."

"I could have been the Unseelie King," he said. "It should have been me!"

A cold tendril wrapped around my heart.

"This woman," I said. "What was her name?"

I'd guessed the answer, but I needed to hear it from his lips.

"The Queen of Air and Darkness," he said, voice a reverent whisper. "My dear, dearest Mab."

My father had been Mab's boy toy. I was going to be sick.

"What happened to my father?" I asked.

"He risked everything, and left me to pick up the pieces, to rebuild the wisp court after Mab spent her anger tearing it apart, all for his ridiculous love for that child."

"Love isn't ridiculous," I said. "If you weren't so obsessed with power, you might realize that."

"Love is a foolish human emotion that has no place in Faerie," he said. "No place in you."

He was wrong. Ceff and Marvin loved fully, and they were fae. But I couldn't help the retort that burst from my mouth.

"Well, if love is a foolish human emotion, I'm glad to be a half-breed," I said.

I expected anger, rage. Instead, my uncle tipped his head back and laughed. A chill ran up my spine when his eyes caught mine again, trapping me in his ecstatic gaze.

"Oh, my niece, you are many things, but you are not human," he said.

CHAPTER 51

My throat tightened and my chest constricted, leaving me gasping for air. My uncle's words, *you are not human,* making the muscles in my stomach clench. It was a lie. It had to be a lie.

"What do you mean, she is not human?" Ceff asked, eyes shifting to black.

Suffering from iron poisoning, he could barely stand without leaning on his trident, but that didn't stop him from stepping forward, putting himself between me and my uncle.

"I am half fae and half human," I said.

But I wasn't so sure who I was trying to convince.

"Oh, you might seem human," Kade said, waving a hand at me. "You might even have human blood running through your veins, but that is just a technicality, a trick of magic. I don't know how my brother accomplished your present state, but one thing is certain. You were not born human."

"What do you mean?" I asked. "I have a human mother."

I knew my mother was human. She wasn't a faerie hiding behind a glamour. I was sure of it.

"Oh, I'm sure Liam found a willing surrogate to adopt you and pretend you were her own," he said. "Knowing my brother, he probably laid a geis on her so that she could never reveal the truth of your birth."

That hit a little too close to home.

"No," I said. "I don't believe you."

"It doesn't matter what you believe," Kade said. "All that matters is who you are."

He was baiting me. I wanted to ask who I was so badly it hurt, but I pressed my lips together in a hard line. I wouldn't give him the satisfaction.

It was all lies anyway, wasn't it?

"If she's pureblood fae, then who's her mother?" Torn asked, tapping his chin with one claw-tipped finger. "Liam only had one wife, and he never mentioned a lover...oh."

"No," I croaked.

I'd come to the same conclusion as Torn, but it was too monstrous to believe. My father had fled Faerie with a fae child. He'd claimed that he was trying to protect that child. Mab left Faerie soon after to find something that had been stolen from her—the thing most precious to her.

"No," I said, shaking my head.

The only thing keeping my world from shattering into a million pieces was the knowledge that the timeline was all wrong. My father had left Faerie over a hundred years ago. I was only twenty-five. No matter how you did the math, I couldn't be that baby.

"Yes," Kade said, eyes wide. "I recognized you as soon as you stepped foot in Nithsdale. You look so much like her. The resemblance is uncanny."

"No," I said.

"You have her strength," he said. He never blinked. When had he stopped blinking? "Her force of will. Mab is like a hurricane, a violent force of nature, and someday you will be as well. I've seen it in you. Her power. That penchant for violence. The desire to burn the world to ash and recreate it in your own image."

"No," I said. "You're lying...there's no way...I'm not..."

"What?" he asked. "Not powerful enough? Don't be ridiculous. I've seen her power raging inside of you. I've helped to nurture it, helped it to grow. Soon it will break free of your father's sorcery, and then you will truly be the worthy heir to Faerie."

"You're the heir to the Unseelie Court?" Torn asked. He let out a low whistle. "I knew you were a princess—a wisp princess—but heir to the Winter Throne?"

I shook my head. My hands were shaking, and my legs felt like they might give out at any moment.

"I'm not...I'm not old enough," I said. "That baby, if it was even Mab's—which we have no reason to believe—would be nearly two hundred years old. So it can't be me."

Please don't let it be me.

"I admit that I found this perplexing as well, until I recalled Liam's friendship with the kitsune," Kade said.

"Inari?" Torn asked, frowning. "What does she have to do with this?"

Normally, I'd perk up at that name, the private investigator in me coming to the forefront, looking for answers. I knew that Torn and Inari had been lovers, but that things hadn't ended well between them. I'd tried to drill him for information about the kitsune when I found out that she was one of my father's former friends, but Torn would never talk about her. I'd been trying to pry details about Inari from Torn since I learned of my father's existence, but I had a feeling that I didn't want to hear what he had to say next.

"She used to visit our court, before Oberon and Mab left and closed the roads to Faerie," Kade said. "And I finally recalled one of her special talents."

"Weapon crafting, nature magic that increases crop yields...oh," Torn said, eyes wide. "Stasis magic. Inari can put a person in stasis."

"Yes," Kade said. "I remembered a story she once shared about putting a fallen kitsune warrior in stasis while they carried her off the battlefield and to the nearest healer."

"But casting stasis on an injured warrior and casting it on a healthy child are two very different things," Ceff said. "What father would do such a thing?"

"A desperate one," I said.

"Mab would have been looking for an older child, and later a grown woman," Ceff said, nodding as he came to the same realization that I had.

"And one that was pureblood fae," Torn said.

"He was trying to protect you from the Queen of Air and Darkness," Ceff said. "Mab would have jealously guarded her throne. You would always have been a threat, her enemy. He was protecting his child."

"Liam was a fool!" Kade said, spittle flying from his lips. Apparently, he didn't appreciate my father receiving praise. "Who knows what Mab would have done with you? Who cares? Liam had the one thing I wanted, and he threw it all away for a child. He left Faerie, and he took Mab with him."

"I'm Mab's daughter?" I asked, voice a whisper.

"You're the reason she left," he said, glaring at me. "I should hate you, despise you, but I took you in. I taught you how to use your powers. You look so much like her. We could have been together. Finally together."

I made a choking sound, and Ceff stepped closer to Kade.

"We've heard enough," Ceff said.

"Wait," I said. "I have one more question. Uncle, in the years since my father left Faerie, did you ever hear where he'd gone? Or where Mab went to?"

If we'd found a back door to Faerie, that meant there would be others. Word would pass between the two realms. In fact, I suspected that the Unseelie Court had a way of communicating between its branches in the human world and its seat in Faerie.

"No," he said. "He left, and she followed. My dearest left me, for him. Always, always for him."

Ceff raised an eyebrow at me, and I nodded. I was done with Kade's ramblings. Ceff slammed a fist into Kade's temple, knocking him unconscious mid-rant.

"No fair, Fish Breath," Torn said. "I wanted to knock him out."

"I will let you do it next time he wakes up," Ceff said.

"Deal," Torn said, a slow grin stretching across his face. "So what do we do with him?"

"Kill him?" Ceff asked. "Chain him in iron? Banish him from Faerie?"

They were all reasonable suggestions considering Kade's crimes and his penchant for diabolical schemes, but I couldn't condone physically harming my uncle, and I didn't want to send him off to wreak havoc on some other unsuspecting world. But there are other ways to hurt a man such as Kade.

"Is there a way to strip a faerie of his power?" I asked.

Power was the one thing that my uncle held dear. He had stolen so much from me, and I planned to return the favor.

I also wasn't stupid. I may not want my uncle imprisoned, but I didn't want a magic-toting sociopath wandering the world, biding his time for revenge.

"Yes," Torn said, frowning. "But you need a loireag to do the spell."

"Where can we find ourselves a loireag?" I asked.

"There are only two that I've ever heard of, Princess," he said.

"Are they here, in Faerie?" I asked.

"Aye, lass," Skillywidden said, coming to stand near me now that Kade was unconscious and drooling on the floor. "We've all heard tell of the loireag. There be one for each court, Seelie and Unseelie."

"They are used in extreme cases, but it is rare for a faerie to be sentenced to having their magic stripped away," Ceff said.

"So there's one of these loireag at the ice palace?" I asked.

"Yes," Ceff said, but we would have no authority to request a stripping of your uncle's powers. If we present his crimes before the Unseelie Court, there is no guarantee of what they will sentence him to suffer, or that they will find him guilty."

"He kidnapped and bound in iron a kelpie king and a cat sidhe lord," I said. "That must be considered a crime, even here in Faerie, right?"

"No," Torn said. "Kidnapping is par for the course, Princess. It would take Mab herself to veto the court's decision."

"We may not have a faerie queen, but we do have a princess," I said. "Would that work?"

Torn stroked his chin, deep in thought. The sound of his claws raking across stubble made the hair on my neck stand on end. His eyes met mine, and his lip lifted in a grin.

"It might," he said. "It just might."

CHAPTER 52

"Are you sure that you want to do this?" Ceff asked. "Mab has been searching for you for more than a century."

We'd already been over this. I understood his desire to keep me safe, but I was done with hiding. Plus, this gave me a chance to clear my name with the Unseelie Court, and find a punishment for my uncle that I could live with.

"Fish Breath has a point, Princess," Torn said. "You'd be serving yourself up on an iron platter."

I shrugged.

"The entire wisp court already knows my secret," I said. "It's not like my uncle was discreet."

Kade, in his frenzied rage, had outed me in front of every wisp who'd been in attendance in the Great Hall. His rant cost me my anonymity. No point in trying to cover it up.

I'd come to Faerie for the truth. I might as well embrace it.

"You are the rightful heir to your father's throne," Ceff said. "You have more political clout than Kade, since this court is your birthright, not his. You can order your people to silence."

"Do you really think that would work?" I asked, lifting an eyebrow. "Because I don't. It's human nature, and fae nature, to gossip. Finding out that the wisp princess is also the winter princess is pretty big news, even for Faerie. People will talk, no matter what I threaten them with."

"But if you order..." he said.

"No," I said, holding up a gloved hand. "Let's be honest. I'm a stranger here. Kade spent his entire life here in the wisp court, but I grew up in the human world. It might be my birthright, maybe even doubly so, to demand their obedience, but I haven't done anything to prove my worthiness as a leader. Hell, I don't want to. I just want to drag Kade's ass to the ice palace, have his magic stripped, prove to the court that I'm no longer a threat to our kind, and return to Harborsmouth."

I'd give up all the pancakes in Faerie and eat ramen for eternity if it meant returning home to my loft apartment with its threadbare couch and musty smelling wall hangings.

"I doubt it will be that simple," Torn said.

"No," I said, letting out a heavy sigh. "It never is."

Ceff stood rigid, and I waited as various emotions—fear, anger, frustration, uncertainty, and resignation—crossed his face. His shoulders slumped, just slightly, and I knew that I'd won the argument, for now.

"Who will you leave in charge of your people?" he asked. "Your father is still missing, and with you gone, who will keep them safe?"

I'd given this a lot of thought, actually. I just hoped that my plan worked.

"I have an idea," I said.

"This should be good," Torn said. "How are you going to find another wisp with royal blood on such short notice?"

"I'm not going to," I said with a smile. "I'm going to teach the wisp court about a little thing called democracy."

"Oberon save us all," Ceff said.

He let out a heavy sigh, but there was laughter in his eyes. He might be a king, but he knew me well enough to recognize when my mind was made up.

Plus, we were fresh out of wisp royalty at the moment, not that my uncle had done all that good of a job leading in my father's absence. Fueled by his obsessions, Kade had led by fear and manipulation, and he'd encouraged competition and paranoia within the royal guard. If it weren't for Kade's jealous machinations, Flavio might be alive right now.

My hands tightened into fists, and I took a deep breath.

"You may want to stand back," I said.

Ceff raised an eyebrow, and then shared a look with Torn who just shrugged, and moved a few feet away. I turned to stride up the remaining steps, and onto the dais. I stripped out of my leather jacket, tossing it onto the throne.

I willed my wings to unfurl, and steadied myself against the buzzing that flooded into my skull. I turned to face the crowd of wisps who'd remained in the Great Hall, waiting to learn their fate. Kade was unconscious, and Flavio was dead, so they looked to me for answers—and I planned to give them that and more.

I would give them their freedom.

I planted my feet in a wide stance, and lifted my chin. My chest tightened, and a small part of me wondered if my father would approve of what I was about to do. Bringing democracy to the wisp court would undermine his authority, his claim to the throne. But I was done with thrones and leaders whose only qualification was the blood that ran in their veins. I wanted more for these people. They deserved to have food to eat and a safe place to live. They deserved to be free from fear, from the tyranny of men obsessed with power.

"My father left Faerie," I said. "For good or ill, he isn't here. My uncle ruled over you with an iron fist and an unkind heart. I will not do the same."

The buzzing roared, a crescendo of thoughts and voices that threatened to overwhelm me, but I soldiered on.

"My first order as your princess is to revoke the rights of my family, of any one family, to lead you, and to instate a new kind of governing power for our people," I said. "I know this is a monumental change, but I have faith in all of you. We as a people are resilient. We glow in the deepest dark. We are wisps."

I held my hands high, tears rolling down my cheeks, as I embraced their cheers. I would only lead them for a day, this day, but I would use my limited time as their princess to bring a positive change for the future.

Through the roaring, I turned and smiled at Skillywidden, and called him to the dais.

"Skilly, do you want to return to Tech Duinn?" I asked, keeping my voice low.

"No, lass," he said, fidgeting with one of his suspenders. "I had hoped to stay 'ere and mind the hearth."

"Even if I leave?" I asked.

"Aye, even then," he said. "I've made friends with the kitchen staff, and I'd be no good in the human world. I'd rather stay in Faerie, if it's all the same to ye."

"I'll miss you, Skilly," I said. "But I was hoping you'd stay. My people need you."

I nodded, pulled a large, cloth-wrapped bundle from my pocket, and handed the adder stone to Skilly. We'd found the stone hidden amongst my uncle's things. He and Flavio had used its disappearance to frame my friends. Now I had other plans for it. The stone represented the power of the wisps, and it would soon become a symbol for change, and a reminder of what can happen when we put our faith in the wrong leader.

"They do?" he asked.

"They do," I said. I raised my voice, my words once again carrying to the gathered wisps. "You will need to elect representatives, men and women you trust, for your new council. Meanwhile, I appoint Skillywidden to aid in decisions that need immediate attention."

"But, Princess, I'm not even wisp!" he said.

"Skillywidden is henceforth known as wisp friend," I said, keeping my voice raised. I winked at Skilly, and he blushed. "He will be an asset to your growing council, and a valuable advisor."

With that, I grabbed my jacket, and stepped down from the dais. Skillywidden frowned, and shuffled his feet.

"What am I supposed to do now?" he asked.

"Help them," I said. "Give them advice when they need it, just as you did for me. In the two years that I've known you, Skilly, you've been a loyal friend. You always gave me good advice, and you have a tender heart. I know that you will help my people, because you can tell the difference between what is fair and just, and what is selfish and cruel."

"The boy," he said.

We shared a look, and I nodded.

"You knew that saving that boy wasn't a failure," I said.

"But to give me this, the ear of ye people," he said. "It's too much."

"It won't be for long," I said. "They'll build a government, in time. But until then, I trust you to do what you can to make things right. And you won't always be on your own. I'll try to return, when and if I can."

"If anybody can, it be you, Princess," he said.

It was true. I was the daughter of the Queen of Air and Darkness. If there were backdoors to Faerie, I'd have access to them. It was just a matter of finding those portals, a job well suited for someone with P.I. training. At least, that was my hope.

I smiled, and nodded.

"There's just one more thing before I go," I said.

"And what would that be?" he asked, eyes narrowing.

I'd asked a lot of him already. I didn't blame him for being suspicious.

"Will you keep the hearth fire burning for me?" I asked. Skillywidden's face relaxed, and he returned my smile. "Aye, lass," he said. "Thought you'd ne'er ask."

CHAPTER 53

"I will not stand for this, I am...*argh!*" Kade yelled, interrupted by a slap to the side of the head.

"Are you sure we can't kill him, Princess?" Torn asked, tilting his head in my direction, and holding an extended claw to Kade's throat. "No one would miss him, and there's a convenient bog right over there..."

"No," I said. We'd been over this, and I wasn't backing down. "He's a delusional creep, but he's my family."

"I knew you cared for me," Kade said, eyes gleaming. "Tell them to unhand me, and we can return to the wisp court where we can rule together..."

"Torn, if you don't shut him up, I will," Ceff said.

"You know how I like it when you talk tough, Fish Breath," Torn said, batting his eyelashes. "But it's my turn to guard the prisoner, and I don't take orders from you."

"Oh, would you all be quiet?" I asked.

My head still ached from my little speech yesterday. Having my wings extended had been necessary for communicating with my people, during the speech and in the meetings we held after, but the subsequent headache had sent me to my quarters without dinner. I'd been too sick to eat, or enjoy the fact that Ceff had shared my bed. Now we were on our way to the ice palace, and I was tired, hungry, and fresh out of patience.

"Like I said, Princess, if you let me kill him..." Torn said.

I sent a fireball whizzing past his shoulder, close enough to singe one of the pieces of bone and fur dangling from his ear.

"Well, that was rude," he muttered.

"So is killing a man," I said. "If he starts ranting again, gag him. Until then, keep your complaining to yourself. I'd rather not attract unnecessary attention."

"Good point," Ceff said. "We do not know what resides in this place."

The thing is, I did know. I'd spent months trudging through the muddy terrain along the edge of this bog, and flying overhead. I'd seen enough to know that we didn't want to encounter some of the bog's more violent denizens.

"Come on," I said.

We were nearly to the boundary, where Nithsdale bordered The Forest of Torment. I wasn't eager to enter the heart of my mother's lands, but the longer we spent in the bog, the more likely we'd encounter a flesh-eating bog fiend or a rabid pack of duergar. Of course, the forest held its own kind of trouble.

"How do you propose we get past the trees?" Ceff asked, giving voice to our newest dilemma.

The bog no longer sucked at our feet, trying to devour us by pulling us into its depths. Instead, the mud here was semi-frozen, moisture forming ice crystals along its surface. We were fast nearing The Forest of Torment and all of its perils, namely trees that drank the blood of Mab's enemies.

To venture into that forest, which formed an impenetrable boundary around her ice castle, was a fool's errand. I guess that made me a fool.

"Don't worry," I said. "I have a little something up my sleeve."

I meant that literally. I suspected that the best way to prove that I wasn't an enemy was to demonstrate my family connection to Mab. Unfortunately, that would require shedding blood in a forest of bloodthirsty trees. I just hope I didn't start a feeding frenzy.

"You do realize chances are good that we'll face certain death," Torn said, eyebrow raised. He'd gagged Kade with a piece of fabric torn from my uncle's cloak, stifling the man's rantings. Kade was just lucky that Torn hadn't used wisp hide, not that I would have let him. "Not that I'm complaining. I do enjoy a challenge."

Torn was just crazy enough to think a field trip through The Forest of Torment was fun, a thrill to break up the monotony of immortality. I shook my head, removed one of my gloves, and slid a dagger from my boot.

"If my plan works, there won't be any dying, not today," I said.

I dragged the tip of the dagger across my palm, and winced. It would have been easier to use the sharp edge of one of my throwing knives, but those blades had seen too much action, and I wasn't prepared to lose a day while I replayed every moment of pain those blades had inflicted. I held my breath, prepared for the visions that did come, but they weren't as bad as I'd feared. Maybe I was finally getting the hang of this faerie thing.

"I take it there's a reason why you just cut yourself, Princess?" Torn asked.

I rolled my eyes. Of course, there was a reason. Blood dripped from my hand, reminding me of another dagger wound I'd had not so long ago. A red cap had stabbed me, but when he licked my blood from his evil, little blade his eyes had gone wide. He'd bowed then, begging for mercy before he ran away. I hadn't understood the red cap's reaction then, but I understood it now. I was Mab's daughter, a fact that some of her minions could taste on my blood.

I hoped that the bloodthirsty trees had a distinguishing palate, or my blood might go from appetizer to the main course.

"Yes," I said.

I strode to the edge of the forest, tilting my head back to gaze up at the trees that grew with their heads together like conspiring demons. A chill breeze sent whispers through the skeletal trees, their bare limbs destined to spend eternity in the torment of perpetual winter.

I held out my fist, and turned my hand, shaking droplets of my blood onto the frost covered ground. The blood steamed in the icy air, sending up a tendril of spectral mist. I shivered, and stepped back as a root burst through the frozen ground to suckle on my meager offering.

Now we just had to wait.

Kade's eyes bugged out, and a moan escaped the makeshift gag that Torn had tied around his face. What did he think, that'd I'd come here to sacrifice him to the forest? That I was sprinkling the earth with my blood to whet the trees' appetite?

"I'm not going to kill you uncle," I said, dryly. "If I was willing to let you die, I'd have let Torn kill you hours ago and saved myself from your ranting."

I turned, and smiled at him. Apparently, it wasn't a very reassuring smile, since he renewed his moaning and struggled against Torn's grip on his arm. I shrugged. I was done with mourning my uncle.

I'd cried most of the previous night, with Ceff a strong presence at my side. He didn't try to stop me, to tell me that everything would be okay. He knew that I was grieving the loss of my uncle, of the family I'd longed for. After the tears came anger, followed by a hollow emptiness. My uncle had broken me, changed me. He'd shattered my heart, but I wouldn't let him scatter the pieces. He'd taken enough from me.

I was done giving him pieces of myself. It was time I started rebuilding my life, and becoming who I truly wanted to be. That person was a P.I. in Harborsmouth with a kelpie husband and some of the best friends anyone could ever hope for. Now I just needed to get home and start living that dream.

I wrapped a bandage around my hand, slid on my glove, and waited to see if my gambit had worked. I didn't have to wait long.

With a terrifying combination of shrieks and groans, the frozen trees parted, leaving us a gleaming pathway.

"Now that looks familiar," Torn said.

It did. The path looked the same as the path of ice that we'd seen when we first entered Faerie all those months ago.

"Perhaps the land recognized you, even then," Ceff said.

"The prodigal daughter returns, so they roll out the icy path home?" I asked. "Like an Unseelie red carpet, or yellow brick road?"

"I would expect nothing less for the daughter of the Queen of Air and Darkness," he said.

The daughter of the Queen of Air and Darkness—now that was going to take some getting used to. I'm pretty sure when little girls dream about being a faerie princess, they don't picture the queen of the bogeymen as their mom. If I thought about it too hard, I'd go nuts, so I shrugged and laughed it off.

I was an immortal, which meant there was plenty of time for rocking in a corner when this was all over—so long as we made it out of Faerie alive.

"Well, if they're rolling out the red carpet, who am I to deny them a princess?" I asked, forcing a smile.

I strode onto the icy path, and into The Forest of Torment. If I did make it home, Kaye was going to have my head.

CHAPTER 54

"Do you think there's a secret knock?" I asked. "Or a password?"

I was going with open sesame, if I had to guess. Torn sighed, and Ceff shook his head.

After hours of freezing our butts off while keeping a death grip on our weapons, and looking nervously over our shoulders, the creepy forest had regurgitated us at the gates of Mab's ice palace. Out of the frying pan and into the fire, but, you know, with less heat. I lifted my chin, surveying my ancestral home. I was trying to channel royal arrogance, but if my uncle's frantic glances were any indication, I'd accomplished more psycho than princess.

It's hard to look confident when your teeth are chattering.

My mother—I'd never get used to thinking that—might be an uber powerful, malicious sadist, but she knew how to impress. Her ice palace loomed high above our heads, towers and thick walls blocking the stars so that the home of the Unseelie Court, Mab's seat of power, seemed to encompass all of Faerie.

It was an impression that only grew as we moved closer, trying to decide how best to enter. The gate and surrounding walls were formed of solid ice that gleamed with eldritch light, and two yetis stood guard. There'd be no forcing our way in. I guess we'd just have to ring the bell, so to speak.

"Oh well," I muttered. "Here goes nothing."

I held my breath as I walked past the tusked behemoths, but they didn't so much as flinch. They were like the Faerie version of Buckingham Palace guards, looking straight ahead without a sound. Their silence was unnerving, so I quickened my pace.

At the gate, I used my dagger to reopen the cut on my palm, careful not to flash my blade at the guards, and shook droplets of my blood onto the shimmering surface where the two doors joined together in the center. So long as my blood continued to act as a key, and Torn didn't do anything stupid like pick a fight with the guards, we might just make it inside the ice palace in one piece.

Whether we ever made it back out again was another story.

I wound a scrap of cloth around my hand to staunch the bleeding, and tugged on my glove. I flexed my hand, making sure the bandage wouldn't impede my ability to fight—if it came to that—and discreetly palmed my throwing knives. If my plan didn't work, and whatever magic my mother had used to ward the gates of her palace had more discriminating taste than the forest, then our only chance to escape was to take out the guards, and run like the dogs of hell were chomping at our heels.

Knowing the extent of Mab's power, and her penchant for the dramatic, they probably would be.

Ceff came to stand on my right, and Torn on my left with my uncle held in an arm lock, as the spectral glow of the gate began to pulse. I grit my teeth, preparing for a fight, but apparently, the flashing light didn't indicate a tripped alarm. We weren't zapped into fae popsicles, or attacked by the guards, though the yetis did begin to move.

The yetis turned in unison, grabbing onto the handles of two wheel-like mechanisms that had been previously hidden behind the girth of their enormous bodies. With a growl and snap of shifting ice, and the clank of chains, the doors of the ice palace gate began to swing inward to reveal a courtyard fit for a queen.

Or, in this case, a princess.

"Are you sure that this is what you wish to do?" Ceff asked, standing rigid at my side.

I knew that he would stand by me, no matter what I chose. I also knew that above all else, he wanted to keep me safe. His concern warmed my heart, just as his solid presence gave me strength, but on this, I wouldn't yield. I'd tried being a ghost, hiding from the fae of Harborsmouth, and I'd hated every second of it.

No, I would present my case to the Unseelie Court, and prove that I was no longer a threat to our kind. I would demonstrate my ability to cast a convincing glamour, and I'd make damn sure that they called off their assassins. The last thing I needed was to survive Faerie only to return home to an arrow through the heart.

But walking through these gates was a monumental step with ramifications of epic proportions. Mab had ruled the Unseelie fae, since the very birth of this world. Her departure, along with that of Oberon and Titania, the rulers of the Seelie fae, had rocked all of Faerie. But my existence? That was a shift in the balance of power that could cause an even greater upheaval—one that might end with me on the end of Mab's sword.

Entering my mother's palace would change everything.

It was a good thing that I was used to shaking things up. I glanced at Torn who was grinning from ear to ear. It's probably the main reason that the cat sidhe kept me as an ally. I was a surefire cure for boredom. Never a dull moment when I'm around, that is for damn sure.

I wet my lips, strode past the shaggy, white furred guards, and prepared to change the history of Faerie forever.

CHAPTER 55

"I request an audience with the Unseelie Court," I said, voice ringing through the courtyard.

A motley group of fae hesitantly approached. More than a few held weapons, though these weren't guards. The predators of the winter lands flanked us, cutting off our escape. No, the fae who scuttled toward us were likely the administration, and if their fidgeting and wary, befuddled glances were any indication, I confused the hell out of them.

Good, that made both of us.

A goblin with a clipboard waddled over. She lifted some kind of writing stylus, and arched a brow as she looked me over.

"Do you have an appointment?" she asked.

She looked down her bulbous nose, taking in my muddy boots and blood smeared pants. At least I was wearing black. Otherwise, she'd probably be horrified at the state of my dress. As it was she sniffed, and gave me the stink eye. It was all I could do not to laugh.

"No," I said. "But I'm sure they'll want to hear my case once you tell them who's here."

"And who would that be?" she asked, rolling her eyes at me as she lowered the stylus to her clipboard.

"Ivy Granger, daughter of Will-o'-the-Wisp," I said, pausing for dramatic effect. Torn caught my eye, and smirked. He must be loving this. These fae were in for the gossip of the century. "...and daughter of Mab, the Queen of Air and Darkness."

I never understood the phrase, "you could hear a pin drop", until now. The acoustics of the frozen courtyard had elevated the shuffling of feet, clanking of weapons, and constant whispers as the fae had speculated about their strange visitors. But now the courtyard was devoid of sound.

"Now may I *please* have an audience with my court?" I asked, edging my voice with haughty annoyance.

The goblin dropped her clipboard, and ran into the palace. The other fae, including the apex predators who'd been guarding our retreat, close at her heels.

"I'll take that as a yes."

CHAPTER 56

The Unseelie Court was a vertigo-inducing inversion of the Great Hall of the Wisp Court I'd grown familiar with. Where the Wisp Court had held its proceedings on the moss-covered stone bottom of a cavern glowing with moonlight, beside a pool of water teeming with life, the Unseelie Court gathered on a drafty precipice, high above a dark, lifeless pit.

Balconies ringed the pit, giving palace residents a bird's eye view. Unfortunately for me, petitioners to the court had to make their way across a narrow path that cut through the dark like a knife's edge, leading to a circle of stone that sat like an island in the greasy darkness. Mouth dry, I tried not to look down as I made my way to the speaker's stone.

I had no idea why Mab had built her palace on top of a vertical shaft that likely led straight to Hell, but I imagined that this path kept the number of petitioners to a minimum. I bent my knees, and closed my eyes as another gust of frigid wind blasted me, freezing my eyelashes and threatening to tip me over into the bottomless pit. Maybe this was a trap, a way for Mab's minions to get rid of the potential usurper to the Unseelie throne. If so, I had to commend their creativity, and their moxie.

Ceff walked a step behind me, a solid wall of muscle at my back. After months in captivity, he was leaner, and the muscle more defined, but that didn't detract from the threat he posed to anyone who dared strike out against me. In fact, I'm pretty sure that two years bound in iron had lent a steely glint to his eyes that hadn't been there before.

Ceff wasn't the only hard-eyed demon in my entourage. Torn was having a bit too much fun dangling my uncle over the precipice, as they followed behind us. At Kade's whimper, I shot Torn a glare over my shoulder.

"Stop playing with Kade like he's a mouse, and get your ass over here," I said.

Torn grinned, showing his teeth.

"As you wish, Princess," he said. "My ass is yours to command."

I sighed, and turned back to face the council members who'd assembled in front of us across the pit. I imagine that distance gave them a false sense of safety, but it wouldn't save them from a well-placed fireball. Not that I planned on immolating council members. The council had the final word of the Unseelie Court, and right now, I needed to be in their good graces.

"What is the purpose of the case you bring before us today?" a somber man asked.

He had a long, gaunt face and spindly hands that never stopped moving, as if he were dangling those hands out of a car window, surfing on waves of chill air.

"I bring two issues before the court," I said.

"That is...most unorthodox," a stout boggart grumbled.

"And I'm not your typical petitioner," I said, arching an eyebrow at the council.

Council members shifted noisily in their stone chairs, and I fought a smile. I wasn't looking forward to a family reunion, but being Mab's daughter sure had its perks.

"Then state your case, or rather cases," Somber said.

I nodded, and took a deep breath.

"First, I request that my uncle, Lord Kade of the Wisp Court, be stripped of his magic," I said.

More than one council member gasped, and whispers and cries broke out from the balcony above us. A troll pounded his fist on the arm of his chair, and the room once again went silent.

"What crime is Kade accused of that we should sentence him to such a harsh punishment?" Somber asked.

"Treason," I said. "He knew of my birthright, and yet he kidnapped my friends, lied to me, and tried to manipulate me to become his...consort. I believe that ultimately, he wished to take Mab's throne, perhaps in revenge for her rejection."

It was all true, but for a moment a pang of guilt tightened my gut. I disliked airing out my family's dirty laundry, but this was the only way to strip Kade of his magic— the only way to allow him to live.

"That is a weighty charge," Somber said.

"Yep, I know," I said. "So I'll give you a minute to wrap your heads around it."

Ceff shot me a wry look, and I lifted my shoulder in a one-armed shrug. The faster we finished this business, the better. Mab's ice palace, and an audience with the council of the Unseelie Court, was making my skin crawl. If being pushy got this done faster, then I'd push. I wanted to go home.

"If he is truly guilty of treason, is stripping him of his magic enough of a punishment?" an elegant highborn faerie asked.

I held up a hand, gesturing to interrupt.

"I have also exiled him from his ancestral home of Tearlach and the wisp lands of Nithsdalc," I said.

The faerie nodded, and I held my breath as the council's sibilant whispering continued.

"We will grant you your wish, Princess," Somber said. "But that is our final favor. Think on this before you bring another issue to our attention."

Great, that didn't sound ominous or anything. I guess being princess wasn't all it was cracked up to be.

"I appreciate the warning, but I will address the court with one more issue," I said.

The council members shared meaningful glances amongst each other, and nodded.

"You may continue," Somber said.

"I was deemed a traitor," I said, and the entire room gasped. It was like the entire pit drew in a breath and sucked it into the void. Yeah, looks like I'd been right and they hadn't put two and two together, realizing that the Ivy Granger who was Mab's daughter was the same half human Ivy Granger they'd ordered to be executed in the human world. Now to see what they were prepared to do about it. "But I can prove that I am not a threat. I will not break the One Law. I will not betray our secret to the human populace."

"That is why her name was so familiar!" a banshee wailed, pointing a hooked finger at me.

More than one faerie glared at me with venom in their eyes, and maybe their fangs. For the moment, I was glad of the pit that spanned between us.

"Look," I said, keeping my voice low and calm. "I can prove my ability to create a glamour. This was all a misunderstanding..."

Their voices rolled over each other, and my mouth snapped shut. I'd have to wait them out, if they even let me speak again, but there was one thing I could do while I waited.

I reached for my power, drawing it up through my body and out through my skin. The fire burned, but I embraced it, letting it wrap around me.

I remembered the heat shimmer that my uncle had likened my glamour to, and bit my lip. If only he'd remained my mentor, and not a madman driven by power, lust, and revenge, but that was water under the bridge. What mattered now was proving mastery over my magic, so that the court didn't decide to have me executed on the spot, princess or not.

I drew forth my power, wove it into a complex skein of fire magic, and draped the glamour around my body. When I opened my eyes, the world still seemed the same, my body was still my own, but my efforts must have paid off. Every faerie, from the harpies perched on the ornate balconies to the centaurs circling the stone council seats, stood rigid, attention focused on the woman who now looked even more like her mother.

According to Skilly, my human glamour looked exactly like Mab's. I'd thought it was an unlucky coincidence at the time, but now I knew that it was a result of my birth—and it presented an opportunity to gain the attention of the council.

My friends and I might have known what to expect, but the rest of the room was unprepared. I'd stunned the palace residents once again into silence. If I kept this up, I might get a complex.

I was almost relieved when the shouting began anew. The noise wasn't doing anything to improve my headache, but at least they were no longer gaping at me. The inside of some of those mouths were a sight best left to the imagination. If these fae were any indication, Faerie was in dire need of dental care.

I smiled, and nodded. I'd achieved my goal. I had the council's attention, now to plead my case. I held a hand up, and the noise began to lessen.

"Within this glamour my...otherness is contained," I said. "The glowing of my eyes and skin—a gift of my father—are not at risk of being seen by humans."

"But we were told..." Somber said.

"Do you doubt my abilities?" I asked.

I put one hand on my hip, and looked at him archly. The entire council blanched. I guess I really did look like Mab.

"No, no, Mistress," he said, bowing obsequiously.

"Then I am free to return to the human world?" I asked.

"Yes, of course, Mistress," he said. "We will send word to the Moordenaar, terminating the contract for your execution."

"See that you do," I said.

I looked around the room, but when I caught Torn's smirk, I had to struggle not to laugh. I was playing up my connection to Mab, but it was time to wrap this up.

"Is that all, Mistress?" Somber asked.

"Actually, I have a question," I said. I paused, and tilted my head. "How do you send your messages to our allies in the human world?"

"Well...there is the scrying pool for sending missives to the Moordenaar," he said. I frowned. That wasn't all that helpful. "And though the roads to Faerie are closed, there is the portal, for when we need to send representatives of the court to the human world, or they to Faerie."

"A portal from this court to the human world?" I asked.

It was as I'd guessed. There were more backdoors to and from Faerie, and Mab had one here in her palace. It made sense. Now to exercise my royal powers, such as they were, and gain access to this portal—and go home.

"Yes," Somber said. "But it is for court business only."

"Well then," I said. "I guess we have one more order of business."

Somber let out a weighty sigh, and the negotiations began.

CHAPTER 57

"Can you send us anywhere in the human world?" I asked, following our guide through one of the many corridors of my mother's palace. The place was a maze of ice, but anything was better than being suspended above a bottomless pit prone to wind gusts.

"Within reason," Somber said.

"What are you thinking, Princess?" Torn asked.

"I'm thinking that I have unfinished business," I whispered to Torn. I turned to the gray skinned faerie, and bowed my head. "It is my wish that you send us to the Braxton junkyard on the outskirts of Harborsmouth."

The faerie raised a thin eyebrow, but didn't comment on my choice of destination. I guess he thought it unwise to challenge the princess.

Somber sighed, and waved his fingers in the air in a complex pattern. When he was finished, he slid his hands into the wide sleeves of his robes, and nodded.

"It is done," he said. "Follow this path to the ash tree, circle it three times widdershins, and step through the portal."

I guess he wasn't going with us. Since the path led down into The Forest of Torment, I couldn't really blame him.

"The tree is the portal?" I asked.

I didn't want to walk face first into a solid tree, only to find out I was supposed to step onto a rock, toadstool, or patch of grass. When in Faerie, it was best not to assume.

"Yes, you must pass through the tree to enter the human world," he said. He looked me up and down from head to toe. "Forgive me if I hope you do intend to stay there."

With that touching farewell, Somber spun on his heel and stalked away.

"Friendly guy," Torn said.

I shrugged.

"I have that effect on people," I said, a wry smile on my lips. "Come on, let's go home."

The frost covered path, no more than a narrow game trail, led through a break in the hedge maze of Mab's rose garden, down a steep embankment, and into the forest.

The footing was treacherous, but at least we weren't trying to navigate this with my uncle in tow. After he was stripped of his magic, Kade was given a choice. He could leave the palace to fend for himself with no magical powers, or remain as a palace servant. He decided to stay.

My uncle was no fool. His chances for survival would have been slim outside the walls of the ice palace. Not that he would enjoy life as a lowly servant.

Kade had fallen far, but he was still alive. I'd held his life in my hands, and I'd allowed him to live. He had an eternity to make amends for his evil deeds, but what he did with the life that I'd granted was up to him. I'd done what I could, what I'd had to, and now it was time to move on.

It was time to go home.

"Torn, can you give us a moment?" Ceff asked.

Torn shrugged, and nodded. After looking us over, and deciding we weren't worth eavesdropping on, he turned and walked further down the trail.

Ceff ran a hand through his hair, and sighed. But when his eyes met mine, they were glowing green with passion. My lips parted, and he leaned closer.

"Before we left Harborsmouth, we made a promise to each other," Ceff said. "Now that we're going back, I have to ask you a question about that promise, and I need you to give me an honest answer."

Ceff started to say more, but I held up a hand. I needed to say this, needed to clear the air.

"A lot has happened since that day," I said. "I've changed, and...we now know the truth about my biological mother. So if you're having second thoughts, I won't hold you to the promise that we made."

There, I'd said my piece. I'd given him an out, a way for us to end things gracefully. My hand went to my stomach.

I was going to be sick.

"I love you, Ivy, and learning the truth of your parentage has not changed my feelings toward you," he said.

He moved closer, and I blinked. He slipped his hand into mine, and squeezed. I was wearing gloves—the action didn't trigger my psychometry—but I didn't need visions to see the way Ceff felt about me. His love was written in the lines of his face and the desire in his eyes, but I still had to ask. I needed to hear it from his lips.

"It hasn't?" I asked.

"No," he said, smiling down at me. "If anything, I love you more. Not for your power or status, but for your strength. You are a survivor, Ivy. We both are."

I flinched, remembering a recent moment of weakness.

"I wasn't that strong," I said. "I-I-I gave up on you."

"You were tricked by a man who has been manipulating people for a millennium," he said.

"But I shouldn't have believed him," I said. "Not for a second. How can you forgive me?"

"He was your family," he said. "We all have a blind spot when it comes to family."

He had a point. His ex-wife Melusine had been his blind spot, and Kade was mine. I guess in a twisted way that made us even.

I nodded, letting him know that I accepted his argument, though I'd likely never shed all of my guilt.

"Do you still wish to marry me?" he asked.

Ceff stared at me, his eyes glowing with passion, and with hope.

"Yes, Ceff, yes," I said. "I've never been so sure of anything in my life. Yes. I want to marry you, and I don't want to wait."

"There is no rush," he said with a pleased laugh.

"Is next month rushing?" I asked.

"Next month?" he asked, eyebrow raised. "We have forever, and we are already rushing our engagement. Are you sure you want to become married so soon?"

"Yes," I said. "I'm ready to begin forever."

We walked hand in hand down the frost covered path. We would face the portal in the same way that we would face our future—together.

CHAPTER 58

I stumbled and retched, bile rising to burn my throat. The sleeve of my jacket vibrated as Torn and Ceff shuddered in unison.

I was struggling not to puke on my boots when Torn let go of my arm. He jumped back, and hissed as if the leather jacket burned his fingers.

"Did you have to take us through one of Mab's personal portals, Princess?" he asked, glaring at me with his slit pupil eyes. "My stomach feels like it's filled with angry spider fae hatchlings."

That did it. We'd encountered spider fae when we'd traveled to Emain Ablach. That seemed like a lifetime ago, but the creatures had left an impression that I would probably carry to my grave.

With images of spider fae dancing in my head, I threw up. I managed to miss getting vomit on our clothes, not that I would have any regrets puking on Torn right now. The cat sidhe lord had a knack for getting under my skin.

"So tell me again why it was so important that we arrive in a junkyard of all places?" he asked.

I wiped my sleeve across my mouth, and surveyed the world around us. Somber had been true to his word. The portal had deposited us in the middle of Jinx's father's junkyard. I'd never been so happy to see those twisted scraps of plastic and metal. And flitting through the gaps in that metal were tiny glowing lights.

The wisps were still here, their bodies pulsating with a sickly shade of green.

My head was pounding, but I pushed away my own discomfort. I may have put the Wisp Court into the hands of Skillywidden and the wisp people, but that didn't strip me of my duties as princess. Plus, I'd taken on a job here, and I planned to finish it.

I pulled off my jacket, and stripped down to my sports bra. I inhaled deeply, filling my lungs, and drawing my power up through my body. When I felt ready to burst with magic, I extended my wings.

The wisps' voices were muffled, the proximity to iron dulling my abilities, but I reached out with my magic, and opened my mind. Thoughts and words rushed in, and a tear rolled down my cheek. These wisps had suffered so much.

But I was about to set things right.

My uncle had taught me some healing magic, in particular how to heal wisp physiology. I'd never attempted to heal more than my own scrapes and broken bones, but I had the knowledge, and it was time to put it to good use.

"Come," I said, a smile touching my lips as I raised my hand palm up. I let my voice resonate with power, using my wisp magic to communicate with them. "Come, my cousins, let me heal you from this sickness."

The wisps came closer and, with my magic opening a conduit between us, I could hear their cries for help. With tears streaming down my face, I sent my power into the wisps, cleansing their bodies of the taint of iron. It was such a simple thing now that I knew how to tap into our connection. Talking to and healing these wisps was as strenuous as walking a city block, nothing more.

Within minutes the wisps were glowing a bright healthy yellow hue. Ceff brought over a plastic container of water that he found while I worked, and set it on the ground at my feet. Even Torn shared the remainder of the rations he had in his pockets, setting the food beside the water with a shake of his head.

"You did it, Princess," he said. "You saved them."

"We did it," I said.

I looked at Ceff, my heart swelling at the secret I still needed to share with Jinx when I arrived home. I smiled, and turned back to the wisps who were darting in and out of the water.

I knew that these wisps needed more than this healing. They needed a home, and food, and safety. I decided then that I would do everything in my power to give them those things, and more.

"We did it, together," Ceff said, a smile on his lips.

I nodded, wondering once again how I'd come to have such amazing people in my life. I'd spent so much of my life alone—my childhood, the months in Faerie—but I didn't have

to do things on my own anymore. I had people that I loved,
who, by some miracle, loved me in return.

I smiled, and slid my gloved hand into Ceff's.

"Together we can do anything."

EXCLUSIVE SNEAK PEEK
Keep reading for a sneak peek of
HOUND'S BITE

The night was broken by howls that sent icy claws skittering down my spine.

"What the Hell is that?" I asked, gloved hands reaching for my blades.

Ceff lifted his hands apologetically, mouth struggling to form words in a way that wouldn't upset me. I could read his discomfort in his stiff posture and the tightening of the skin around his eyes.

Torn had no such concern for my feelings.

"You didn't think you could enter Faerie without consequences, did you, Princess?" Torn asked with a mocking sneer.

So much for friendship. Apparently, returning to Harborsmouth had brought out Torn's snarky side.

The doors to Faerie had been sealed by Mab, Titania, and Oberon when they disappeared more than a century ago. The faerie paths no longer led to the Seelie and Unseelie lands. Lucky for me, I'd found a key to a hidden back door.

At least, that key had seemed like a stroke of luck at the time. I'd needed a way into Faerie, to the wisp court that promised clues to my father's whereabouts, not that my journey had been easy. Nothing worth fighting for ever was.

The ability to come out of hiding? That was worth fighting for. I was tired of slinking around the shadows of my city.

The problem was that, even though I'd been raised human, the supernatural gifts I inherited from my father, Will-o'-the-Wisp, continued to grow like wildfire—burning me in the process. With no one to teach me how to control my growing powers, I'd broken the one rule that all fae live by. I used my powers in public, unglamoured, and risked exposing the secret of our kind to humans—a crime punishable by death.

It didn't take the fae uppity ups long to send out a faerie hit squad to take me out. The Moordenaar, a group of elite assassins, shot me full of poisoned arrows. I died. Thankfully,

I had a magic apple up my sleeve—an apple that resurrected the dead, and not in a creepy, zombielicious kind of way.

So yeah. I died, but I got better. Take that faerie assassins. Ivy Granger, 1. Faerie assassins, 0.

With the fae believing I was dead, I used my father's key to enter the wisp court. As I said, it hadn't been easy. I did things there that were sure to give me nightmares—more than I already had—but I'd foolishly believed that the worst was behind me.

Surviving a trip through the land of the dead and into Faerie and back again—homicidal relatives and all—had left me hopeful. I'd learned how to control my powers. My friends and I had survived. Heck, I'd only been back a few minutes and already I'd managed to heal the wisps who'd been living in Jinx's father's junkyard of their iron sickness. It was starting out to be a good day.

I should have known better.

But I had so many reasons for being hopeful. I was returning to Harborsmouth after demonstrating my newfound control to the Unseelie Court. The ruling fae had decided that I was no longer a threat to their existence. That meant no more hiding. For once, no one was trying to kill me. Even my relationship with Ceff was a good place. My life was supposed to go back to normal.

Another hungry howl pierced the night, and I grimaced.

"This is no time for games, Torn," I said. Getting an answer from a cat sidhe was like following the metal ball in a game of Mouse Trap. I was pretty sure that Torn was allergic to straight answers, but I was sick of playing the mouse. Our journey to Faerie had been an exhausting one, and I was short on patience. The sooner we fought the big baddy coming our way, the sooner I could drop into my bed. "Did we wake the Hound of the Baskervilles, or what?"

Ceff and Torn exchanged a meaningful look, faces grim. I flashed Ceff a grin, hoping to lighten the mood, but he shook his head.

"Torn was right," Ceff said. "It would seem that our trip to Faerie was not without consequences."

"What consequences?" I asked, throwing my blade-laden hands in the air. "Will one of you just tell me what is out there? A heads up might make killing the howling monster a little easier. Knowledge is power, yada yada."

"You will need more than mere blades to fight that enemy," Ceff said.

I ground my teeth while mentally stabbing a picture of my cryptic boyfriend with my "mere blades."

"Are you saying we should run?" I asked, eyebrows raised. "Because you should know me better than that."

"What he's saying, Princess, is that you woke up something too big for the three of us to defeat alone," Torn said.

That made me pause. We'd fought faerie queens, pyro demons, a lovesick necromancer, and a psychotic lamia, to name a few. I may not have come through those battles unscathed, or with all my guts still on the inside, but with my friends at my side, and a new arsenal of wisp powers at my fingertips, I felt nearly invincible.

I looked to Ceff, hoping he'd grab his trident and join me for some quick monster cleanup. I may not be on the clock for this one, but I didn't let hungry fae prowl the streets of Harborsmouth. And if Torn was right, I'd somehow let this one follow us out of Faerie. No way was I turning tail, no matter how tired I was.

But Ceff didn't reach for his weapons.

"We need allies," he said.

"And larger weapons," Torn said, with a wink.

The cat sidhe looked excited, which was a clue that I wasn't going to like the answer to my next question.

"And what monster do we need to gather our allies and weapons against?" I asked.

"Haven't you guessed yet, Princess?" Torn asked, eyes gleaming. "We're not just facing one howling beast."

Ceff turned to me, closing the space between us. In the moonlight, I could see my reflection in the dark pools of his kelpie eyes—eyes that were tight with worry.

"What are they?" I asked.

Ceff's voice was low and reverent, and tinged with the taint of fear.

"The Wild Hunt."

Ivy Granger World
Don't miss these great books set in the world of Ivy Granger.

Ivy Ganger, Psychic Detective Series

Shadow Sight
Welcome to Harborsmouth, where monsters walk the streets unseen by humans...except those with second sight, like Ivy Granger.

Blood and Mistletoe: An Ivy Granger Novella
Holidays are worse than a full moon for making people crazy. In Harborsmouth, where many of the residents are undead vampires or monstrous fae, the combination may prove deadly.

Ghost Light
Holidays are worse than a full moon for making people crazy. In Harborsmouth, where many of the residents are undead vampires or monstrous fae, the combination may prove deadly.

Club Nexus: An Ivy Granger Novella
A demon, an Unseelie faerie, and a vampire walk into a bar...

Burning Bright
Burning down the house...

Birthright
Being a faerie princess isn't all it's cracked up to be.

Hound's Bite
Ivy Granger thought she left the worst of Mab's creations behind when she escaped Faerie. She thought wrong.

Hunters' Guild Series

Hunting in Bruges
The only thing worse than being a Hunter in the fae-ridden city of Harborsmouth, is hunting vampires in Bruges.

E.J. Stevens is the author of the HUNTERS' GUILD urban fantasy series, the SPIRIT GUIDE young adult series, and the award-winning IVY GRANGER urban fantasy series. She is known for filling pages with quirky characters, bloodsucking vampires, psychotic faeries, and snarky, kick-butt heroines.

BTS Red Carpet Award winner for Best Novel, SYAE Award finalist for Best Paranormal, Best Horror, and Best Novella, winner of the PRG Reviewer's Choice Award for Best Paranormal Fantasy Novel, Best Young Adult Paranormal Series, Best Urban Fantasy Novel, and finalist for Best Young Adult Paranormal Novel and Best Urban Fantasy Series.

When E.J. isn't at her writing desk, she enjoys dancing along seaside cliffs, singing in graveyards, and sleeping in faerie circles. E.J. currently resides in a magical forest on the coast of Maine where she finds daily inspiration for her writing.

CONNECT WITH E.J. STEVENS

Twitter: @EJStevensAuthor
Website: www.EJStevensAuthor.com
Blog: www.FromtheShadows.info

www.ingramcontent.com/pod-product-compliance
Lightning Source LLC
Chambersburg PA
CBHW070856250626
47159CB00003B/1083